ISLAND ESCAPE

An Isle of Man Romance

DIANA XARISSA

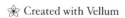 Created with Vellum

AUTHOR'S NOTE

This book is set in the amazingly beautiful Isle of Man, and the location plays a large part in the story.

The Island is located between England and Ireland in the Irish Sea. While it is a Crown Dependency, it is a country in its own right, with its own currency, stamps, language and government.

This is a work of fiction. All of the modern characters are a product of the author's imagination. Any resemblance to actual persons, living or dead, is entirely coincidental. Similarly, the names of the restaurants and shops and other businesses on the Island are fictional.

The historical sites and landmarks on the Island are all real (Castle Rushen, Peel Castle and Rushen Abbey), as are the Manx Museum, the House of Manannan and the Wildlife Park; however, all of the events that take place within them in this story are fictional.

The Manx History Institute does not exist. Manx National Heritage is real and their efforts to preserve and promote the historical sites and the history of the Island are extraordinary. All of the Manx National Heritage staff in this story, however, are fictional creations.

The historical characters mentioned within the story (the Seventh Earl of Derby and his wife) did exist.

While the Isle of Man has its share of ghosts, spirits and Little People (fairies), to the best of the author's knowledge the ghost of Charlotte de la Tremouille does not haunt Castle Rushen. That's fiction, too.

I

Katie Kincaid sighed as she looked out the airplane window. All that she could see below her were clouds, clouds and more clouds. Somewhere, down there, was London. Katie had wanted to go to London for her entire twenty-nine years of life. Now she was finally getting the chance to do so. She would be landing in London in only a few minutes.

Unfortunately, she wasn't staying. Katie pressed her nose to the window glass and squinted, twisting her head to the left and right, trying to focus on something underneath the piles of clouds that blocked her view. Surely she should be able to see something by now, she thought to herself. They had been made to sit upright in their seats, tray tables neatly folded away, many minutes ago. Surely that meant that they were about to land.

The plane seemed to circle around yet again and then began to drop noticeably lower in the sky. Katie strained to get her first glimpse of England. She could hardly believe that she was actually here. All the years of trying to work out a way to get here, and now she was really here and it wasn't at all like she had imagined. The flight had been far too long and incredibly tedious for a start. For some reason she had expected it to feel more exciting. She was flying across the ocean to a whole different country. She should have felt excited and amazed. After the first hour or so, however, she had just felt bored and restless.

She shifted restlessly in her cramped seat. She had dressed for comfort in a pair of worn jeans and an oversized T-shirt and her feet were encased in her comfiest pair of shoes. In spite of all of that, she still felt uncomfortable and stiff after the long journey. A friend had suggested that she dress up, in hopes of being upgraded, but Katie had decide it was more important to be comfortable if she wasn't upgraded than uncomfortable in a larger seat.

Katie had gone straight from high school to college, earning a bachelor's degree, then a master's, and finally a doctorate without a break. She had immediately taken up a teaching position at the same university where she had earned her doctorate. Having never really lived outside of the academic bubble, she still tended to dress and act like a student much of the time.

The pilot's voice crackled over the plane's loudspeakers

"Sorry about this, folks, but there isn't too much to see this morning. Fog and heavy cloud are about all that is out there right now. I'll remind everyone to move their watches forward five hours. It is three minutes past six in the morning in London and we should be on the ground and at the gate by half past."

Katie looked at her watch. She had excitedly reset it as soon as she'd boarded the plane, thinking herself worldly now that she was on "London time." She looked back out the window again, but still couldn't manage to actually see anything. She leaned her head on the wall of the plane and sighed again.

The long journey and the miserable weather had conspired to make her revaluate her summer plans. She thought now that she might have been too hasty in booking this escape. Maybe she should have just stayed put and sorted out her life instead of running away and leaving life to, hopefully, sort itself out behind her.

Half an hour later, still without seeing much more than a few roads and runways from the air, Katie struggled through the gate of the airplane and into Heathrow airport. She followed the flood of passengers down seemingly endless corridors, beginning to wonder if she had actually landed in England or was simply walking there from New

York. She joined what she hoped was the shortest line at passport control and watched enviously as many of her fellow passengers breezed quickly through the much shorter "European Union Passport Holders" lines.

"Never mind." The man behind her had seen the same thing. "They won't have the luggage off the plane yet anyway. Those guys aren't actually going anywhere any faster than we are."

Katie smiled at the man and felt a little bit better. It was finally her turn to have her passport checked and stamped and Katie felt a flutter of excitement as she turned over her brand-new passport to the man at the desk.

"Good morning," he told her, his English accent making Katie suddenly feel far from home. "Can I ask why you are visiting the United Kingdom?"

"I'm actually here to do some studying," Katie answered with a smile. "But I'm not staying in London. I'm flying on to the Isle of Man from here."

"Studying on the Isle of Man?" He grinned. "Motorbikes or abnormal cats?"

Katie had to laugh. Not many of her friends back home knew anything about the Isle of Man, but the few that had heard of the place all said pretty much the same thing. The motorcycle racing and tailless cats were the Island's claims to fame.

"Actually, not either, sorry," she told the immigration official. "I'm actually a specialist in Early Modern English History. I'll be studying what was happening on the Island during the English Civil War period."

"Right, well, welcome to the United Kingdom. I hope you enjoy your stay," he told her as he stamped her passport and handed it back to her.

"Thanks, I hope so, too," she replied with a big smile.

She was suddenly excited again as she absorbed his welcome. She was actually really truly in Europe and she was going to be here for nearly three months. She tucked her passport away and went in search of her luggage with a huge smile on her face.

The smile transformed that face. At first glance Katie was only conventionally pretty, but when she smiled her large brown eyes lit up and gave her face animation that made more than one tired male passenger look twice. A great figure and long wavy brown hair completed a package that was far more attractive than its owner realized.

Katie made her way through the "Nothing to Declare" channel after baggage claim, hoping that she looked as innocent as she actually was. She passed through the doors into a huge concourse that took her breath away. For a moment she felt completely overwhelmed by the crowds of people that seemed to be standing everywhere, all talking and calling to one another, shouting hellos to new arrivals and pulling each other in all directions. Katie took an unconscious step backwards and was rewarded by having a luggage cart driven into the back of her heel. She leapt aside quickly, muttering apologies to the angry woman shepherding the overstuffed cart and three small children into the chaos.

Katie took a hesitant step forward and sucked in a deep breath. "English air," she thought to herself giddily as she began to try to sort out the confusion in front of her. As she studied it, she realized that the disorder was actually far more organized that it first appeared and she began to understand how things were arranged.

Directly in front of her was the exit into the main concourse and she made her way slowly in that direction, following the rest of the crowd, most of whom seemed to have clear destinations in mind. To the right it seemed that families were being reunited, some of whom mustn't have seen each other for many years, if the shrieks and tears were anything to go by. On the left stood a long line of bored-looking men and women, most wearing shirts bearing the names of various taxi and car rental companies, holding signs with people's names on them.

Katie glanced down the row and spotted an absolutely gorgeous guy who looked incredibly out of place among the ordinary looking taxi drivers. The casual uniform-style shirt and trousers he was wearing only showed off an obviously toned and well-maintained body. He was at least six feet tall, with dark hair that was obviously carefully styled to fall sexily across his forehead. As he brushed the hair from his eyes, Katie felt their sapphire blue gaze catch her own.

Katie stopped suddenly in the crush, earning her ankle another whack from a different luggage cart. Somewhere in this mess was supposed to be someone with a sign with her name on it, she remembered, forcing herself to look away from the stranger. The Manx History Institute had promised to arrange a connecting flight for her, and someone was supposed to meet her and make sure that she got on to it.

She turned her head and started checking the names on the signs. As she looked down the row, she found herself catching the eye of Mr. Gorgeous. He smiled at her and then winked. If men that look like that drive taxis in London, I'm moving for sure, she thought to herself. Her eyes reached the end of the line and Katie realized she hadn't seen her own name.

A slightly hysterical giggle welled up as she suddenly began to wonder what she would do if she couldn't find the right person and ended up stranded in London on her own. She thought about the fairly useless credit cards in her wallet that were all but at their limit, run up to pay for a wedding that had never happened.

Katie gave her head a quick shake. She was overtired and her imagination was running away with her. She stopped again, this time being careful to move out of the way of the other passengers before doing so. Then she started again, checking each name on each sign. The job was made easier by the fact that the numbers of card holders had fallen as the newly arriving passengers connected with their pre-booked taxis and cars.

Katie found her eyes irresistibly drawn upwards as she worked her way down the line. She smiled and flushed as she realized that the good-looking man was watching her as well. She reached the end of the row and frowned again. One more time through and then I'll have to find a phone and call someone, she told herself. This time she forced herself to concentrate, ignoring the handsome stranger and the crush of people around her.

When she finally spotted her name, she realized why it had taken so long. Someone had neatly lettered "Dr. K. Kincaid" on the sign, where she had been expecting something far less formal. Katie smiled in relief and headed towards the sign. When she looked up from the formal wording, however, she found herself nervous for another reason. It was inevitable that the man holding the sign was Mr. Gorgeous himself.

"Hi," Katie smiled her brightest at the man, unknowingly raising his interest in her another few notches.

"Hello, there," he smiled back, moving sideways from her to keep the sign he held in clear view of the departing passengers. "Come here often?" he teased her.

"Wow, I was hoping for better lines from the English." Katie surprised herself by flirting back. She wasn't usually the type, but being so far from home made her feel brave. Or maybe she was just so tired that she wasn't behaving normally.

"I can do better," the man smiled daringly at her. "Maybe I can buy you a coffee or something? The only thing is, I'm waiting for some stuffed-shirt professor from America who is coming over on a study trip. If you don't mind waiting for a few minutes, I'll find Dr. Dull and we can all get a drink?"

Katie smiled wickedly. "How do you know Dr. Dull will be that bad?" she asked innocently.

"Oh, they all are," the man answered confidently. "The Manx History Institute brings historians over at least once or twice a year. It is usually my job to collect them from London and fly them to the Isle of Man. They are all the same, noses in books, only interested in the past. I haven't met one yet that I would willingly talk to for more than ten minutes."

"Oh dear, I'd better talk fast if I only have ten minutes." Katie laughed and then held out her hand. "But then we haven't been introduced. I'm Doctor Kathryn Kincaid, Katie to my friends. But you can call me Dr. Dull if you prefer."

Katie laughed harder at the look of total astonishment that crossed the man's face. He blushed and stammered for a long moment before collecting himself.

"I don't believe it," he shook his head at her. "A woman that looks like you shouldn't be a historian. You should be doing something far more interesting with your life than studying dead people."

Katie smiled, refusing to be offended by the comment. "History is what makes us who we are. There is nothing more interesting than studying people and what makes them do the things that people do. The more you study the past the more you realize that we haven't changed much. I study ordinary people and the first thing you learn is that even if they lived four hundred years ago, they still did all the things that we do now. They went to work, they fell in love, they had families, and the more we can understand about them, the more we can understand about ourselves."

She flushed under his concentrated gaze. "Sorry about the lecture. I'm passionate about what I do and I do get carried away some times. Especially when I'm jetlagged and tired," she tried to explain.

"Don't be sorry. Most of the historians I've met tend to be as exciting as the dusty old books they study. You actually make it sound quite interesting. I'm delighted to find someone who is passionate about their work."

Somehow the man managed to make the last sentence sound quite erotic and Katie found herself blushing under his watchful eye.

"By the way, I'm Finlo Quayle, owner and operator of Quayle Airlines. We run the only chartered passenger service to and from the Isle of Man."

"Nice to meet you," Katie said formally, suddenly nervous that their flirting was getting carried away.

"Well, let's get underway, then, shall we?"

They had been standing in the middle of the airport concourse for the long exchange and now Finlo took the handle of Katie's luggage cart and began to lead her away from the muddle that was international arrivals.

Katie struggled to keep up with Finlo as he steamed through the crowd.

"Hey, you might know where you are going, but I don't. And you're taller than I am. Besides which, I haven't slept for I don't know how long and I've got jet lag. Could we slow down a bit?" Katie bit her lip, knowing that she sounded like a grumpy child.

Finlo just laughed. "Sorry about that. How tall are you?"

"I'm five foot seven," Katie answered automatically, and then wondered why she had responded to the impertinent question.

"That means I've got seven inches on you. I suppose it is only fair that I slow down a bit." Finlo smiled and fell into step beside Katie, taking care to match his pace to her own.

"Sorry if I sound out of sorts," Katie offered. "I'm unbelievably tired. The journey was far harder than I expected it to be."

"We have a bit of a long walk, I'm afraid," Finlo told her. "Chartered flights leave from the farthest terminal from here. We can get a bus, if you need to, though."

Katie shook her head. "If we have time, I don't mind walking. It feels good to walk again after all that time squashed into an airplane seat."

"That is the beauty of flying Quayle Air," Finlo grinned. "We take off when I'm ready, not before, so we have all the time you need. You could have flown one of the standard commercial airlines, but my way is so much nicer."

"It must cost more, though," Katie answered. "My whole trip is being paid for by the institute, through their special grant program. They made all the flight arrangements. I would have thought that they would have found the least expensive way for me to travel."

"I give the institute a special deal," Finlo explained. "The Island is a small community and there are a lot of special arrangements for things that are mutually beneficial. Besides, my cousin runs the institute and I have to provide really good rates for family or my mother would disown me. If there were any more Quayles on the Island, I would be bankrupt."

Katie smiled and the two walked slowly through the crowded airport. Katie was busy trying hard to ignore how attractive she was finding the man walking next to her. She had enough problems in her life at the moment. She didn't need any added distractions. Finlo, meanwhile, kept flirting. No doubt he was used to attracting women everywhere that he went, but Katie wasn't interested in being one of his conquests.

He led Katie through the crowded airport and into a much quieter area. Here only a handful of people were rushing around and they all seemed to know exactly where they were going. Katie paused for a moment to catch her breath. The long night of traveling was beginning to catch up with her and she rolled her head back and forth to try to stretch the aching muscles and wake herself back up.

"Here," Finlo spoke in her ear. "Let me see if I can help." His hands came down warmly on the back of Katie's neck and he began to slowly and methodically work the exhausted muscles. Katie could feel the tension in her spine draining away and her knees suddenly felt weak underneath her. She closed her eyes and for a long moment surrendered to the wonderful warmth and pressure that was Finlo's touch. She breathed out a long sigh and then dragged herself back to reality.

"Thanks," she told him, stepping away from further temptation, "but I mustn't hold you up all day. I'm sure you have lots of other things to do besides flying me to the island."

"There aren't many things I would rather do than spend time with a beautiful woman," Finlo smiled easily, "but you look totally done in, so maybe I should concentrate on getting you somewhere where you can have some sleep. We can work on getting better acquainted once you're recovered from your travels."

His smile made it obvious that getting to know her better was something that he was looking forward to and Katie felt herself blushing and feeling flustered again.

"I am really tired," she told him, really trying to reassure herself that that was why she was behaving uncharacteristically.

Katie had never been very good at flirting or the dating game. It had never really mattered. She hadn't dated much in high school and then she had fallen madly in love with a teaching assistant at the university where she had earned her bachelor's degree. They had been together from her freshman year there until three months ago. Now, suddenly single for the first time in ten years, Katie didn't think she was ready for a man like Finlo Quayle.

Finlo led her down a long hallway and outside. A sudden gust of cool air surprised Katie. "Wow, it isn't as warm here as it was at home," she told him.

"Wait until we get to the island," Finlo answered. "Because of its location, it never gets particularly warm or cold. If it hits the seventies in the summer, we all run around in shorts, trying to get a tan and complaining about the heat."

Katie giggled. She lived and worked in southern Maryland, where summer temperatures reached triple digits and most people spent all of their time in front of their air-conditioning units avoiding the sun.

"But you don't get a lot of snow, either, do you?" she asked.

"No, not much. Not any most years, actually. Once in a while we get a half an inch or so and everything stops for a day while everyone looks out at it and wonders what to do."

Katie laughed now. "We get a couple of feet every year at home," she told Finlo. "And we still go out and go to work and everything. I won't be here come winter, of course," she added as an afterthought.

"What a shame," Finlo answered, in full flirting mode again. "But at least you will be seeing the island at one of its most beautiful times of the year. In the winter, while we don't get snow, we do get a lot of rain and high wind."

"All those poor small children." Katie grinned. "You can't build a rainman or a windman. What do the kids do all winter long?"

"I guess they stay inside and watch telly," Finlo answered. "Children aren't really my thing," he told her with a wink. "I haven't felt the need to procreate, at least not yet. Maybe I just haven't found the right woman yet?"

Something in his eyes suggested to Katie that he was measuring her up for the role. Something in his attitude told her that he was just talking nonsense in an attempt to get her into bed. While Katie had little personal experience of men, she had been teaching college-aged boys for over five years and she had a pretty finely-tuned ear for lies and half-truths. She hesitated for a moment, wondering how best to reply. Finlo saved her having to figure it out by stopping short next to a small plane.

"Here we go. This is my baby. Well, one of them anyway." He grinned at Katie. "Maybe my planes are the reason I don't have kids?"

He grabbed Katie's bags and loaded them into the open cargo area of the plane. "Climb up and hop in."

Katie climbed the short flight of steps up the door of the airplane. As she stuck her head inside the tiny cabin she was surprised to find someone already seated in the back.

"Oh, sorry," she said in a flustered voice. By now Finlo had shut the cargo door and had followed Katie up the steps.

"Never mind him," Finlo told Katie. "That's just Jack, my co-pilot, navigator and air hostess."

The man rose lazily to his feet. He was taller than Finlo by several inches and in the tiny airplane cabin he seemed almost as wide as well. He looked to be in his sixties with broad shoulders and a full head of long gray hair. His green eyes twinkled at Katie as he reached her.

"Air hostess, my arse," he told Finlo. "He's damn lucky I keep working for his pretend airline. I could work for one of the big ones and actually get paid what I'm worth." This time he spoke to Katie, but clearly the words were intended for Finlo.

"Ha! You do get paid what you are worth. Exactly nothing," Finlo answered. Katie could tell this was a conversation that they'd had frequently.

Finlo turned to Katie and smiled at the confusion on her face. "Jack is an old friend of the family," he explained. "He retired from an international carrier about two years ago and is bored at home, so a couple of times a week he flies with me. It works out well for both of us, because he gets a break from his wife and I get a cheap qualified co-pilot."

Finlo turned back to Jack. "This is Dr. Kincaid, by the way. She's coming to the island to do some research at the institute."

"Pleased to meet you, Doctor," Jack grinned. "I have to say that when I was at school the professors didn't look anything like you. Then again, I've never met anyone visiting the institute that looks like you either."

"Stop flirting and start the ground checks," Finlo told Jack in a mock-stern voice.

"Aye, aye, captain," Jack mocked straight back. He winked at Katie as he made his way past her into the cockpit of the plane.

"As you are our only passenger today, you can have your choice of seats," Finlo told Katie. "They are all window and aisle seats, of course."

Katie turned and looked at the cabin of the small plane. There was a narrow aisle with seven seats on each side of it, each one positioned next to a tiny window. The seats were small, but Katie thought they looked slightly larger than the ridiculously cramped ones that had been on her transatlantic flight. At the rear of the cabin there seemed to be a small toilet on one side and some storage cabinets on the other. Katie sank down into the closest seat, tiredness catching up with her again.

"I'm afraid there won't be much to see out the window for now," Finlo told her apologetically. "There is a lot of fog here and I'm pretty sure there will be a lot on the island as well."

"Never mind," Katie answered. "I'm not sure I could keep my eyes open to look anyway."

"Just relax, then. We have a few pre-flight checks to get through and then we just have to wait for clearance to take off. The flight itself will only take about an hour. We should be landed at Ronaldsway in less than two hours, if we can get a take-off slot without too much trouble and the worst of the fog holds off."

"Sounds good," Katie felt like her voice was coming from far away. All of her earlier excitement had faded now and exhaustion was wining out over her desire to see London. Finlo found a blanket in an overhead compartment and placed it over her. Katie murmured her thanks, barely audibly.

Twenty minutes later, with all the pre-flight checks completed, Katie was fast asleep in her seat.

2

"Sorry, Mark, I'll be up in a minute," Katie mumbled as she shifted in the seat, trying to steal a bit more sleep.

Finlo touched her arm again. "Katie?" Finlo spoke softly. "It's Finlo. We're here, on the Isle of Man."

Slowly the words penetrated Katie's fuzzy brain and she began to try to bring herself awake. As she woke, she realized what she had said and wondered if she had actually spoken Mark's name out loud or if that had been part of a dream. She opened her eyes and looked curiously at Finlo. Surely he would say something if she had called him by someone else's name.

Finlo merely smiled at her and then gestured out the window.

"We're here, safely landed on the Isle of Man. Welcome, on behalf of Quayle Airways. For the record, you didn't miss much. There was fog and cloud from take-off until landing."

"I can't believe I slept," Katie told him as she struggled to her feet. "I've never managed to sleep on an airplane before."

"You were exhausted. Traveling across the ocean will do that. And I bet you weren't sleeping well before you left, either. You were probably too excited about your big adventure." Finlo smiled at her.

"No," Katie answered. "I haven't been sleeping well." Though not only for the reason that Finlo suggested.

"You may find that the Island's air is a great cure. Many people find, when they first arrive, that all the sea air helps them sleep. You do get used to it after a while, though," Finlo told her.

"Sea air? I hadn't thought of that." Katie smiled. "Right now I'm so tired that I can't believe I will ever have trouble sleeping again."

She knew, however, that once she was over her initial tiredness, all the things that had been keeping her awake would be back. She just hoped that the three months on the island would help her recover. Time cures all, she told herself for the millionth time. The next three months would provide her with lots of time to forget about what she had left behind.

"Now I've got a question for you," Finlo told her. "Do you want to go straight to the institute and get some rest or would you prefer a short driving tour of the island?"

Katie felt a wave of excitement wash over her. She had been too tired to think about it, but now she suddenly realized that she was actually here, on the Isle of Man. She had wanted to visit for years. Here she could do some serious research, with actual and original sixteenth and seventeenth-century documents. Even more exciting, she could visit the places that were mentioned in the documents. Castle Rushen, Peel Castle, Rushen Abbey. She ran through a mental list of the places she most wanted to see. Katie suddenly felt wide-awake and could barely contain her enthusiasm.

"Oh yes, please," she told Finlo, her eyes sparkling. "I would love a quick tour."

"No problem," he grinned at the dramatic change in her. "I give lots of tours to our visitors. We won't actually stop anywhere, but I'll drive you around and point things out. You can start to get a feel for the island and where things are."

Katie nearly jumped out of her seat and began to gather up her things. She was down the steps as soon as Finlo opened the door and took a deep breath of the fresh sea air. Manx air, she thought to herself.

Small islands and other minor kingdoms and principalities had always fascinated her. It amazed her how their history could mirror that of their larger neighbors for years or it could go off in a totally different direction entirely. The Isle of Man was a particular favorite for some reason that Katie had never quite figured out.

Perhaps it was because it had managed to maintain its independence for centuries in spite of its larger and more powerful neighbors. True, it was a Crown Dependency, but it had its own stamps, currency and, most importantly, government. Tynwald was the world's oldest continuously operating parliament and it still met once a year in the open air where all of the previous year's laws were read out in public and anyone on the Island could present a grievance to the government.

The idea of being able to complain directly to the President of the United States was unthinkable, but perhaps the U.S. would be a better place if a similar thing could happen somehow there as well.

Katie had studied English and European history for her Master's Degree, focusing on islands like Man and the Channel Islands. For her doctorate she had studied the Isle of Man more intensely, specializing in those times when its larger neighbors had most influenced the Island's history.

From Viking invasions to Scottish rule, through the English Civil War to Revestment, when the rulers of the Island sold some control of the Island to the English Parliament as they struggled to cope with smuggling, Katie had been continually captivated by the rich history of the Island. She had always loved the idea of visiting England and seeing all of the places she had studied over the years. As she finished her doctoral research, she decided that the Isle of Man was definitely top of the list.

While she'd pored over maps and photos of the Island with great interest, she'd never been able to save up enough money to fund a trip outside the U.S., in spite of years of trying. Her parents had done well to fund her years of study, from undergraduate work through to her doctorate, but they couldn't afford to pay for a trip to Europe either.

A grant opportunity to study the island during the Civil War period had finally arrived at just the right time. The Manx History Institute was working on an extended history of the island and they were eager to find someone to do some new research into that period. Katie had been ecstatic when she received the letter confirming that she had been selected. The grant would pay for her to travel to the island, provide accommodation for three months and also pay her a small stipend that would help to cover the cost of meals and transportation for her during her visit.

In exchange, she had agreed to contribute a chapter to the extended history. Katie was convinced that she would be able to provide a great deal of original and interesting material to that volume. She could hardly wait to get started. On a personal level, the trip had come up at just the right time. The best way to deal with the crisis at home was to get away for a while and a three-month study trip was an ideal excuse to do so. Now, actually standing on the ground on the Isle of Man, Katie could barely contain her impatience as Finlo finished shutting down the plane.

Finlo smiled as he watched Katie tapping her foot impatiently. "Come on, then," he told her as he collected her bags from the ground where Jack had unloaded them. "I can see you are eager to get going." He quickly led her through the small airport and out into a sunny but cool day.

"But don't I have to go through passport control or something?" Katie asked.

"No, there's no passport control here. As long as you are cleared into the United Kingdom you can come and go from the island without any problems."

"But don't I get a stamp in my passport from the island, then?" Katie sounded disappointed.

Finlo laughed. "I'm really sorry," he told her, "but I don't think the island has a special stamp for its visitors. I'll have a word with my M.H.K. the next time I see him and let him know that you complained, though."

Katie knew he was talking about his "Member of the House of Keys" which was the island's parliament. It would be like Katie talking to her senator if she ever happened to meet him. What was exciting was that, on a small island like this, Finlo might actually know his M.H.K. personally.

She smiled. "Sorry, I'm being silly. I've just never traveled abroad before and I was looking forward to going home with a whole bunch of stamps in my passport to show off to my friends."

"Well then, we will just have to make sure you do some more traveling, won't we?" Finlo answered easily.

"I'm not sure how much time I'll have." Katie didn't want to encourage the man too much.

She was determined not to get her heart broken again, at least not so soon after the last time. Finlo Quayle seemed like the type that broke women's hearts without a second thought. "I'm here to do some very intense research. And I have to write a chapter for a book before I go as well," she told him seriously.

"I'm sure you can manage some fun as well," Finlo told her, not seeming at all discouraged as he led her through the parking lot to his expensive sports car. "Here we are," he told Katie as he used the remote to unlock the doors. "Hop in."

Katie looked over the tiny and obviously expensive car. "Are you sure my bags will fit in?" she asked doubtfully.

"No problem," Finlo answered as he unlocked a large van that was parked next to the sports car. "Jack can take your bags up to the institute and drop them off. He lives in Douglas anyway, so it isn't even out of his way. Then they'll be waiting for you when you arrive."

Finlo finished loading Katie's bags into the back of the van just as Jack arrived.

"The plane is all checked in and locked down," he told Finlo. "I'll drop the bags off and I'll see you tomorrow around ten."

"Great, thanks, Jack," Finlo shook hands with his friend and climbed into the driver's seat of the high-priced car.

"Thanks for taking care of my bags, then," Katie spoke over the top of the car as she prepared to climb in. "I really appreciate it."

"Not a problem," Jack answered as he climbed into his van and drove away.

Katie slid into a buttery-soft leather seat that seemed to mold to her contours. A sigh slipped out as she realized the car probably cost more than she made in a year. Clearly there was good money in owing an airline.

Finlo grinned at her. "It is a great car," he told her. "A real indulgence, but I'm worth it."

Katie smiled at the arrogance in the remark. Finlo's mocking grin made the remark far less offensive than it might have been.

"Buckle up and we'll get underway," he told Katie.

Katie fumbled with the seatbelt and then sat back. "I'm ready," she told Finlo, barely suppressed excitement in her voice. She was going to see the Isle of Man.

Finlo smiled and started the car's engine. It roared to life with an expensive growl and Finlo drove expertly out of the airport car park. He was silent as he negotiated the tight corners in the car park and then the exit gate but began the tour as he drove to the roundabout that marked the entrance and exit to Ronaldsway Airport.

"To the right is the road to Douglas," he explained to Katie. "I'll just take a short detour left, down into Castletown, and run you past Castle Rushen."

Katie struggled to control her excitement. Castle Rushen was medieval in date and Katie had never seen any standing structures that were that old. Not only was it old, but it was also the site of several important events in the history of the Island, most notably where the Earl of Derby and his family stayed during the Civil War. Katie intended to spend a lot of time at the castle, soaking up its atmosphere. She was sure that it would add another dimension to her research.

Finlo drove easily through the ancient narrow streets of the former capital of the Island. The village looked charming and picturesque to Katie as she looked first one way and then the other as they drove. Suddenly, in front of her, was Castle Rushen. Katie found herself frowning.

"I thought it would be more isolated from the town," she blurted out. "I mean, it is lovely, but I thought it would be surrounded by a moat or something. I don't know what I mean. I saw lots of pictures but none of them made it look so close to the rest of the town."

Finlo smiled. "I'm sorry if you're disappointed. It really is a very nice example of a medieval castle, even if it hasn't got a moat or anything. Peel Castle is actually on its own little island. Maybe that will impress you more."

Katie frowned. "I didn't say I wasn't impressed," she argued. "Just that it wasn't exactly what I was expecting. I'm sure it is wonderful inside and I really can't wait to see it. I'm not disappointed, just surprised."

Finlo drove through a tiny parking area and then pointed to a small building in front of them. "There is the Old Grammar School," he told her. "It was originally a church, but was used as a school from 1570 until the 1930s."

Katie gasped. "1570? That is less than a hundred years after Columbus discovered America and well before the first colonies were set up there. It's strange to think that my country wasn't even being settled yet, and there was already a school here. I've really focused on the Derbys and the castles in my initial research, but maybe I need to think about the more ordinary people as well."

Finlo drove back through Castletown, pointing out the Old House of Keys and the Nautical Museum as they went. Katie felt herself being drawn deeper into her enthusiasm for the island and its unique history and culture. If she'd had even a tiny bit more energy she would have insisted that they stop so she could actually visit some of the sites that Finlo was pointing out to her. On the way out of Castletown, he drove past Rushen Abbey and Katie twisted her neck to try to see around the gates to get a view of the ruins of the ancient abbey.

"There is not much to see there, really, though the archaeologists do their best," Finlo told her. "There are only a few ruins left, though there is a small scale reconstruction of how it might have looked when it was active and archaeologists dig there all summer long. You can usually drop in and find someone in a pit to tell you about the latest finds. They have special open days to encourage everyone to come and see what's new in what is old, if you see what I mean."

Katie laughed. "Rushen Abbey is a bit too early for the research I'm here to do, but it fascinates me all the same. Again, it's something really old. And it is definitely on my 'must see' list for my visit."

Finlo smiled. "Are you sure you will have time for research?" he teased her. "It sounds like you want to sightsee more than anything."

"I can't do one without the other," Katie argued. "Seeing the sights will help me to put my research into context. It will help me really understand how the Island worked. At least, I hope it will."

The last sentence was said under Katie's breath as she looked around at the Manx landscape that was flashing past the car windows. Katie had seen pictures of the palm trees, but somehow seeing them for real made the place seem even more magical.

They sped back past the airport now and along a winding road. Katie sat back and relaxed for a moment. Finlo slowed down suddenly.

"Wave to the Little People," he instructed Katie, as he waved out his side window towards the side of the road while they were passing over a small white bridge. Katie quickly followed his lead and waved in the direction of the bridge. As they passed over it, Katie could see a tree that seemed to be covered in notes and ribbons.

"What was that?" she asked curiously.

"Fairy Bridge," Finlo answered in a serious voice. "It is where the Little People live, we never call them fairies, even though the bridge is called Fairy Bridge. Everyone on the island knows that you have to wave or at least nod hello to them as you pass over the bridge or you will have bad luck."

Katie started to laugh, but stopped short when she realized that Finlo was serious. "What was going on with the tree, then?" she asked.

"People leave notes and presents for the Little People," Finlo answered. "I've never done that, but I do make sure I always say hi."

Katie found herself torn between finding the whole thing ridiculous and thinking it was a lovely idea.

"I think you'll find that most people on the Island, whether they're superstitious or not, make a point of saying hi to the Little People," Finlo told her, still obviously taking the whole thing seriously.

"Okay," she replied doubtfully.

"When I was ten," he continued, "we had a school trip to Castle Rushen and everyone on the bus waved when we passed over the bridge. All except for George Greene. He was from 'across,' as we call England, and he laughed at us. The next week, on the very first day of the summer holidays, he fell down some steps and broke his arm in two places. He spent the entire summer holiday in a cast and didn't get to have any fun. We all figured he got what he deserved."

Finlo grinned at the amazed look on Katie's face. "I'm not sure if the Manx are more superstitious than the average American or not, but I am sure we all believe in the Little People."

Katie smiled at him and shook her head. "I don't walk under ladders and I'm not crazy about Friday the thirteenth," she told Finlo. "So I suppose I can't really say much about your Little People. I think the whole idea is charming, anyway, whether I believe in it or not."

They both fell quiet for a short time then, both lost in their own thoughts. Actually, Finlo may have been lost in thought, but Katie was struggling to stay awake. Finlo looked over at her after a few minutes and smiled.

"I think we can leave the rest of the tour for another day," he told her. "You look totally done in and I think you need to get to the institute and get some sleep. My services as a tour guide are always at your disposal, though. Please don't hesitate to ask."

"Thanks," Katie answered him. "I might just take you up on that."

They drove in silence then for the rest of the short distance into Douglas and to the building that housed the Manx History Institute.

3

The institute was housed in the middle of a row of old Victorian terraced houses that stood proudly right on the seafront in central Douglas. Katie watched the waves crashing into the beach for a moment as Finlo parked along the wide promenade than seemed to run for miles in each direction, curving along to match the contours of the beach. The terrace was now mostly made up of hotels and boarding houses and each one had been painted to suit the personality of its owner.

Katie looked in surprise at the pink, blue and green houses that were all joined together but seemed to each have their own individual personality. The institute building itself had been painted a very subdued cream color that seemed drab when compared to its more colorful neighbors. Katie supposed that it was appropriate for an academic building, but she couldn't help but wish that someone had been a bit more adventurous with the paint choice. She loved the brightly colored buildings that marched cheerfully along the seafront, seeming to welcome visitors and residents alike.

Katie made her way up the steps to the front door of the institute, casting a last look over her shoulder at the Irish Sea. The tide was in and the water seemed to be splashing dangerously close to the wide promenade full of children on bikes and scooters, adults pushing strollers and older men and women walking carefully with sticks. Katie knew she would enjoy the view even more once she'd had some much-needed rest.

Finlo shouted "hello" as he walked in the front door of the building and after a moment a voice answered back. "I'm in the office."

Finlo grinned and opened the first door to the right along the short hallway that opened off the front door.

"Hey, Ealish, I have your new professor here," Finlo announced as he swung the door open wide and ushered Katie inside. "Katie Kincaid, this is Ealish Christian, the Assistant Director of the institute."

Katie smiled at the young woman who was sitting on the floor in the large room they had just entered. The room was clearly used as an office, with a large desk along the wall in front of them, just in front of the window. The desk contained all of the usual office equipment, including what looked like a state-of-the-art computer. File cabinets dominated the left wall, with piles of papers threatening to spill off the tops of every cabinet. The right side of the room was lined with book-shelves, all crammed to bursting with books and magazines.

The limited floor space was covered in piles of papers. Ealish Christian sat in the middle of the mess, with a large pile of papers on her lap. She smiled as Katie and Finlo walked into the room and then started to get up from the floor.

At first glance, Ealish looked to be in her mid-twenties, with long straight hair worn in a simple low ponytail. She wore little or no makeup and was dressed in jeans and T-shirt advertising Manx National Heritage. A closer look revealed the beginnings of smile lines developing around her mouth and at the corners of her eyes and the odd gray hair mixed among the rich brown tones on her head. Katie guessed that she was closer to thirty-five than twenty-five.

"Oh, please don't get up on my account," Katie told her, watching the other woman struggling to stand with piles of papers in her lap and all around her.

"I won't, then, if you're sure you don't mind," Ealish laughed. "Now I'm down here, I'm not sure I'll ever be able to get myself out. I'm feeling a bit swamped in paper, though, so I will have to get up eventually."

Katie smiled at the older woman. "If I can help, just let me know how," she offered.

"Thanks, but Jane should be back any minute now and she can help me finish the sorting. Jane is the office secretary, by the way. She'll be able to help you with lots of things, once you get settled in. She only works part-time, so we often end up with piles of papers that never seem to get sorted or filed. I offered to help her tidy up the filing, but every time we start something another emergency seems to come up and things just get thrown together into a pile for later." Ealish shook her head.

Katie grinned. "I know exactly what you mean. My office back home is full of piles of papers. I never seem to find time to file anything."

The two women smiled at each other in understanding. Katie felt much better about her three months on the island now. She was fairly certain that she had already found a woman who would be a good friend.

"Ealish, I'll leave Katie in your capable hands," Finlo interrupted. "I've got to get back to the office and get some paperwork done."

"Thanks for collecting her from London for us," Ealish answered him. "Bill us as usual."

Finlo nodded at Ealish and then turned to Katie with a dazzling smile. "Once you get settled in, I hope you'll let me take you on the rest of the tour," he told her, taking her hand and, instead of shaking it, holding it tightly. "I'd love to show you more of my home."

Katie blushed under his intense gaze, feeling sparks flying up from their clasped hands. "I'd like that," she finally muttered, pulling her hand away gently.

"I'll call you in a few days." Finlo promised, reaching a hand up to brush a stray hair off her cheek. As he turned and walked out of the room, Katie let out a breath that she wasn't aware she'd been holding. All of her tiredness seemed to flood back as if Finlo had been somehow supplying her with energy.

"Watch that one," Ealish spoke from the floor. "All flowery words and promises he is, but only in the beginning," she told Katie.

Katie felt stung. She hadn't encouraged Finlo, but she'd enjoyed the casual flirting and didn't see the harm in it. She didn't like being told what to do, especially by a total stranger. Before she could reply to the warning, however, Ealish shouted past her.

"He's gone now. Come on down and meet Katie."

A few seconds later, Katie heard footsteps and then the door was pushed open more widely. The young woman who came through it was strikingly beautiful and Katie immediately felt how grubby and unattractive she must look after her long journey.

"Hi," the woman smiled at Katie and held out a perfectly manicured hand. "I'm Jane Robbinson, the institute secretary. I hope I'll be able to help you while you are here."

Jane looked no more than twenty-one with silky smooth skin that was enhanced by expertly applied makeup. Her hazel eyes looked enormous under dark lashes and her long blonde hair was casually, but skillfully styled. She was slender, with a tiny waist, but still curvy and was dressed in a stylish business suit that managed to look professional but still sexy.

Katie's first thought was, meanly, that the girl should have been called Barbie, such was her resemblance to the iconic toy. The name Jane somehow seemed insufficiently glamorous for such a beautiful young woman. Katie realized suddenly that she was staring and not speaking.

"Oh, I'm sorry," she spoke rapidly to hide her confusion. "I'm really tired and I think at least half of my brain has shut down. It is nice to meet you. I'm not sure how much help I'll need while I'm here, although at the moment, I feel like I need help just walking and talking."

Jane smiled kindly. "Traveling is hard work," she agreed. "I've never been further than Blackpool and even that tired me out."

Ealish stood up now and handed her pile of papers to Jane. "Here, dear, you find a place for these and I'll show Katie to her room. I think the best thing for everyone is if she has a long nap."

"Sounds heavenly," Katie agreed at once. She was looking forward to getting to know both Ealish and Jane better, but for now sleep was the only thing that held any appeal.

Katie followed Ealish up two flights of stairs, struggling to listen to and remember what she was being told.

"Jane runs the office on the ground floor, where we just were. Behind that is a small kitchen area with tables that we use for small meetings. You can just about squeeze eight people in there if they are all good friends. The first floor has the administrative offices. William Corlett, the institute director, has his office there and so do I. There are two other offices on that level that are shared between the five associates who teach courses through the institute. You can have space in one of those offices as well, while you are here, if you don't want to be working in the flat all the time."

She paused for a minute to let Katie catch her breath before she headed up the next flight of stairs. "Up here, we have a large conference room that can seat about twenty. We also use it as a classroom for the courses that we teach when we have more students than will fit in the room downstairs."

Ealish paused now in front of another door. "This is the door to the top floor flat." she told Katie. "It has its own lock and key and a separate entrance from the back of the building so that you don't have to come in through the main building if you don't want to."

She handed Katie a ring of keys and then used one on her own ring to open the apartment door. "I'm sorry we can't give you a key to the front door of the building, but we've had too many go home with our visitors. When you go in and out after hours you will have to use the back door. If you prefer, while you are staying, I can give you my spare key to this door and the one in the back. Then you will be the only one that can get into the apartment."

Katie smiled. "And then, if I lock myself out, I'm stuck, aren't I?"

Ealish grinned. "We do prefer to keep a key, for that very reason. But I like to offer as well. Some researchers are very secretive about what they are doing and don't want anyone to have access to anything."

"I'm not secretive, but I am possessive," Katie answered. "Someone stole some of my research once before, so I keep everything on my laptop very well password protected. My cousin is a computer expert and he's taught me a lot about how to protect and keep my work safe. My only worry about you having a key is that you will find out how messy a housekeeper I am!"

"As long as you leave the place in reasonable condition when you leave, what you do while you are here is up to you. And that includes whether you dust or hoover or wash up or not. It also includes having visitors. You have your own entrance and the institute shuts at five anyway, so for the most part your private life is just that."

She looked hesitantly at Katie. "In the past, however, it has been deemed helpful for our guests to inform us if they are having people to stay for more than a day or two. I would be grateful if you would let me know if, say, your parents are coming to visit for a month or a boyfriend is moving in with you."

Katie smiled. "My parents can't afford to come for a month or even a weekend, unfortunately. And at the moment I can't imagine anyone besides me will be staying upstairs. I will let you know if anything happens to change that."

"Thanks." Ealish answered. "You wouldn't believe the kinds of things that have gone on in the past," she told Katie. "When you are rested up and want to waste an afternoon, I'll tell you some horror stories."

"I'd like that," Katie answered. "I suspect I will be one of your most boring guests ever."

"Boring can be good," Ealish smiled. "At least the police won't be coming to get me out of bed to deal with complaints if you're boring!"

"Police complaints? Goodness, that does sound interesting," Katie smiled.

Ealish grinned back. "It all makes a good story now, but it wasn't fun at the time. One night after you have your body clock sorted out, we can get a couple of bottle of wines in and I'll tell you the whole story. I'll tell you a few stories about our favorite airline pilot as well, explain why I warned you about him."

"I will definitely look forward to that," Katie answered. "But you don't really need to warn me about Finlo. I've sworn off men for the foreseeable future."

"Well, if you don't mind talking about it, we can include your reasons why in our drunken evening," Ealish suggested.

"I don't mind, especially if I can have a glass of wine or two before I start," Katie answered with a smile.

"Right, let me get you upstairs and show you where everything is before you fall asleep on your feet."

Ealish turned the door handle and pushed the door open. Immediately behind the door was yet another flight of steep steps. Katie followed Ealish to the top and then stopped to get her bearings. Her two suitcases had been set neatly on the floor near the top of the stairs.

"Jack dropped those off on his way past," Ealish told Katie, waving a hand at her bags. "At least you were saved having to drag them up all the stairs."

"I hope you didn't have to do it." Katie was appalled at the idea of someone else having to do such hard work on her behalf.

"Oh no, don't worry about that!" Ealish laughed. "Jack and William carried them up and Jack was happy to be repaid with a cup of tea and a chocolate digestive."

As Ealish spoke, Katie looked around slowly. At the top of the stairs was a small landing, just about big enough for Katie, Ealish and the suitcases. A single step up took Katie through an open door into the apartment.

The door led to a large room that was furnished with a comfortable-looking couch and two chairs. The pieces didn't actually match and none of them were new, but they were all clean and neat. A low table had been placed in front of the couch that was centered between two windows on the furthest wall from the door. In the corner nearest to Katie was a small stand that held a television and a DVD player. Katie moved into the room and turned slowly, taking it all in.

"This is the lounge or living room, call it what you like," Ealish smiled. "The telly only gets the basic channels and reception is a bit hit or miss. If you are a real telly addict, I can talk to William about whether or not we could have a satellite dish installed. You would have to pay for it, though, and I'm not sure that they would let you have one for such a short time."

"It doesn't matter," Katie was quick to reply. "I'm not much of a television watcher and I don't plan on wasting much time on it while I'm here. I've only got three months and I have a lot of research to do and then a whole chapter to write. Television will be a very low priority. I assume the DVD player works if I get desperate for something to do?"

"It worked the last I knew," Ealish answered. "There are a few old movies rattling around in a box in the bedroom. I think we have a complete set of all the videos about the island as well, so if you are really bored you can have a look at some of them."

Katie smiled. "Actually, I probably would enjoy that, when I'm not out seeing the real thing!"

"There isn't a telephone up here, either. We used to have an extension of the institute's line in here for guests to use, but one guest spent hours tying it up with endless calls to his girlfriend so we finally removed it. There is a phone in the conference room downstairs that you are welcome to use. We never lock that door. If you call the U.S., though, you will have to charge it to your credit card."

Katie nodded. "I will probably stick to email to talk to my family, anyway," she told Ealish.

"If you want to get a mobile phone to use while you here, I can help you get that sorted out tomorrow or whenever."

"I don't think I want one," Katie grinned. "The less people can bother me while I work the better."

Ealish grinned back at her. "Well, let me know if you change your mind." She walked across the large room and began to open the doors along one of the walls. "Here's the kitchen," she told Katie.

Katie walked over and looked into the small room. Again everything was dated, but looked clean and functional.

Ealish continued. "There is a microwave as well as a traditional cooker and hob. There is a kettle and a toaster as well and the fridge is under the counter behind the table."

Katie looked it all over. One wall was taken up with the cooktop and oven, what Ealish had called a "cooker and hob", as well as a sink. The counter on that side was cluttered with small appliances, with a microwave fighting for space with the toaster and kettle. There was a small table with two chairs pushed up against another wall to provide an eating area. A single window took up much of the wall above the table. A short counter ran along another wall, with cupboards underneath. Katie looked twice, trying to locate the promised refrigerator, finally realizing that it was the small white box hiding between the cupboards.

She had had a similar unit in her college dorm when she was younger. She opened it and found a carton of milk, a couple of cans of cola and a bottle of white wine inside.

"I thought you might need a drink of something once you arrived," Ealish explained. "I've put bread and a few other staples in the cupboard as well."

"It is just so tiny," Katie found herself speaking her thoughts aloud. "The fridge, I mean. Not the apartment."

Ealish laughed. "All of our American guests are amazed at the size of the fridge, but many English families live with a fridge this size, even large families."

Katie shook her head. "I guess, with the language and everything, I sort of forgot that I was in a foreign country. But some things are totally different from home."

"There is another fridge like this in the kitchen downstairs, so if you really need to keep more things cold than you can fit in here, feel free to use some of the space in there as well. As long as we can fit a carton of milk for tea in it, you can use what you need of the rest of the space," Ealish offered.

"Thanks, but I really can't imagine that I'll need that much room. Mostly my fridge at home holds drinks and leftover takeout food."

Ealish moved back out into the main room and opened the next door. "Here is the loo," she told Katie, stepping back to let Katie have a look.

Katie grinned. That was one English word she knew for sure. The loo was the bathroom. The room was small, but seemed to have all of the standard equipment, including a shower over the tub.

"And here is the bedroom." Again, Ealish stood out of the way so Katie could look inside. This room was larger than the kitchen had been, but smaller than the main room. A double bed filled nearly all of the space, with a large wardrobe against the wall taking up most of what was left. A small bedside table with a lamp on it completed the furnishings. Again, nothing was new, but it was all clean and well-looked after.

"I'm sure I'll be really comfortable here," Katie told Ealish.

She was actually delighted with the small apartment. It was nicer than she'd hoped. When they had offered her the use of it, she had worried that it would be a single tiny room in a cramped corner of the building. Having an entire floor and a separate entrance felt quite luxurious.

"We're happy to let you use it," Ealish answered. "When we have visiting researchers it is nice to have a place where they can stay. Hotels can get very expensive after a short while and I know what sort of salaries academics get. We are hoping to be able to buy the boarding house next door in the foreseeable future. The plan is to use that as apartments for visiting academics. Then we can turn this apartment into more office and classroom space for the institute."

Katie could tell that Ealish was excited about the idea. "Of course, it all comes down to money, or lack of it," Ealish concluded a bit gloomily.

"Like everything else in academia," Katie answered with a grin.

"Yes, I suppose so," Ealish smiled at her. "Now I'll leave you to unpack and get settled in. It's lunchtime and Jane and I usually get sandwiches from the coffee shop on the corner. Would you like anything or are you going to get some sleep?"

Katie hesitated. "I think, actually, I would prefer to get some sleep before I do anything else," she began slowly. "I can't believe that I'm actually not hungry. I'm usually always hungry. But right now I'm just too tired to be hungry."

Ealish smiled. "Right then, you get some sleep and if you wake up before five, I'll be downstairs. After that you'll probably be on your own. There is a list of telephone numbers by the phone in the confer-ence room if you need anything. Otherwise, I'll be in at nine o'clock tomorrow morning."

She headed towards the door and then turned back. "If you go out the back door of the building and down the alley towards the promenade and then turn left, about four doors down is a hotel with a coffee shop that does takeaway. You can get sandwiches and things until eight o'clock at night. We only have one pizza delivery place, and that number is by the phone as well. They deliver until midnight. Otherwise, there are always biscuits and tea and coffee in the kitchen downstairs, if you fancy a little something but don't want to go out. We never lock the kitchen, either."

Katie smiled at Ealish. "Thanks for all that. I'm sure I'll be fine. I'll crash out for a few hours and then come down and you can tell me all of that again so I remember it."

Ealish frowned. "Do you want me to write anything down for you? Directions to the closest coffee shop or anything?"

"Don't be silly," Katie answered her new friend as she led her towards the door. "Even if I sleep until the middle of the night and then wake up starving, I have bread and milk, thanks to you. I won't starve to death before you get back in the morning!"

"I'll leave you to it then," Ealish smiled at her. "Come down when you get up or else I'll see you in the morning."

"Thanks for everything," Katie told her, her eyes feeling heavy and gritty and desperate to close.

Katie followed Ealish down the stairs and made sure that the door was shut and locked behind her. Then she climbed back up and opened her suitcases. She quickly found an oversized T-shirt and crawled into it. She grabbed her makeup bag and headed into the small bathroom.

Unlike most American bathrooms, with countertops and cabinets, this bathroom had a pedestal sink. Katie looked around. Where could she keep all of her toiletries? For now, she simply dropped the bag on the floor after she'd dug out her cleanser. She grabbed a washcloth from the pile of towels on the side of the bath and gave her face a thorough cleaning.

With the makeup that had been applied more than twenty-four hours earlier scrubbed off, Katie felt better than she had in hours. She quickly brushed her teeth and her hair before heading back into the main room. She went from window to window, pulling all of the curtains shut and then slipped into the bedroom.

Katie shut the curtains on the single bedroom window, frowning, as they seemed to do little to block the sunlight that was still coming in. She pulled back the covers and sheet and climbed into the spacious bed. Her head hit the feather pillow and Katie sighed deeply with satisfaction. Whatever else happened to her on this visit, she figured she would sleep well in this incredibly comfortable bed.

Her brain seemed reluctant to shut down, however, and Katie found herself lost in thoughts about Finlo Quayle. Her mind endlessly replayed his gorgeous eyes and the feel of his touch as he'd massaged her neck at the airport. Katie groaned and tried to think of something else.

Her brain mocked her by filling itself with memories of Mark. Katie flipped over crossly, determined to think of something other than men and the trouble that they caused. Katie forced herself to focus on where she was and why and a small bubble of excitement at the job in front of her was Katie's last conscious thought for many hours.

❦ 4 ❧

When Katie woke up, the room was totally dark and she was completely disoriented. She sat up with a start and looked around the unfamiliar space in confusion. The clock on the bedside table read 21:43 and Katie struggled to understand what that meant or even where she was.

As the clock changed to 21:44, Katie's tired brain finally clicked into gear and she remembered where she was and why. She stretched and climbed out of bed, brushing her hand along the wall, searching for a switch to turn on the overhead light. Katie blinked at the sudden brightness that filled the room and then she looked at her watch to try to figure out the time and was then surprised to find that it was nearly ten o'clock. She had slept for nearly twelve hours and had missed her chance to spend any more time with Ealish that day.

Katie sighed and padded out of the bedroom and into the main room of the small apartment. She flipped on the television, struggling to find something to watch on the few channels that were actually available. After a few frustrating minutes, Katie decided that the television was a wasted effort.

She paced back and forth across the room, trying to figure out what to do next. She had a paperback that she had started already somewhere over the Atlantic, but it had failed to hold her interest on the plane and she doubted it would do so now. She also had a magazine and a book of logic puzzles, but neither held any appeal.

She felt restless and ready to start the day. Unfortunately, it was nearly ten o'clock at night and the rest of the island was heading to bed. Katie sighed again and decided that she might as well try to get her body clock in sync with the rest of the island and head back to bed. There was only one problem with that decision. Now that she was awake, she was absolutely starving. There was no way she could get any sleep until she'd had something to eat.

Katie padded into her tiny kitchen and began to search for food. She could barely remember the dreadful airline food that she had eaten shortly after take-off so many hours earlier. They had offered something for "breakfast" just before landing, but Katie had been too excited and too tired to try it. Now she felt like she could eat anything and everything.

Ealish had mentioned a coffee shop nearby, but the thought of getting dressed again and brushing her hair seemed like way too much effort. She dug out the loaf of bread and popped two slices into the toaster. She slid the handle down and watched in surprise as the bread popped back up immediately. She looked at the tangle of cords behind the toaster. Something was plugged into the electrical outlet above the small appliances, but apparently it wasn't the toaster. Too tired to try to sort out the mess of cords and plugs, Katie sank down at the small table and tried to think.

"Biscuits", she suddenly remembered. Ealish had told her that there were biscuits in the kitchen downstairs. And biscuits to the English were cookies to Americans.

"I hope there are some chocolate chip ones," Katie thought excitedly as she headed for the stairs.

The promise of chocolate renewed her energy in a way that toast never could have. Katie unlocked her door and shuffled down the remaining two flights, still dressed only in an oversized T-shirt, her feet bare. The large building was dark except where a few lights must have been left on for security reasons. The main light in the entrance hall was lit so Katie was easily able to find her way around when she reached the bottom of the stairs. She turned to head down the short hallway to the institute kitchen and ran straight into someone who was just coming out of it.

"HELP!" Katie screamed loudly, struggling to get away from the dark figure that was now holding her tightly to him. After a moment of sheer panic, Katie realized that whoever was holding on to her was laughing quietly.

"This is NOT funny," she shouted at the trespasser, struggling to break free from the hold. "Who are you and what you are doing in here?"

She knew that the emergency number on the island was 999 rather than 911, but she couldn't remember where she'd seen a telephone or figure out how to get away from the intruder to make the call.

"Sorry," said a deep male voice, and then Katie was released.

"You must be Dr. Kincaid," the intruder continued, laughter still evident in his soothing tone. "I don't think I've ever met any of our researchers under such, um, interesting circumstances before."

Katie's brain was still in fight or flight mode and it took her a moment to make sense of what the man was saying. " Who are you?" she finally sputtered out.

"I'm William Corlett, the Director of the institute," he replied.

Katie thought suddenly that she might have preferred a burglar to meeting her new boss under these circumstances.

"Come on in the kitchen and I'll make us both a cup of tea," he offered gently. "I was just raiding the biscuit tin, and you look like you could use a biscuit and a hot drink."

Katie followed William in silence, struggling to figure out the right thing to say in the awkward situation. William switched on the kitchen light and Katie blinked in the additional brightness. While he was busy filling the kettle and finding clean mugs, Katie sat down in one of the comfortable chairs that dotted the room and studied him silently.

He was much younger than she'd been expecting. All of her correspondence with the institute had been with Ealish, who was responsible for coordinating researchers. Katie had imagined that the Director would be an old, gray-haired university professor with forty years of teaching under his belt. The man now making her tea looked to be in his mid-thirties. He was about six feet tall and was far more muscular than any professor she had ever seen before.

Katie's knees felt weak when she remembered the strength in the arms that had briefly held her. William turned towards her and handed her a cup of tea. For a moment neither spoke as they each hugged their mugs and studied one another.

William wasn't strikingly handsome, but he was definitely attractive, in spite of the fact that he looked very tired. He was obviously working late and tiny lines were evident in the corners of his eyes. The eyes themselves were an amazing grayish green color that reminded Katie of the sea that she had stared at so eagerly earlier in the day. His hair was a rich brown shade and it needed combing rather badly.

Katie had to hold her mug more tightly to resist the urge to reach out and straighten the few stray strands that stood out at odd angles. She guessed that when he was working he unconsciously ran his fingers through his hair.

"You look tired," Katie spoke almost without thinking.

"I am tired," William agreed with a warm smile that made Katie flush. "I've been working late on the final draft of a report that needs to get to the publishers in the next twenty-four hours. I think I've just about cracked it, but I still need a few more hours to finish it."

"Can I help?" Katie asked. "I'm a pretty good typist if that is any good to you." She found herself wanting to help William for all sorts of reasons, not least his incredibly beautiful eyes.

"I wish you could. Unfortunately, it is all typed up and ready to go, I'm just checking and rechecking for mistakes. Unless you are an obsessive expert on Manx archaeology, you aren't going to be able to spot those." William smiled again and Katie felt another rush in the pit of her stomach.

"Sorry, I'm not much of an expert in anything at the moment," she told him. "Hopefully, in three months' time I'll be an expert on the island during the Civil War period."

"We could certainly use an expert in that," William told her as he pushed off from where he had been leaning on the counter. "Now, how about a biscuit or two?" He held out a large tin that was nearly full of cookies.

Katie looked into the tin and frowned. She had been eating cookies her whole life but none of these looked familiar. "Okay," she said to her companion, "tell me what they all are and I'll try some."

William laughed softly, a sexy sound that flustered Katie yet again. "Where is your sense of adventure?" he asked Katie. "Just try one and see what you think of it."

Katie blushed. "I'm not all that adventurous with food," she told him. "And what I really want is something chocolate. I'd hate to dig through the whole pile trying to find a chocolate one if there aren't any in there."

William's eyes burned into hers for a moment. "Not adventurous with food. That leaves a lot of other areas for adventure still open."

He smiled at her, sending her heart racing and her eyes to the floor. Katie was suddenly aware that she was only wearing a large T-shirt and panties. She wished she had thought to pull on a bathrobe before she came downstairs. She hadn't been expecting to run into anyone, least of all an incredibly sexy man.

"If it is chocolate you are after, you need some of the special biscuits," William told her. He turned around and dug through a cupboard.

While he was searching, Katie tried to pull down the hem of her shirt, painfully aware that she hadn't bothered to throw on a bra.

"Here we go," William told her as he turned back around. His eyes smiled, as he looked her up and down. Her belated attempts at modesty had not been lost on him.

"Ealish always keeps a box of these hidden in the back of the cupboard for emergencies," he told Katie, holding out a box to her.

Katie took the box and used it to cover her knees as she studied it. The front showed a pile of various types of cookies, all smothered in a rich coating of chocolate. Katie turned the box over and found a "menu" with a photo and a description of each type. Katie felt her mouth begin to water as she read the various descriptions.

William laughed as he watched her reading the box. "If only I get a woman to look at me that way," he teased as he took the box from her and opened it.

"Please help yourself. I'm going back upstairs to get a bit more work done. Stick your head in and let me know when you go back upstairs, okay?"

"No problem," Katie answered absent-mindedly, as she studied the list again, wondering where to start.

William shook his head and left the room, muttering darkly about men being replaced by chocolate in the evolutionary game.

Katie held her breath until she heard his footsteps overhead, and then she let out a big sigh. She gave up pretending to study the biscuit packet and sat back in her chair. That man was a dangerous package. He was attractive, but not too good-looking for his own good. Even worse, he seemed like a really nice man, who knew exactly how much to flirt before stopping.

Katie figured she could resist the rather more obvious charms of someone like Finlo Quayle, but a man like William Corlett was more worrying. He seemed to be exactly her type: charming, funny, and he could make a cup of tea and find chocolate biscuits in the middle of the night. Katie gave herself a mental shake. She wasn't going to waste any of her short time on the Isle of Man with men. Even the nicest and most wonderful of them couldn't be trusted. She'd learned that in the hardest possible way. Chocolate biscuits, they were the way forward, she told herself sternly.

Half an hour later, stuffed full of more biscuits than she could count, Katie made her way up the stairs. She paused on the first floor and looked around. There were four doors that opened off the small landing, but only one door stood open, with lights blazing. She peeked around the corner.

William was sitting with his back to the door surrounded by papers. Katie realized that he hadn't heard her approaching and took a moment to study the office. There wasn't much to it, besides shelves of books and piles of paperwork. One section of bookshelves held boxes labelled with site names and Katie guessed that they would be full of archaeological finds from those sites.

What was missing in the office was anything of a personal nature. There were no photos of William with a wife, girlfriend or lover. There weren't even any plants. All offices needed a few plants in her opinion. Katie frowned. Maybe William was too dedicated to his work. She'd met a lot of academics like that over the years. She watched him for another minute and then self-consciously knocked on the door.

He didn't look up and Katie waited a moment and then knocked again more loudly.

"William? Mr. Corlett?" Katie wasn't sure what to call the man who was, at least on some level, her supervisor for the next three months. "You wanted me to tell you when I was going back upstairs."

Katie wondered now if he was hard of hearing or something. She was about to speak again, when he spun around in his chair. He blinked at her twice as if trying to regain focus.

"Oh, sorry," he told her. "I was lost in a bit of pottery there. Have a good night then. I'll probably see you tomorrow."

He was clearly immersed in his research and Katie suspected that he'd forgotten she was even in the building before she'd knocked. She shrugged and called "good night" over her shoulder as she climbed the rest of the stairs to her apartment.

She felt a bit let down over the dismissive way that he'd treated her as she said good night. While she had no intention of getting involved with anyone during her stay, she wouldn't have minded a little more harmless flirtation. She locked her door tightly behind her and climbed the last few stairs slowly. She felt the events of not only the last twenty-four hours or so, but also the last several months, catch up with her and threaten to overwhelm her. Full to bursting of tea and chocolate biscuits, she climbed back into the soft bed carefully and flopped down on the pillow.

"Okay, Katie," she told herself in a stern voice, "no dreams about Mark or Finlo or William. Tonight you need to dream about how happy you will be being single and on your own. No one to have to cook and clean for, no one to shave your legs for, just yourself to please."

Katie shook her head as an evil little voice whispered, "No one to cuddle up with, no one to make you tea in the middle of the night, no one to travel the world with." Katie shushed the little voice and rolled over on to her side. She squeezed her eyes tightly shut and forced herself to relax. As tiredness caught up with her, she felt herself finally falling back to sleep. Her last conscious thought was wondering whether William or Finlo would be the better kisser, though she had no intention of finding out.

Katie had set her alarm for seven, but she was awake by six, her body clock still nowhere near aligned with her new location. She took a long hot shower and dressed carefully in a pair of dressy pants and a new top. She spent extra time fussing with her hair and makeup, determined to make everyone forget how awful she must have looked the previous day.

At five past nine, she headed down the stairs, carrying her briefcase containing her laptop, pads of blank paper and a dozen pencils. She raced past the first floor, feeling embarrassed at the thought of seeing William again after the previous night's encounter. A large box held the door to the office open and the front door to the building had been left ajar, allowing cooling sea breezes to waft down the hallway and cool the heat coming in the windows from the brightly shining sun.

Katie stuck her head into the office cautiously, calling "hello" as she did so.

"Oh, good morning," Jane replied, looking up from her desk. "You must have been really tired yesterday. We thought you would come back down, but you never did."

"I was exhausted," Katie agreed, walking into the room. "But I'm feeling much better now and I'm eager to get started on my research."

"Ealish is in her office if you want to talk to her about anything," Jane grinned. "William hasn't come in yet, but by the look of things, he was here late last night, eating all the posh biscuits."

Katie blushed. "Actually, I was eating them, I ran into William about ten o'clock last night and he said it was okay to help myself. I was starving but too lazy to go out and get any real food."

Jane smiled. "It doesn't matter. Ealish or I will get more the next time we are shopping. William has a bad habit of eating them when he works late, so we are always buying more boxes. Did you manage to get some breakfast this morning?"

"Yes, I had some toast."

Katie had spent ten minutes untangling cords and then figuring out how to make the toaster work, but once she'd done that part, making toast had been easy.

"Ealish left me some cereal as well, but I'm going to need to get to a grocery store soon or else the rest of those chocolate biscuits will be in grave danger," she told Jane.

"There is a ShopFast right behind us two streets back. That's the big locally owned supermarket chain," Jane told her. "They should have everything you need and it isn't too far to walk with bags."

"Maybe I'll try to get there this afternoon," Katie replied. "I'm really anxious to get to the museum for now and start looking at some of the documents I've preliminarily identified as useful."

"The museum is only a few doors down, but they don't open until ten," Jane replied. "So you might as well go and have a chat with Ealish if you don't feel like grocery shopping straight away."

Katie frowned. "Not until ten? I didn't realize that. I suppose I should check in with Ealish anyway."

"Go on up. I'll buzz her that you are coming so she can hide the magazine and try to look busy with work," Jane laughed. "If it still isn't ten when you finish with her, come back down and we can have a chat until ten. You can tell me your life story."

"Thanks," Katie grinned. "But that wouldn't take more than two minutes and you would probably fall asleep midway through it!"

Jane grabbed her phone and buzzed Ealish to let her know that Katie was on her way up as Katie headed for the stairs. Katie paused on the landing, unsure of which office belonged to Ealish, as all four doors were tightly shut this morning. Suddenly one of the doors flew open and Ealish popped her head out.

"Good morning," Ealish called out in a cheery voice. "Glad you see you looking as if you feel a bit better."

"I'm feeling lots better, thanks," Katie replied, trying to inject some of the same enthusiasm into her own voice.

"Don't mind me," Ealish told her. "I'm a morning person. I'm always really cheery and full of energy first thing, but I slump after lunch. Most people would rather talk to me after lunch as I'm more calm and less relentlessly cheerful."

Katie had to laugh at Ealish's own description of herself. "I think I can just about manage 'relentlessly cheerful' this morning," she grinned at Ealish.

"Good, come on in and sit down, then," Ealish offered, opening her door wide and gesturing Katie into the room.

Katie stepped over the threshold and smiled. The room was very like William's and indeed like most academics' offices. Piles of books vied for space with piles of paperwork. A computer was perched on the end of the desk and its keyboard was being used to hold a book open to a particular page. Ealish lifted a stack of books off a chair in the corner of the room and motioned Katie into it.

"I'll just drop these over here," Ealish muttered as she looked around the room for a place to relocate the books she was now holding.

Katie had to laugh as she watched Ealish struggle. "Maybe we should just go down to the kitchen and have a chat there?" Katie suggested after a few moments. "Then you can put the books back on this chair."

Ealish laughed as well, dropping the books onto her own desk chair and pushing the hair that had fallen out of its rubber band off of her forehead.

"Come on, then," Ealish agreed. "We can eat up some of the biscuits that William opened last night as well, before they go stale."

As they headed down the stairs, Katie felt obliged to confess to being the late-night biscuit raider. Ealish only laughed again.

"Right," Ealish smiled once they had sat down with a plate of biscuits between them and a cup of tea each. "What shall we talk about?"

Katie smiled. "Well, I'm eager to get started on my research," she told the other woman. "Is there anything I need to know before I get to the museum?"

Ealish thought for a minute. "You need to talk to Marjorie Stevens. She's the head librarian and archivist. She's been in charge of the records over there for nearly twenty years and she knows exactly what she has and what she doesn't. She should be able to point you in the right direction. The problem is finding time to talk to her, because she's such a busy person. I suggest you go over at ten and try to get an appointment with her for some time today. Then forget about looking for anything until after you have talked to her. You will only be wasting a lot of time and effort trying to find anything anyway."

"That sounds like good advice," Katie replied. "If she can't see me right away I'll head to ShopFast and get my shopping done first. All this traveling has made me lose track of days. It is Friday today, isn't it?"

"Yes, so we aren't open tomorrow, but the museum is. You should be able to get some research done if you want to. Personally, I think if you get a chance to meet with Marjorie today, you should take the weekend off and start fresh on Monday. That way we can have a bottle of wine and a laugh tonight and get to know each other better. Of course, it is up to you."

Katie hesitated. She was very eager to get started on her research, but she didn't want to offend Ealish. Besides, it had been years since she spent a night drinking and gossiping with the girls. While she had been involved with Mark, he had discouraged her from spending time with her girlfriends. This trip was important for her career, but Katie was also hoping it would help her get herself back on track emotionally. A night of drinking and bonding with Ealish might just help with that goal.

"Wine and laughter sound like the perfect evening," Katie agreed with Ealish. "I'd love a chance to get better acquainted. Maybe Jane can come as well and we can all tell all of our deepest secrets and complain bitterly about men!"

Ealish laughed. "That's exactly the sort of night I had in mind," she told Katie. "I'm sure we can get Jane on board as well. To bashing men and drinking too much." She held up her teacup in a mock toast to Katie.

"Cheers," Katie laughed as she tapped her mug into Ealish's.

"Good morning, all," a voice called from the doorway. "Nice to see everyone in such a good mood this morning."

It was William, and he looked as if he was wondering what Ealish and Katie were finding so funny this early in the morning. Katie's eyes cut over to Ealish's and the two women burst out laughing, making William look uncomfortable.

"Right, well, I'll get to work then," William told them curtly. "At least someone should be doing something productive around here," he said, grabbing a biscuit and then turning and leaving the room.

"Oh dear," Katie sobered instantly. "You're not in trouble because of me, are you?" she asked Ealish worriedly.

"Oh no, no worries. William is just grumpy because he is over-tired," Ealish answered. "But he is right, I should be working. Shall we agree to meet in your flat at six then?" Ealish asked.

"Six is fine," Katie answered. "When I get to ShopFast I'll get a frozen pizza or something so that we can eat as well as drink. Should I get white wine or red?"

"I prefer white, but I've no idea which is correct with frozen pizza," Ealish laughed again. "Get whatever you like and I'll bring a bottle of my favorite, as well. And I'll invite Jane and tell her to bring a bottle, too."

Ealish left Katie sipping her tea and nibbling yet another chocolate biscuit. Before she knew it, it was ten o'clock and time to head out to the library to begin the hard work that was the real reason for her being there.

$\mathscr{E}$ 5 $\mathscr{E}$

Ealish had been right that Marjorie was very busy, but she managed to find an appointment for Katie at two o'clock that afternoon. With the morning suddenly free, Katie headed back down the street to the institute building. Armed with directions from Jane, she headed into the city itself for a look around central Douglas and a chance to do some shopping.

Her first stop was a branch of the local bank, where she traded in some traveler's checks for a pile of brightly colored Manx money. As she tucked it carefully into her wallet she reminded herself sternly that, even though it looked like play money, it was very real and actually in short supply. Then she walked the length of the pedestrianized street of stores, peering into shop windows and wandering into the most interesting looking stores for a closer look.

She spent a happy ten minutes, studying the various chocolates available at an amazing chocolate store. She finally selected a handful of assorted truffles, the price of which seemed entirely reasonable until she converted pounds to dollars in her head and realized what she had really spent. She justified the expense as a special "first day in a new country treat" and then headed off to the supermarket, determined to spend as little as possible.

An hour later she felt as if her head was spinning as she waited in the checkout line. She only hoped that she could use what she had in her cart to make something edible back at her apartment. She had walked into the store convinced that the island was a lot like home. Now she had confronted a number of differences that had left her feeling unsettled and incredibly homesick.

She looked again at the bags and boxes she had selected. She hoped that "plain flour" was something like the "all purpose flour" she bought at home. "Granulated sugar" seemed the safest best for mixing into her tea and coffee, though she did wonder at "caster sugar" and "Demerara Sugar". At least the "icing sugar" was in a clear plastic bag, so she was fairly sure that it was what she would call "confectionary sugar", which obviously wouldn't do for mixing into hot drinks.

She looked over her shopping again and reminded herself that she was in a foreign country. Things were bound to be different here. She just needed to remember that. As she transferred her shopping to the moving belt she tried to add everything up to figure out how much she had spent. Even with her quick math work she was still surprised at the size of the grand total.

Katie paid for the shopping out of the money she had just received and frowned when she saw how little she had left. She would have to be very careful for the next week until she was due her first stipend payment. Loaded down with shopping bags, Katie headed back to her apartment, planning to use the back entrance. It was closer and it also meant she would be spared having her shopping looked over by anyone that happened to be in the institute when she arrived. Katie was used to her privacy and she wasn't sure how living on top of a public building was going to work out. She couldn't complain, however, as she couldn't afford any alternative.

Katie walked as quickly as she could through the winding alleyways that led to the back of the institute. She was lost in thought and struggling with the heavy bags and consequently missed seeing William until she ran straight into him.

"Oof," she breathed out as she crashed into his arms, only just managing to hold onto her overfull bags of shopping.

"Steady on there, Katie,"

Katie could hear suppressed laughter in his voice yet again.

"Sorry, I didn't see you coming. I was trying to get my car open," he steadied Katie on her feet and then took a step backwards. Katie saw now that he was standing next to a rather old and battered-looking car that might have been white when it was new, many years earlier.

"Sorry," Katie told him, trying to ignore her suddenly racing heart.

She worried that the sudden jump in her heart rate was more due to the closeness of the man in front of her than the shock of the encounter and she frowned to herself. "I wasn't watching where I was going. I was thinking about other things," she explained.

"No harm done," William's eyes twinkled at her. "Let me help you with those bags."

Katie protested, but William ignored her and took several of the heaviest bags from her fingers. Katie quickly used her now free hand to unlock the door to her apartment, and William followed her up the stairs and set her bags down in the middle of the living room floor.

"There's only one parking space for the building at the back there," William explained. "As our guests rarely ever bring their own cars, I usually use the space. I'm here the most and it saves me having to worry about parking. Jane and Ealish have permits that let them park on the promenade when they need to, though Ealish can easily walk to work from her flat and Jane often walks when the weather is fine."

"Thanks for helping with my shopping," Katie smiled at William, unsure of what else to say.

"I'm happy to help," he told her. "I'll just be on my way, then. Ealish said you were going to try to arrange a meeting with Marjorie for today. Have you managed it?" he asked her as she followed him back down the stairs so that she could lock up behind him.

"Yes," Katie answered, checking her watch. "In fact, I only have an hour to grab some lunch and then I'm due back at the museum."

"Good luck with Marjorie. She should be a big help to you," William smiled and waved as he walked back to his car and climbed inside.

Katie made her way back up the stairs, annoyed with herself for letting the man get her flustered yet again. She quickly unpacked her shopping, added another bottle of wine to the one already in the fridge and checked her appearance. Her carefully done hair and makeup had disintegrated in the sunshine and exercise of the morning and Katie frowned at what she saw. She quickly threw together a sandwich and ate it standing in the kitchen. Then she brushed her hair back into place and reapplied powder and lipstick in an attempt to look professional for her meeting.

At two o'clock she presented herself at the museum library, notebook in hand, ready to meet with the formidable Marjorie Stevens. By three o'clock, when she left the library, Katie was feeling deflated. Marjorie was happy to have someone on the island who was interested in the Civil War period and was prepared to tackle some research into it, but she'd quickly set Katie straight as to the difficulty of the job she was facing.

The good news was that there were piles of documents and records from the period. The bad news was that nothing was indexed or catalogued, let alone transcribed and readily available. What Marjorie could offer her was a pile of boxes full of books, loose papers and miscellaneous documents that dated from the period. What she was hoping to get back was a list of what Katie had found. Katie was used to working from transcribed copies of original documents. This would be a very different sort of project.

Marjorie had provided her with a few photocopies of a handful of documents from the period and Katie could see right away that she was going to have problems. The writing was virtually impossible to read to her untrained eye. She was going to have to learn how to read seventeenth-century handwriting before she could tackle the original documents.

Katie walked back into the institute feeling like she had bitten off more than she could chew. She couldn't imagine how she could possibly manage to learn enough in the next three months to be able to write an entire chapter about Manx history. Learning to read the old documents would probably take three months on its own. Katie sighed as she climbed the front steps to the building. Applying for the grant had been an impulsive decision, based on wanting to get away from home and from Mark. Now it seemed like she might live to regret her impulsiveness.

She entered the building in a gloomy mood and stomped past the open office door and straight for the stairs.

"Hey, how did it go with Marjorie?" Ealish called from the office where she was busy photocopying.

"Not great," Katie turned and stepped into the office. Jane was filing and William was signing a pile of letters and putting them into envelopes. Three sets of eyes now focused on Katie, as she stood framed in the doorway.

"Wasn't Marjorie helpful?" William asked, frowning.

"Oh, she was as helpful as she could be," Katie answered. "I just didn't realize how difficult the handwriting was going to be to read. I suppose I thought everything would be neatly transcribed and indexed and I would just have to dig through the lists of documents to find the ones I wanted. Instead, Marjorie has about ten boxes full of miscellaneous documents and even she isn't sure what is inside most of them."

"The library simply doesn't have enough staff to do what really needs to be done with the materials they hold," William told her. "When they're lucky enough to have a research student or a volunteer, they get a few boxes indexed, but they tend to trust students and volunteers with the more modern materials only. The seventeenth-century documents that you need to look at are irreplaceable. Marjorie doesn't let just anyone even look at them. I doubt she has ever had anyone on staff who was actually capable of reading and transcribing them."

"So do you have any suggestions as to what I might do?" Katie asked him, determined not to give up at the first obstacle. "How I can learn to read the documents quickly so that I can do the research?"

"I don't know how quickly you can learn," Ealish spoke up. "But I'm happy to help you as much as I can. My area of expertise is actually earlier, the fourteenth and fifteenth centuries, but I can read seventeenth century handwriting as well. I can certainly give you some tips and help you out with a few documents."

"Helping Katie is great," William smiled to soften his words. "But remember that you have a full-time job here. You can't do Katie's work for her."

"I can do what I like after work, though," Ealish spoke quickly as she saw Katie's face fall. "Besides, seventeenth-century hand isn't all that difficult once you get your eye in. I bet you'll pick it up quickly enough. And anyway, I'm sure there is plenty of material that you can use that won't be a problem. If you want to do any demographic analysis, for example, the parish registers are all transcribed. There aren't many from that early, but there are some and you'll be able to use them easily. Don't worry too much for now. You have three months and I know there is a lot of material available. I'll bet that you find enough material for your chapter plus a lot more."

Katie smiled gratefully at Ealish. "Thanks so much. I'm not sure it will be that easy to 'get my eye in' as you put it, but I'm feeling a lot better," she told her and the others.

"Marjorie told me she had a few documents she had copied to get you started. Did she give you anything?" Ealish asked.

"Yes, but I can't make sense of them at all," Katie confessed.

"I think you need to take the weekend off and then we can make a start on Monday morning," Ealish told her. "I've got a space in my diary at nine on Monday so you can come in for an hour and we can tackle the documents that Marjorie gave you. I'm sure I can help steer you in the right direction from there."

Katie was touched by the other woman's willingness to help. "Are you sure it is okay to use up your time during office hours?" She glanced over at William, worried that he might object.

William just laughed. "I don't mind Ealish giving you an hour of her time. Part of her job is to look after the researchers, after all. I just don't want her spending all of her time working on your transcriptions, that's all. I think Ealish is right. You need to take the weekend off and explore the island a bit. You will feel more optimistic once you are settled in and have caught up on your rest. How about..."

William was interrupted there by the front door opening suddenly and a loud voice shouting, "Hey, anyone here?"

Finlo stuck his head around the door and beamed at everyone. "Hey, Ealish, you look great today," he began.

"Jane, love, how are you?" he asked as Jane colored brightly and resolutely turned her back on him.

"William, everything good?" He smiled at the other man and then turned to Katie who was standing just inside the door.

"Katie, just the woman I wanted to see. I couldn't figure out how else to find you, so I came here looking for you. I have a big party of pensioners to fly home tomorrow, but I have Sunday off, so how about we have a proper tour? I'll take you around the castles and we can grab lunch somewhere nice? Pretty please?" He turned the full wattage of his dazzling eyes and smile onto her and Katie found herself feeling powerless to resist.

"I would like to see the castles and more of the island," she found herself agreeing.

"Great, I'll collect you from here at half-nine and we can be at Castle Rushen when they open at ten." He dropped a kiss on the top of her head and called a quick "bye" to everyone as he left as suddenly as he had arrived.

Katie stood open-mouthed when he had gone, feeling completely overwhelmed by the man.

"What time is half-nine?" Katie asked weakly as Finlo disappeared.

Ealish laughed. "We do speak totally different languages, don't we? Let's see, half-nine is nine-thirty and a diary in America is an appointment book. Pensioners are people past retirement age. Does that clear up all the Brit-speak from the last ten minutes?"

Katie grinned. "I hope so."

"Well, I suppose I should be getting back to work," William stood up and quickly disappeared up the stairs.

"Me too," Ealish followed him. "See you at six," she told Katie as she raced up the stairs.

"Did I say something to upset William?" Katie asked Jane.

"Finlo usually has that effect on him," Jane answered. "But I'll tell you all about it tonight. Especially if you are going out with him on Sunday."

"It's hardly a date," Katie answered quickly. "He is just being nice and showing me around."

"You don't know Finlo," Jane replied. "He never does anything to be nice."

With Jane's words echoing in her ears, Katie headed up the stairs herself. She was beginning to feel quite tired again, and decided that it would be good to lie down for an hour before Ealish and Jane arrived for their wine and pizza.

Katie felt much better a few hours later when the women arrived. Ealish brought two more bottles of wine and Jane brought a third. Katie was quick to open the first bottle as she turned the oven on to heat up for the pizzas.

"Right, Katie first," Ealish demanded. "Tell us your life story. Everything interesting, please!"

Katie laughed. "About the only thing interesting that has ever happened to me is that I've got to come to the Isle of Man to do some research," she told the others. "Up to now, I've led a very dull life."

"Oh, come on, that can't be true," Jane insisted. "What about all those gorgeous hunky American men? I can't believe you haven't had loads of boyfriends?"

"I wish," Katie grinned, pouring herself a glass of wine. "Would you believe that I've only had one serious boyfriend in my whole life? And he turned out to be a lying, cheating, scheming, manipulative creep."

"Now that's what we mean," Ealish shouted as she gulped wine. "Tell us the whole story, please, please!"

Katie took a big swallow of her own wine. She liked Jane and Ealish, but she wasn't sure she was ready to tell them the whole sorry story. Maybe she needed another glass or two of wine first. She said as much with an apologetic smile, but Jane and Ealish only laughed and encouraged her to drink a little faster.

"While we wait for the wine to hit, Jane can tell you about Finlo," Ealish said decisively.

Jane shook her head. "Steady on there, Ealish, I think I need another glass of wine as well before I start divulging all my secrets."

Ealish sighed dramatically. "Honestly, you two are just postponing the inevitable. Right, then, shall I tell you both all of my secrets then, while I wait for the alcohol to loosen your tongues?"

Katie grinned. "Go on then, spill," she demanded.

"Yes, go on, Ealish. If there is anything you haven't already told me," Jane grinned. "Ealish and I have been friends for over a year, ever since I took the job here," she explained to Katie. "I've heard most of

Ealish's stories many times over, but I'm always a little drunk when I hear them, so I usually forget some of the juicy details. And Ealish's stories always have juicy details."

Katie laughed. "This should be fun, then."

Ealish spent the next hour regaling the other two with stories from her past. Growing up on the Isle of Man had limited the selection of men available to her, but once she'd headed across to the University of Liverpool she had made up for lost time. Jane and Katie laughed until they cried as Ealish told them about being caught nearly naked in a little used section of the library, being propositioned by a senior member of the history department who tried to convince Ealish that going to bed with him would help her to write a better thesis, and moving into a large and luxurious home to live with her first serious boyfriend, only to find that his parents had been on holiday for the two months they had been dating, but still very much lived in the house she was now occupying.

Ealish was a natural storyteller and she didn't mind making herself look ridiculous if it made the story funnier. Katie forgot all about cooking the pizzas until suddenly her tummy rumbled loudly and she realized that they hadn't eaten anything yet. She dashed into the kitchen and threw the pizzas in the now red-hot oven, setting the oven timer so that they wouldn't forget to take them out. She grabbed another bottle of wine on her way back to the others.

Having heard so many of Ealish's stories, it would have been rude not to tell her own and Katie was feeling more than ready to tell the others about Mark now. They'd finished one bottle of wine and were working through a second, but Katie didn't feel terribly drunk, just rather happy. She was enjoying the company of other women for the first time in a long time and she felt like she hadn't laughed so much for years.

"Okay," she announced as she sat back down. "I suppose I should just tell you about Mark and get it over with."

"Go on, then," Ealish spoke kindly, clearly realizing that Katie's story wouldn't be funny or easy for her to tell.

"I think my first mistake was not dating more in high school," Katie began slowly. "I went out with a few boys but I didn't really date anyone more than once or twice. I'm not sure if I put them off because I had such serious academic plans or if there just wasn't enough chemistry or what. I suppose it was obvious to them that I wasn't going to jump into bed with them, so they didn't see much point in asking me out a second time."

"Ah yes, teenaged boys," Jane laughed. "They're about as subtle as sledgehammers when it comes to what they want."

Katie laughed. "Well, I made it clear they weren't going to get it and, consequently, I didn't go out much. So I went off to college pretty naïve. And I met Mark during Freshman Orientation Week. He was a senior, in his last year of undergraduate work and he seemed so grown-up and mature to me then. He was studying history as well. He was interested in the same sorts of things I was interested in. He seemed just perfect. By the end of my freshman year, Mark and I were actually engaged. I was only nineteen, but I was so sure he was the man I wanted to spend the rest of my life with, that I was over the moon." Katie shook her head at her own stupidity.

"We all think we know everything when we are nineteen," Ealish winked at her. "You should have seen the knuckle dragger that I was dating when I was nineteen. I didn't dare bring him back to the island to meet my parents. They would have disowned me."

Everyone laughed and Jane refilled the wine glasses. Just then the oven timer began to sound and everyone crowded into the tiny kitchen to fill plates with slices of pizza. Once all three girls were comfortable in the main room again, pizza balanced on laps and wine glasses to the ready, Katie continued.

"Mark did his Master's Degree and his Doctorate at the same school where I was studying, so we never had to be apart. He finished his dissertation the year after I finished my Bachelor's Degree, while I was working on my Master's. It all seems so long ago, really. He was hired immediately by the history department to teach and he was on track for tenure. I finished my doctorate a few years later and we were all set to get married and live happily ever after."

Katie paused there and ate a slice of pizza thoughtfully. Things had gone wrong somewhere in that space of time. Katie had already spent hours going over and over again the various things she might have done differently. Now, with a little bit more perspective she wondered if she really wished she'd done things differently any longer. Looking back now, maybe she and Mark were better off apart. Maybe they shouldn't have stayed together as long as they did.

Katie sighed and then realized that Jane and Ealish were watching her expectantly. She laughed. "Sorry, I got lost in thought there," she told them. "Somehow, sometime after I finished my degree, and before we actually got down the aisle, everything went wrong. I'm still trying to figure out exactly where."

"Well, maybe if you tell us the rest of the story, we can help you figure it out," Ealish offered. "We have a fresh perspective, as such. Maybe we will see something you didn't."

"I'm going to tell you the story anyway," Katie grinned. "Fresh perspective or not, but it will be interesting to see what you think." She took a deep breath and then continued.

"After I finished my doctorate, I joined the history department as well, and got on the tenure track. We were the perfect academic couple, really, both teaching and researching and helping each other along. I became a very popular professor with the students. Mark wasn't as popular with the kids, but he was good at research and very good at getting his work published. We were both on track to get tenure and have long happy careers with the same university where we had both met and studied."

Katie paused again for a big sip of wine. "Anyway, after a year or so we started planning an extravagant wedding. I had the big white dress, we had a sit-down dinner for over a hundred people planned, a great local band, everything really, all ready for the 15th of June, this year." Katie paused again, watching her audience for reactions.

"But that's next week," Ealish exclaimed, as she and Jane both looked shocked.

"Yep, I was supposed to be getting married next week," Katie admitted with a rueful smile.

"You didn't chuck it all in because of the grant to come here, did you?" Jane asked, sounding shocked.

Katie laughed. "No, I applied for the grant after the wedding was cancelled," she reassured her. "I needed to get away, somewhere

where I wouldn't have to see sympathy in everyone's eyes as they said hello."

"So what happened?" Ealish spoke quietly. The mood in the room was suddenly serious.

"Oh, nothing terribly unusual, I suspect," Katie tried to sound flippant, but only managed bitter.

"Just before Christmas, the head of the department called me into his office. Someone had raised some concerns about the possibility of one of the students cheating. That isn't that unusual, actually. A lot of kids try to get away with things, especially with all the stuff available on the Internet these days. The schools have to work hard to stay on top of it. Anyway, the girl in question was in one of my classes and her roommate had reported that she had seen exam questions from my final exam in their room the week before the exams were given. The head wanted to know where copies of the exam questions had been kept, and who might have had access to them. And he also wanted me to read over some essays that the girl had submitted to another professor in the history department. The head was convinced that the girl was plagiarizing something off the Internet, because the essays were too well-written to be the work of an undergraduate." Katie stopped and drew a shaky breath. The story had been easy to tell so far, really, but this was the tough bit.

Jane and Ealish both smiled encouragingly and Ealish patted Katie's hand. "You don't have to tell us, if you don't want to," she said, though it was clear from her voice that she was dying to hear the rest of the story.

Katie had to smile at that. "You would never forgive me if I stopped now," she grinned. "Besides, I need to tell you. I need to be able to move on and talking about it will help."

"If you're sure," Katie could hear the relief in Ealish's voice.

"I'm sure," Katie took a deep breath and big drink of her wine and plunged into the rest of the story. "Anyway, when I read the essays I was shocked because I recognized them very well. They were practically a word-for-word copy of an article I had just submitted for publication. The only question was how this undergraduate had managed to get a copy of my article, when it wasn't even published yet."

Jane shook her head and Ealish muttered under her breath. Katie was pretty sure they had already guessed the rest of the story.

"Yep, Mark. The essay in question had been written for Mark's class. And he knew quite well that it was plagiarized because he had proofread the article for me before I had submitted it. Once the head called him into the office, he was good enough to confess everything, which I suppose I should be grateful for. It could have been a lot worse if there had been a full investigation. But I wasn't prepared for what he was going to confess. I thought that she had broken into his office somehow and stolen the exam questions and my paper. I guess I was naïve, but up until the very last possible moment, I believed that Mark would be able to explain everything and that everything would be okay."

"Men are bastards," Jane shouted, guzzling the rest of the wine in her glass and hunting around for the bottle.

"Do you want to finish the story or should we guess the rest?" Ealish shook her head.

"Oh, I'll finish," Katie was determined now. Mark had hurt her badly, but in telling the story she felt herself growing stronger.

"Though I'm sure you've figured out what I couldn't see until Mark told me himself. He had been having an affair with the girl. She was more than ten years younger, a student of his, and, let's face it, not very bright. But he had seduced her, or allowed himself to be seduced by her, and then he found himself in a real mess. He had stolen my exam questions for her, he had stolen my paper and let her use it as her own essay, and he had helped her cheat in another class as well."

Jane leaned over and refilled Katie's wine glass and all three women took a long drink before Katie continued.

"Obviously, everything blew up then. Mark was fired. I dumped him immediately and cancelled the wedding. We had bought a house together and it took months to disentangle our lives. In the middle of all of the chaos, I remembered that I had seen something in some journal about the Manx Institute accepting grant applicants for the summer. I had read it the first time and thought that it was a shame I would be on my honeymoon during the summer and couldn't apply. Now I had nothing to stop me. I threw the application together in between moving out of the house and selling my dress on the Internet. I never actually expected to get the grant, but I needed to be doing something that was forward-looking in the middle of all that sadness."

Katie stopped now and blinked back the tears that were threatening to gather in the corners of her eyes.

"What an unmitigated, first class, grade-A, arsehole," Ealish shouted.

"I can tell you exactly where it all went wrong," Jane told Katie. "When you got mixed up with that slime ball in the first place."

"I can't believe that he did that to you after all those years together," Ealish told Katie. "Thank God you didn't actually marry him or have children."

"Yes," Katie replied. "I am glad now that we didn't actually make it down the aisle or have children. As awful as it was, it could have been worse. But now you see why you don't need to warn me about Finlo. I have no intention of having my heart broken again. I've given up on men for at least a year. I'm going to dedicate myself to my career and forget all about falling in love."

All three girls then burst out laughing, though Katie had been totally serious in her declaration.

Jane poured everyone more wine and then spoke quietly. "My story doesn't seem so bad, after yours," she told Katie sadly. "And mine is pretty straightforward. Finlo came on really strong, flirting and telling me I was wonderful. After a while, I started to fall for him in spite of everyone warning me about him. We dated for about six weeks and then he dumped me for someone else. That is the whole story. He isn't even with her any more. They only lasted about three weeks."

Ealish gave her friend a hug and turned to Katie. "Finlo is a great guy and if you can stay friends with him you'll be fine. But once you start to fall for his big blue eyes and his charming manner, you're in trouble. He doesn't have a faithful bone in his body. While he is with you, you'll feel like the only woman in the world, but once he gets tired of you, and it doesn't take long, he'll drop you so fast your head will spin. Basically, once the thrill of the chase wears off, he gets bored."

"Are you speaking from experience as well?" Katie wondered.

"Oh no, I'm not Finlo's type," Ealish laughed. "I'm not nearly sweet enough for him and I can see right through his particular brand of charm. It feeds his ego when women fall for him. They are all convinced that they'll be the one to change his womanizing ways. So far, none of them have been."

Katie shook her head. "I'm not interesting in even trying. I couldn't hold onto a man that was the faithful type, so I've no chance with a womanizer."

"Mark wasn't the faithful type," Jane told her. "He might have stayed faithful for years and years, but clearly he was going to stray at some point. At least he did it in time for you to apply to come here."

"Yes," Katie grinned wickedly. "I suppose I should send him a thank-you note!"

All three women laughed at that and then settled down to have some more wine. Time passed quickly, and many hours later, when the wine was finished and Jane and Ealish were ready to walk home, the three women were firm friends. They would all be terribly hungover in the morning, but they definitely agreed that it had been worth it.

❧ 6 ❧

Saturday passed in something of a blur for Katie. She was still not fully recovered from her trip and the late night and subsequent hangover didn't help. After a very late breakfast, she headed out and took a long walk on the promenade. She first walked the short distance to the Sea Terminal and watched as a large ferry sailed away from the island. She could see cars and people on board, as well as massive truck containers. After it disappeared into the distance, she slowly walked the entire length of the promenade to the far end. There she could see the remains of the Summerland complex that she had read about when she had been studying the island. It had been torn down recently, and Katie wasn't sure what was going to replace it.

She stood for a long time at the end of the promenade watching the waves crash up onto the rocks. In spite of her pounding headache and the tiredness that she still couldn't seem to get over, she felt a sense of well being settling over her. That feeling had been missing for many months, since she'd found out about Mark, and she was reassured to have it back. The last several months had been difficult, but Katie felt now that she was finally moving past it and getting on with her life. Mark had moved away from Maryland and taken a job doing research for a television company.

They had sold the house and Katie had used her share of the money to pay off as much as she could on her maxed-out credit cards. She had moved into a small rented apartment and then moved right back out again when she'd left for Europe. Now all of her things were in storage at her parents' house in Pennsylvania. When she got home, she would have to start looking for an apartment or a small house. She still had her job. Mark's confession had proven her innocence in the whole sorry matter. She had worked throughout the whole crisis, teaching her classes and trying to avoid feeling self-conscious as everyone pointed and whispered about her. The worst of that should be over by the time she got back, however. Now Katie just had to learn to live without Mark in her life. So far, it was proving far easier than she'd expected.

Eventually Katie made her way back to the small apartment over the institute. She made herself a quick meal and watched some television. She spent a short time looking over the papers that Marjorie Stevens had given her, but no matter how much she looked at them, she couldn't make out more than a word or two. She spent half of an hour looking over some of the tourist guides to the island that she had collected over the years, so that she would be ready for her tour in the morning. Finally she curled up with her half read novel and her expensive truffles. When she finished the book she took herself to bed early, determined to be well rested when Finlo arrived.

Katie was up and dressed in jeans and a T-shirt when Finlo drove up outside the back of the institute. She had pulled her hair into a somewhat haphazard ponytail and on the way out of the apartment she grabbed a denim jacket. She had found over the past few days that there was often a chill in the air, even when the sun was shining.

"Good morning," she called to Finlo as she locked up the door to her apartment. "I was afraid it was going to rain today."

"I wouldn't have allowed it," Finlo told her as he leapt from the car to hold her door open for her. "There is too much to see outdoors. I couldn't possibly have let it rain."

Katie giggled at his nonsense and felt young and carefree for the first time in years. She and Mark had been together for so long that they'd already felt like an old married couple. While Katie had enjoyed that feeling of comfort and security, flirting and dashing around a foreign land with a handsome stranger made her feel more alive than she had for a long time.

"Well, thank you for that careful bit of planning," she told Finlo, still laughing. "If you could arrange for the sunshine to stay for the entire three months that I'm here that would be great," she teased him.

"We need rain, too," he answered her with a dazzling smile. "A lot of the island is agricultural, but I'll do my best to keep rain to a minimum while you are here."

He climbed back into the car and took a moment to fuss over Katie's seatbelt. "I need to make sure you're safe," he told her in a serious voice as he double-checked that the belt was tight.

The gesture felt quite intimate in the enclosed space of the small car and Katie found herself holding her breath. Her heart was racing and she felt light-headed and giddy but not at all like laughing. Her limited experience of men suddenly seemed a huge disadvantage when faced with a man as sophisticated as Finlo.

He looked into her eyes and she was sure he could see the fear, uncertainty and excitement that were bubbling inside of her. "All set?" His voice was quiet and seductive.

"Sure," was all that Katie could choke out, certain that she was blushing furiously.

"Then let's go," Finlo snapped his own seat belt on and then pulled out into the traffic. "I've changed our plans slightly. I hope you don't mind," he told Katie with a sideways glance.

Katie was disappointed, as she was particularly eager to see Castle Rushen, but she did her best to hide it. "No problem, whatever you want," she told Finlo.

"Well, I thought, since we had already driven by Castle Rushen and Rushen Abbey, that we would start in the west of the island today, instead. I thought we would hit Peel Castle and the House of Manannan and then grab lunch on our way north. We can drive through Ramsey and Laxey and then head south. We should have time for a short stop at the abbey and then finish up at the castle. Is that okay?"

Katie smiled at Finlo. The day sounded wonderful and she told Finlo that excitedly. Then she settled back in the amazingly comfortable seat of the luxurious car and forced herself to relax. Finlo drove steadily through Douglas, pointing out a few interesting sights as they drove.

The main Douglas-to-Peel road was part of the world famous Tourist Trophy (TT) motorcycle race course and Katie was amazed that people actually raced motorcycles along the fairly narrow road that was packed with houses and businesses. Katie marveled at the wide black and white stripes that covered every inch of the curb along the road's edge. She couldn't imagine having to repaint those every year. Finlo pointed out the remains of St. Trinian's chapel as they sped along and Katie craned her neck to make out the ruined church.

"I think it is fourteenth-century," Finlo told her. "It's been in ruins for hundreds of years. Technically, Manx National Heritage owns the site and an access route to it, but the field it sits in belongs to a farmer and in order to visit you have to make arrangements with him. Not that there is anything to see besides crumbling walls," he explained.

"Fourteenth-century?" Katie smiled excitedly. "I would love to be able to walk around something that old."

"Peel Castle has older sections," Finlo reassured her. "And we can spend as much time as you like walking around that without annoying any farmers or sheep."

Katie found herself barely able to contain her excitement. After all the years of reading about and studying the place, the island was finally hers to explore.

"On your right," Finlo's voice interrupted Katie's thoughts. He slowed the car and pretended to be a proper tour guide. "You will see Tynwald Hill. This is the site where, even today, the world's oldest continuous parliament meets annually." Finlo paused and then winked at Katie.

"They meet a lot more than annually, of course, but they have a proper building in Douglas for most of their meetings. They only meet here on the 5th of July. Everyone on the island is welcome to come and hear the laws from the previous year read out. And anyone who has a complaint or concern can present a petition to the government. Democracy in action, live and interactive, once a year at least."

Katie looked over at the small green mound that was Tynwald Hill. While what it represented was exciting, the stepped hill itself was fairly unremarkable. Steps led up between the taller platform sections and Katie could see a handful of people climbing the steps and posing for photographs.

"I'll have to come back and get my photo taken at the top before I go home," she spoke more to herself than to Finlo.

"Not a problem," Finlo replied. "And you'll be here for Tynwald Day as well. You should think about coming out and seeing the spectacle for yourself. It isn't just about boring government stuff. There is a fair with cake stalls and performances from local bands and all sorts of excitement."

Katie grinned. "Sounds like fun. I'll have to see if I have time."

After that it was only a short distance to Peel and Finlo drove expertly through the narrow streets that Katie couldn't imagine trying to negotiate herself. He parked behind a large building and as they walked around it, Katie could see that there was a Viking longboat that seemed to be coming out through the large windows at the front. Life-sized sculptures of Vikings seemed to be pulling the ropes in an effort to pull the boat through the wall and on to the ground outside. Katie stared at the display for a long time, enchanted by the clever construction.

"Come on," Finlo walked ahead and held open the door. "The House of Manannan has won all sorts of awards for its displays. I can't wait to see what you think of it."

Katie followed him eagerly. She had read about this museum and she couldn't wait to see if it was as good as everyone promised. It was more than an hour later when they emerged back into the sunshine and Katie was, if possible, even more excited than she had been as they went in.

"That was amazing," she told Finlo as they retreated to his car. "I've never been in such a wonderful museum. Children must love it. Though I suppose it might be a bit scary in parts, for the littler ones.

Still, the amount of history that they will learn, without even realizing it, is incredible."

Finlo laughed. "I'm glad you liked it," he told her. "I've never seen anyone so excited by a museum. None of that stuff was actually really old, you know, just re-creations and the like."

It was Katie's turn to laugh. "I know. Wait until you see how excited I get by the stuff that is really old," she told Finlo.

His eyes lit up at the remark. "Well, that is something to look forward to," he answered, taking her arm and giving her a look that was loaded with sexual innuendo.

Katie blushed and tried to change the subject back to the museum they had just left. "The displays were really good, though. And I really liked the Viking ship in real water. So much was interactive as well, which must be great for kids. And I really liked the room with the big windows so you could see Peel Castle. I could have sat there all day, watching the sea and the boats with the castle sparkling in the distance."

"Wouldn't you rather actually go to the castle?" Finlo teased as he held Katie's door open for her. "We can go back in and just sit and watch it, if you would prefer."

Katie held back a sigh. "You know what I mean," she told Finlo as he climbed into the car. She had already made sure that she had her seatbelt buckled, and she made a point of checking it as Finlo looked over so that he would be certain it was tight enough. That didn't stop him from reaching across her to check for himself. The car seemed to shrink until there was barely room for two inside and Katie held her breath as she felt her body react to Finlo's touch. As he sat back into his own seat, he brushed his hand across her cheek and winked at her.

Katie suddenly worried that she was playing with fire spending time with Finlo. Their innocent trip around the island now seemed charged with electricity and Katie wasn't sure she was ready for the experience. Mark had been nearly as inexperienced as Katie when they started sleeping together all those years ago. Katie had always felt that their sex life was fine, but Mark had never made her feel electrified by a single touch. Katie sat back and deliberately turned her head away from Finlo. She reminded herself that he was just playing with her and that if she succumbed to his charms he would soon be off looking for the next conquest.

Finlo chuckled quietly as Katie turned away. "Would I be right in assuming that you have been warned about me, then?" he asked as he started the car.

"Should I have been warned about you?" Katie asked back, not wanting to repeat what Jane and Ealish had told her.

Finlo chuckled again. "Just remember that there are two sides to every story and you will have heard only one. I'm sure Jane doesn't have a nice thing to say about me, but the truth is that we dated for a while and it didn't work out. That doesn't make me evil or even a wild womanizer, but Jane and Ealish seem to want to paint me that way. All I would ask you to do is give me a fair chance. Judge me by the way that I treat you, not by the way I'm supposed to have treated others."

Katie knew it was all probably just a line, but it sounded convincing and it seemed fair. "I'll take everything I've been told with a grain of salt," she told Finlo. "But it really doesn't matter, anyway, because I'm not looking for a man. I've just come out of a long-term relationship that went disastrously wrong and I have no intention of getting myself mixed up in another one."

Finlo grinned wickedly at her. "That sounds suspiciously like a challenge to me, young Katie," he told her, "I always love a challenge."

"You would be wasting your time," Katie insisted to him. "Let's just be friends and leave it at that, can't we?"

Finlo pulled into the parking lot for the castle and parked. He turned to Katie and pulled her hand into his.

"No, Katie, my dear, I don't think we can just be friends. I'm attracted to you and I always go after the things that I want. Consider this fair warning that I will be making a play for you. How you deal with that is, of course, up to you. But I will tell you that I'm used to getting what I want."

With that he leaned towards Katie and planted a gentle kiss on her lips. The kiss wasn't demanding or aggressive, it was soft, almost affectionate and incredibly brief. Katie found, to her dismay, that she was enormously disappointed when Finlo didn't push things any farther. Instead he let go of her hand and climbed out of the car.

"Come on then, history lover, Peel Castle awaits," he told her as he swung her door open for her. Katie looked up at the castle and completely forgot how badly she'd wanted Finlo to kiss her moments earlier. The castle loomed large over the car park and Katie could barely keep herself from running along the wall to the stone steps that marked the entrance.

Finlo followed at a more leisurely pace and Katie had already paid her admission and grabbed her electronic guide to the castle by the time he caught up to her. She quickly followed the markers to the first listening post and pushed the buttons on the guide. As the voice on the guide started to share the history of the castle with her, she put some space between herself and Finlo and began to relax.

The next hour flew by as Katie followed the electronic guide around the entire site. She marveled at structures that had been built in the eleventh century and were still standing, at least in part. She spent a long time in the ancient chapel, reading inscriptions on stone markers that marked burials that were far more recent than the building itself. She revisited the area where the Derbys had had their apartments, so many years earlier. Then she stood for a very long time at the highest point she could find along the castle walls, watching the waves crashing onto the rocks below her. It was there that Finlo finally caught up with her after she'd visited every spot on the electronic guide and found herself wandering back to once more watch the waves.

"Look," Finlo said by way of greeting. "Just there, do you see little brown heads? Those are seals, playing in the sea and on the rocks."

Katie looked hard at him to see if he was teasing her, and then studied the water again. After staring intently where he was pointing, Katie could just make out the tiny bobbing heads in the sea. She found herself laughing, amazed and captivated by the view. "Seals," she exclaimed. "I didn't know you could see seals from here."

"It is a really beautiful view from here," Finlo agreed. Then he looked attentively at Katie. "I'm really glad that I got to share it with you."

Katie had been afraid that he was going to say something corny about how she made the view better. Instead his words had been perfectly chosen to make her feel special. Katie found herself blushing again and wishing that he would kiss her. As soon as she realized what she was thinking she was furious with herself, but before she could move Finlo seemed to read her mind. The wind was blowing softly and the castle suddenly seemed irredeemably romantic.

Finlo leaned towards her and kissed her. Again, it was a soft and gentle kiss, a bit more intense than the one in the car, but nowhere near as satisfying as the kiss that Katie found herself wanting. As he pulled back from her, Katie found herself sighing in frustration. It took every bit of her will power not to pull Finlo into her arms and kiss him with the passion she was fighting.

Finlo laughed softly. "I told you I'm used to getting what I want," he reminded her gently. "I'm hoping it will be what you want as well." Then he took her hand and led her around the castle, pointing out things that she missed the first time and things that the guide hadn't mentioned.

"How come you're so well informed?" she wondered as he pointed out the exact location where the pagan lady burial was found.

"I thought I told you that my cousin runs the institute?"

"Hang on, William is your cousin?" Katie hadn't made the connection.

"Yep, his mum's my dad's sister," Finlo smiled. "I do a lot of digging with them when I'm not too busy."

"Digging? What sort of digging?"

"Archaeological digging. I did my degree in archaeology at university. My parents promised me that if I graduated, they would pay for flying lessons. As soon as I finished, I started flying and I never went back to archaeology, at least not formally."

"But you do some work for the institute?"

"Strictly as a volunteer. You may not have realized it yet, but the institute is seriously under-funded. I suppose that isn't unusual. Most academic institutions probably struggle to find the money to pay for all the things they want to do. The institute holds several archaeological digs every year. If they had to pay for staff to carry them out, they could only have one, or maybe not any. So they rely heavily on volunteers. Most are enthusiastic amateurs with no background in archaeology. I'm sure William would let you have a go if you wanted to," Finlo explained.

"A go at digging at a real archaeological dig?" Katie felt a flutter of excitement. While archaeology had never interested her as a field of study, the chance to try doing it seemed irresistible.

Finlo laughed. "Yes, a real dig. As I said, most of the volunteers are amateurs, though many have been helping for years and are more valuable to the institute than I am, even though I studied archaeology. Have a word with William and see if he can include you at Rushen Abbey this summer. I'm sure you would love it and William would be grateful for the extra help."

Katie nodded eagerly. "I'm sure I would love it, too, but I'm not sure I'll have time," she frowned. "I have a lot of my own work to do."

"Well, at least you can come one day and have a look around," Finlo told her. "We can stop there today and see the place, but the digging doesn't start until July. Maybe by then you will be doing so well with your research that you'll have lots of time to spare."

Katie shook her head. July still seemed far away, but the chance of her being ahead by then seemed impossible.

"I know you are enjoying the view from here," Finlo continued. "But we really should get moving if we are going to see Rushen Abbey and Castle Rushen before they shut for the day. It's already lunchtime."

Katie was surprised. She had lost all track of time while tramping around the castle ruins and she suddenly realized that she was starving. She followed Finlo out of the castle, stopping at the entrance to try to memorize everything she could see.

She buckled herself in quickly after Finlo opened her door and held her breath as he climbed in and smiled at her. "Buckled up tight?"

"Yes, nice and tight," she answered quickly, torn between not wanting him to check and wanting to feel his hands on her again.

"Good," was all that Finlo said as he turned the key in the ignition and pulled out of the parking lot. They rode in silence for several minutes. Finlo was busy concentrating on negotiating the tight corners and narrow roads of Peel. Then he pointed the car north and relaxed in the driver's seat.

"I would have checked your belt," he grinned wickedly at Katie, "but I'm hungry and I was afraid if I leaned across you again you might grab me and try to take advantage of me. Goodness only knows how long that would take, and I need to eat."

Katie turned bright red. She was speechless and she sat in silent outrage for a long minute, desperately trying to think of a suitable crushing reply.

"Don't feel too badly," Finlo added. "I'll give you another chance later."

He winked outrageously at her and Katie found herself laughing in spite of herself. A few minutes later they pulled to a stop at a small building that was surrounded by a large car park. Katie looked for a sign that would indicate where they were.

"Lunchtime," Finlo told Katie as he helped her from the car.

"Where are we?"

"It is a pub," Finlo answered. "They do pub food, but it is really good pub food. Would you rather go somewhere nicer? This just happened to be on the way and I know the food is good."

"I'm happy to eat here," Katie answered. "I just wondered what the place was called."

"Oh," Finlo was silent for a minute as he studied the front of the nondescript building. "I have no idea," he finally admitted with a laugh. "It's just the pub on the Ramsey road. I'm sure it has a name, but I don't know what it is."

Katie laughed. "Well, I hope the food is more memorable than the name, then," she told him as they walked to the door.

Inside, Katie blinked hard. Outside the summer sun was dazzling, but the inside of the pub was gloomy and dark. As her eyes adjusted, she looked quickly around. The pub was smaller than any restaurant she had ever visited in the States. There were maybe ten tables, all pushed together in a corner. A long narrow bar filled the rest of the room, with half a dozen stools dotted along its length. The room was about half full of people and Katie forced a smile onto her face as she realized that nearly everyone had stopped what they were doing to look at the new arrivals.

"Hey, Jimmy," Finlo called out, raising a hand in greeting to the man behind the bar. "Can we get a table for two?"

"Sit anywhere empty," the man called back. "Bangers and Mash on special today," he added as he turned back to the bar and resumed filling glasses.

"Thanks," Finlo lead Katie to a small table against the back wall. He leaned over to grab a menu off another table as they went. "Have a look at the menu and see what sounds good," he told Katie. "If you don't know what something is, just ask."

Katie sat down, grateful to be hidden in the gloom. It had felt like everyone was staring at her, though she couldn't imagine why anyone would. She looked at the menu in her hand. It had been hand-written and then photocopied and laminated, apparently many years earlier if the stains and smudges of food and drink that covered it were anything to go by. Katie read through a list of sandwiches, baked potato fillings and hot meals. She had no idea what she should order.

"What are you having?" she finally asked Finlo, hoping for guidance.

"I'm going to have the Bangers and Mash," Finlo answered. "I'm really hungry and a hot meal sounds better than just a sandwich."

"Bangers and Mash?" Katie remembered that the man at the bar had said that was today's special. "Maybe I should try that, too."

"Shall I order two, then? Do you want vegetables as well?"

"Yes, please," Katie smiled.

"And a drink?"

"Oh, a cola, please."

Finlo was gone for a few moments, placing their order and then he returned with their drinks.

"Cheers," he said as he clinked her glass with his own.

"Cheers," Katie echoed as she looked around the tiny room. "How does a restaurant this small stay in business? I mean it is so small, they can't be making much money, can they?"

"It's a family concern," Finlo answered. "Jimmy's father and mother ran the place for forty-odd years. Jimmy took over about two years ago when his parents retired. They still come in from time to time to check that Jimmy isn't running the place into the ground or making too many changes. The place is a Manx institution, and the Manx like to support their own. Overheads are low because they own the property and Jimmy and his wife do all the work and they grow a lot of the food on the family farm."

Finlo shrugged. "I've never really thought about it. I suppose they aren't getting rich, but money isn't everything to everyone. Big American restaurant chains wouldn't understand, but some people actually like to feed people good food rather than just make money."

Katie smiled at him. "That's good, coming from a man who drives a car that cost more than I'll make in the next two years," she told him, feeling the need to score a point after the emotional morning.

"Ah, I did say some people. I'm not one of them, of course. I prefer profits to good causes every day. I suppose that is why I didn't stick with archaeology. University professors don't make a lot of money. I'm much happier being in business for myself and having control over my income."

Katie smiled. "Some of us like to think that we are making a difference when we educate the leaders of tomorrow," she told him, a little primly.

"Wouldn't you rather be one of the leaders today?"

"Politics aren't my thing," she told him with a shake of her head.

"You don't have to be involved in politics to be a leader," Finlo argued. "Heads of big business are leaders in other ways. Look at Richard Branson or Bill Gates. Their actions change the world in lots of ways."

"I suppose," Katie mused. "I guess I'm just not that ambitious. I would rather do the job I love, and do it well, than make lots of money."

Finlo shook his head. "There are too many toys to buy, and too much fun to have. Besides, I love my job enormously. I can't imagine that I could do anything else and have as much fun as I do. But I do it for a profit, not just for the fun."

Katie opened her mouth to reply but she was interrupted by the arrival of their food. The conversation was instantly forgotten as Katie looked at the plates that were piled high. The sausages were smothered in rich brown gravy, the fluffy white mashed potatoes provided a tasty looking contrast and the steamed vegetables looked as if they were struggling to stay on the overfull plates.

Everything was deliciously fresh and tasted better than homemade, and as Katie finished she couldn't remember the last restaurant meal that she had enjoyed that much.

"I can't believe how good all of that was," Katie said as she finished her last bite.

"I'm really glad you liked it," Finlo smiled softly. "I hope it is the just the first of many experiences I can share with you."

Katie wanted to laugh at the corny remark, but the look in Finlo's eyes was so serious that she couldn't. She even found herself starting to believe that he was sincere.

"Have you saved room for pudding?" Finlo asked after a moment. "They do an amazing chocolate cake with a melting center."

Katie shook her head reluctantly. "I wish I could try that," she told him. "But I am absolutely stuffed. Maybe another time."

"That sounds promising," Finlo told her with a wink. "We should get back to the tour, then, if you're finished. There's lots more to see and only so many hours left before everything shuts up for the night."

Katie quickly collected her bag from under her seat and followed Finlo from the pub. She felt fat and lazy now that she had eaten so much and she thought maybe a short nap would be better than continuing the tour. When she thought about where they were headed, however, she felt her excitement returning. Rushen Abbey would be interesting for a short visit, but Castle Rushen was the one thing she really wanted to see.

Finlo drove her through the towns of Ramsey and Laxey, pointing out a park here and a museum there and then the huge water wheel in Laxey that used to work for the mines. Katie felt like she spent the entire drive craning her neck, first one way and then the other, trying to see everything that she could. Finally they drove back across the Fairy Bridge and Katie was quick to wave to the Little People.

Finlo pulled up in the parking lot at Rushen Abbey and stopped Katie as she started out of the car. "We really need to spend no more than an hour here, if we are going to have time to see Castle Rushen properly," he told her. "If you would rather, we can skip the abbey for today and just head to the castle. I'm sure you'll have other chances to see the abbey."

Katie was torn. The abbey was on her list of things to see, but the castle was essential. She was hoping that she would get a real feel for the Derby family's life on the island by spending some time at the castle and actually visiting the rooms that they had used during the Civil War. Rushen Abbey had been long closed by the time the Seventh Earl had taken up residence during the English Civil War.

Finlo laughed. "I can see the indecision dancing all over your face," he told her. "I'll decide for you if that will make your life easier."

Katie shook her head. "It's okay," she answered. "I'm just not feeling one hundred per cent yet after the traveling. I think, if you don't mind, we will skip the abbey today and concentrate on the castle. As you say, I'll have other chances to see the abbey, but I don't think I could sleep tonight if I didn't get to the castle."

Finlo laughed again. "It's just an old building," he told her dismissively. "I don't understand why people get so excited about it."

Katie looked at him hard, wondering if he was teasing. He looked serious and she thought for a while about trying to explain exactly what was so exciting about this particular old building. It would probably be a waste of time, she decided. People either loved history or they didn't. If Finlo didn't, then it was his loss.

She buckled her seat belt back together and settled into her seat. Finlo hadn't insisted on checking it when they got back in the car after the pub and Katie wasn't sure if she was relieved or disappointed. Now he leaned across her and checked carefully, brushing his hand across her cheek and lifting her hair from her neck where it was tangled in the belt. His eyes studied hers for a long time and Katie held her breath, wanting him to kiss her and being afraid that he might.

Finlo finally broke the spell by chuckling. "Things will get easier when you stop fighting the attraction and start to enjoy it instead."

"I don't know what you are talking about," Katie forced out between gritted teeth.

"Shall I prove my point now or wait until later?" His expression was suddenly quite serious.

"I thought you said we should get going," Katie tried to distract him and cool the tension.

"You're right. Let's go. We can finish this conversation later, somewhere more comfortable than in a car," Finlo reversed out of the parking lot lazily and drove the short distance to Castle Rushen. He slid into a parking space and turned to Katie.

"There you are. Castle Rushen. I hope it lives up to your expectations."

Katie's eyes were shining and she barely heard him as she looked up at the ancient building. She knew so much about it, had studied it for years, and now she was going to be able to walk around inside of it. She barely glanced at Finlo as she jumped out of the car and headed towards the entrance. Finlo followed slowly.

7

K atie raced up the stone steps that led to the main gate of the castle. She paid her admission and continued across the bridge to the entrance to the main building. She was surprised to be stopped when she was halfway across the bridge.

"Halt!" A voice shouted. "Who goes there?"

Katie froze in place. She didn't know how to answer.

Finlo had caught up with her by now and he laughed loudly. "Bob, are you still scaring the visitors?"

A face peered out from behind the massive door in front of them. The man was dressed in medieval attire and was carrying a massive crossbow. "Finlo? What are you doing here? I would have thought you would have seen enough of this place during the dig last summer?"

"I'm showing Katie around," Finlo gestured at Katie. "She is a new academic doing some research into the Civil War period. I've been taking her on a quick once-around the island."

"Well now, isn't that interesting?" Bob replied, looking Katie up and down. "I might be wrong, but your cousin's been running that institute for a long time now and this is the first time I remember you showing anyone around for him."

Finlo laughed. "I told William when he got the job that I would help him out with anyone who was young and beautiful. Is it my fault that this is the first time he's actually brought someone over here that fits the bill?"

Bob laughed at Katie's blushes. "He's right there," Bob told her. "Most of the folks that come over here to study are late fifties or early sixties and male. We have had a few women, of course. Remember that horrible old spinster lady from Poland?" He nudged Finlo in the ribs. "She was terrifying."

Finlo grinned wickedly. "Apparently she was rather brilliant at transcribing thirteenth and fourteenth-century Latin. Unfortunately, most of the old documents here aren't in very good Latin, more like a combination of Latin and Manx. She couldn't get away from here fast enough."

"So what is your area of expertise?" Bob turned back to Katie.

"Mostly the seventeenth century," Katie smiled. "I'm here specifically to look at the island during the Civil War period."

"It's about time someone had a good look at that," Bob smiled amiably. "I'm guessing you want to have a good look around the castle, then? See the Derby apartments and things?"

Katie's eyes shone with excitement. "Yes, please!"

Bob looked pleased with her enthusiasm. "Come along, then," he told her and he led her across the bridge.

As they passed through the portcullis, he gestured above their heads. "Murder holes," he told Katie who stopped and stared. Above her head, between the two sets of doors, were a number of holes in the floor above. Anyone attempting to invade the castle could be caught between the two sets of doors. Then hot oil could be poured over them, arrows could be fired at them or rocks could be dropped on their heads. Katie shivered at the gory thoughts and hurried after Bob into a large courtyard.

"There is lots to see here and we always recommend that visitors follow the same route. Since the stairs are particularly narrow throughout, we try to keep everyone going in the same direction. The tour starts with a video, and I do suggest that you watch it. It only takes about ten minutes and it introduces the castle quite nicely," Bob paused for a breath and looked questioningly at Katie.

"A video introduction sounds great," Katie agreed easily. She wasn't about to start demanding special privileges. She just wanted to see the castle.

"You're in luck as it is quiet this afternoon. I can start the video whenever you are ready and then, when it is finished, I'll give you a special tour."

Katie followed Bob eagerly into a small room lined with wooden benches. Much to the men's amusement, she chose a seat in the front row. Finlo slid into the row behind her and nodded to Bob that he could start the show. The lights went out and the tiny room was pitched into total darkness for a scary moment, before the video began to play. Katie watched enthralled as a very brief history of the castle played out before her.

After a few moments, she felt Finlo moving closer to her and she had to force herself to ignore him and concentrate on the film. Another minute passed before Finlo's hands began to stroke her back. She tried to move away from him without taking her eyes from the screen. Finlo shifted in his seat so that he was even closer to Katie and his hands settled on the back of her neck.

He began to rub gently, easing the tension that was still present after the long flight of a few days earlier. Katie felt herself relaxing under his touch. Despite her best efforts, she found her eyes closing and her body sinking backwards towards Finlo. She heard him chuckle softly as he slid an arm around her waist and pulled her closer. Katie breathed out a sigh, as she felt powerless to resist the kiss she knew was coming. Suddenly the movie stopped and light flooded the room.

Katie sprang to her feet and moved quickly away from Finlo. The door opened and Bob leaned in. "Sorry about that, there was a glitch in the tape. Hang on a moment and I'll get it restarted."

"Never mind," Katie spoke quickly. "I think I'd rather just get going with the tour, if you don't mind."

Bob nodded. "Okay, you saw most of it, anyway. I'll be right back, I just need to tell Beth on the gate where I'll be."

He left the room and Katie pretended to be absorbed in studying the thick stone walls.

"Saved by the broken film. You won't get away that easily next time," Finlo spoke quietly with determination in his voice.

"I was just about to stop you anyway," Katie insisted, struggling to keep her voice from wobbling.

"You try to convince yourself of that if it makes you feel better. I know the truth," Finlo gave her a satisfied smile and then turned away as Bob walked back into the room.

"Right this way, then," Bob told them, opening a door in the wall next to the video screen.

Katie followed him quickly as he led them up a steep flight of narrow steps. The stairs wound around in a circle with very little headroom as they did so. Katie only just avoided hitting her head twice as they climbed. Finlo was behind her, and he kept reminding her to duck as they rounded another bend. He had to climb almost the entire time with his head down, because of his extra height. The stairs opened into a small room with several signs explaining the things that visitors could see.

"Right," Bob began, "each room has a sign like this that explains how the room was used in the past. Our ideas for how the rooms were used in the very earliest times are educated guesses based on how similar castles were used in other parts of the British Isles. The seventeenth century ones are based on written descriptions of how the castle was being used. Lastly, during the nineteenth century, the castle was used as a prison and we know exactly what each part of the castle was used for during that period."

He showed Katie a large sign that had three separate floor plans for the room in which they were standing. Katie read carefully the various ways in which the room had been used over the years.

"It is hard to imagine how awful this must have been as a prison cell," she commented after she finished reading the descriptions. "It's so cold and dark and small, with only that one tiny window to let in light."

She climbed on to a step and tried to peer out of the tiny window that was more of a slit in the stonework than a proper window. "You can't even see anything, really," she remarked. "The prisoners must have gone mad trapped under these conditions."

"It certainly wasn't a nice place to be held," Bob agreed. "But then, I don't think the idea was to give them someplace nice to live."

Katie had to smile at that, but she shivered when she thought about how gloomy and depressing life must have been in the castle during its years as a prison. She followed Bob through a number of rooms, determinedly ignoring Finlo, who trailed behind, uncharacteristically silent.

Katie was delighted when they finally reached the rooms that had been the Derby apartments during their residence on the island. She stood for a long time in the throne room, imagining how it must have looked and felt all those hundreds of years earlier. Then she reluctantly followed Bob and Finlo around the remainder of the castle.

Their last stop was the medieval kitchens and Katie marveled at the small area where, once, great feasts were prepared for those who lived in the castle. Ovens fueled by wood fires were made of stone and Katie wondered out loud how difficult it must have been to cook anything in the crowded space that obviously lacked electricity or even running water.

"I wouldn't want to try to prepare anything in there," Katie told the others.

"You should come back when we have our special event days later in the summer, when the schools are on their summer break," Bob told her. "We have a couple of medieval enthusiasts who come in and actually prepare typical foods from the day for the kids to see and try."

"Wow," Katie smiled, "I would love to see that. I'll have to try to get back."

"Grab a brochure on your way out," Bob told her. "It gives all the dates for all the special events. We have a group that comes and re-enacts medieval and seventeenth-century battles as well. Those are always good fun."

Finlo rolled his eyes. "You have a strange idea of fun, Bob," he told his friend.

Bob shook his head but didn't bother to reply. Katie looked from one to the other. "How long do I have before the castle closes for the night?"

"About half an hour. We shut at five," he told her.

"I'm just going to run back up to the throne and treasure rooms, if that is okay?"

"Of course. You and Finlo are the only ones here, so you can go up backwards if you want. I'll make sure someone comes to get you at closing time," Bob grinned. "I can't imagine that you would like to spend the night shut up in here, no matter how much you love the castle."

Katie shivered. "No thanks. I'll leave happily at closing time. I just want another look at the rooms the Derbys used. Sorry I'm not wearing a watch. I usually don't bother. If someone could come and find me at five that would be great." Katie raced back up the narrow stone steps, eager to get back to the most interesting rooms in the castle.

She stood for a long time in the throne room, imagining what it must have been like when James Stanley, the Seventh Earl of Derby, was holding court there. Then she moved into the much smaller room behind it, where he would have kept his treasure. The tiny windowless room felt creepy and Katie quickly returned to the larger and brighter throne room.

Katie walked to the center and tried to imagine being presented to the Earl in this very room. She tried a curtsey in the direction of the chairs that were on the raised platform along one wall. Then she laughed at herself. After a closer look at the chairs, she headed back across the room and sank down into a smaller chair that had been put in the room for visitors.

She sat for several minutes trying to soak up the atmosphere of the room. "If only you could talk," she said to the walls that surrounded her. "You could tell me some of the stories that I want to know." She sank back in the comfortable seat and shut her eyes for a moment, stretching out and breathing deeply, trying to draw in the history that encircled her.

When she opened her eyes, she was startled to see a woman in the room with her. Like Bob, she was dressed in period costume and Katie was amazed at the elaborate and obviously expensive detail on her dress. Katie rose to her feet and was about to speak when the woman turned towards her. Katie could instantly see that the woman was crying. Worried that she was intruding in some way, Katie wasn't sure what to do. Clearly the woman hadn't seen her when she came into the room.

"I'm terribly sorry," Katie began. "It must be closing time, mustn't it? I really do have to be going."

Katie was flustered and turned towards the door, but the other woman was already there. She turned and looked at Katie one last time and then she vanished through the door without speaking. Katie blinked hard, trying to figure out what had just happened. She took a tentative step towards the door and jumped as Finlo suddenly appeared through it.

"Come on then, love, it is closing time," he told her. He looked more closely at her and frowned. "Are you okay? You look pale. Have we done too much today?"

Concern was evident in is voice and Katie rushed to reassure him. "No, I was just sitting here and I was startled by someone else coming in. You must have passed the woman in the hallway as you came in?"

"I didn't pass anyone. We're the only visitors in the castle at the moment. Bob is downstairs checking that everything is secure and Beth is shutting up the office. Are you sure you saw someone?"

"Maybe I dozed off and dreamt something," Katie smiled at Finlo. "Never mind. Let's get back downstairs before Bob locks us in."

She followed Finlo out of the room and back down the stairs quickly. Bob escorted them to the main castle door and then locked it securely behind them.

Finlo took Katie's hand now as he led her back to his car. "All the sites are shut up now, so the rest of the night is ours," he told her. "Do you feel like going out for a proper meal or something less substantial after our big lunch?"

Katie frowned as she reclaimed her hand and climbed into the car. "I didn't expect the tour to include meals as well," she told Finlo as she made a big show of fastening and tightening her seatbelt. "I appreciated the tour, but I'm awfully tired, so maybe you should just take me home."

Finlo grinned. "Okay by me. Do you like Chinese? I know a great Chinese that does takeaway, and it isn't far from the institute. I'll call them now and they can have the order ready when we get to Douglas."

Katie frowned. She hadn't intended for Finlo to come back to her apartment with her and she knew that he knew that as well. She wasn't sure how to persuade him to just drop her off. It didn't help that part of her wanted Finlo to come back. Part of her even wanted Finlo to stay the night. Katie frowned harder as that thought crossed her mind. "NO, NO, NO," she shouted at herself, scowling.

Next to her in the tiny car, Finlo laughed. "I bet you are a terrible poker player," he told her. 'I can see all of your thoughts fluttering across your face. I don't want to upset you, so how about this? We get Chinese and go back to your flat. We eat and talk for a bit. Then I go home, with only a good night kiss to keep me warm tonight. I'm happy to take our relationship slowly, but only if you will admit that we're working towards a relationship."

Katie shook her head. "I don't know what we are doing," she admitted miserably. "I've just come out of a very long-term relationship and I'm really not ready to get involved with anyone right now. I don't mind having a Chinese meal with you, and I've had a great day, but I really don't need a boyfriend."

Finlo smiled. "Let's get the Chinese. You'll feel better when you've had something to eat. What do you like or not like from a Chinese restaurant?"

She quickly ran through a few of her favorites. Finlo rang a number that was pre-programmed into his mobile phone and ordered what sounded to Katie like one of everything that they had on the menu. He pulled out of the parking lot and a comfortable silence descended in the car.

Katie was more tired than she had realized. The effects of traveling and drinking too much over the previous week were catching up with her. Finlo drove easily and skillfully, obviously enjoying being behind the wheel of the high performance car. Other than reminding Katie to wave to the Little People, he didn't speak until they reached Douglas.

There, he pulled to a stop in front of the small Chinese restaurant and ran inside. A few moments later he returned, laden down with more bags of food than Katie thought they could eat in a week. He piled everything into the back of the car and then drove quickly back to the institute. They stopped just short of the building and looked at it in surprise. There were cars parked everywhere, and the front door to the building was open. Katie and Finlo watched as a taxi pulled to a stop and three people climbed out. All three were dressed in business clothes and they made their way up the steps and in the front door of the institute. Beside her, Finlo made a noise.

"Looks like a board meeting or something," he said to Katie.

"What does that mean?"

"It means about forty people crowded into the various rooms. The main meeting will take place in the conference room, but then there will be smaller subcommittee meeting afterwards that will be scattered all over the building. We can go in your back door and avoid them, but there will be a lot of noise. Or we can go to my flat, which is just down the road and will, I promise, be very quiet."

Katie didn't know what to do. She really wanted a bit of peace and quiet, but Finlo's apartment sounded dangerous. She shook her head, trying to think of an alternative. Finlo interrupted before she spoke.

"If we go back to my place, the same arrangement still stands. I promise to be good, except for one good night kiss," he promised.

"Your place sounds good then," Katie agreed gratefully as yet another taxi arrived and more people rushed into the institute. She didn't think she could relax in her apartment knowing that there were so many people buzzing around beneath her.

Finlo smiled. "Great, off we go."

He drove further down the promenade, past the section of hotels and boarding houses where the institute was based. After a row of bars and restaurants, there was a large section of expensive-looking apartment buildings. Finlo turned into the underground parking garage of the newest and most spectacular structure. He waved a key card at the automatic gate and it swung open lazily.

"Here we are," he told Katie as he pulled into a numbered space near the exit. "Come on."

He gathered the food from the back of the car and headed off towards a corner of the garage. Katie followed more slowly, looking around in amazement at the rows and rows of very expensive-looking cars that were parked in the underground space. She looked in vain for something resembling an ordinary family car. Nearly every car was a slick and sophisticated luxury vehicle and Katie wondered if there was anything in this garage that cost less than her annual salary. She didn't think so. Finlo had reached the elevator and stood waiting for Katie to catch up. She hurried now, embarrassed at being caught staring.

Finlo only smiled and pushed the call button. They waited in silence for the elevator to arrive. Once inside, Katie could only stare at the internal panel. There were no buttons to push.

"How do you select your floor?"

"You don't have to," Finlo answered, waving his key card in front of electronic eye. The elevator rose smoothly, with the floor numbers flashing past as they rose.

"So it knows which floor you live on?"

"Yep."

"But what if you want to visit a friend on another floor?"

Finlo laughed. "Leave it to you to find a flaw in the system," he told her. "There is another lift for guests and deliverymen at the front of the building. This one is only used by residents when they park in the garage. The front door has a manned security station so that anyone coming in has to sign in. Whoever they are visiting has to confirm that they are expecting them or at least are happy to see them. Then the security team can authorize the front lift to take them to the correct floor."

"Wow," Katie found the level of security quite extraordinary. "Is all this necessary on the island? I mean, should I be worried about the rather flimsy lock on my back door?"

Finlo shook his head. "Don't worry. The island is one of the safest places in the world today. But the guy that built this place had just moved here from London and he put in security that would be high tech even there. It makes most of the residents feel much more important and also helps to justify the ridiculously expensive cost of the flats and the annual maintenance fees."

He stopped there, as the elevator had stopped on the top floor. The door slid noiselessly open and he and Katie stepped onto the thickly carpeted landing. There were four doors off the landing and

Finlo flicked his key card towards one of them. A light on the door switched from red to green and Finlo pushed the door open.

"In you go," he told Katie, ushering her into the apartment in front of him.

He hit a switch on the wall next to the door and light flooded into the room. The door had opened into a huge living area with floor-to-ceiling windows along the far wall. The carpet under Katie's feet was so thick and luxurious that it was almost difficult to walk over. A suite of overstuffed white leather furniture curved around to face a huge multimedia centre with an enormous flat screen television as its centerpiece. Katie took a few hesitant steps into the room and then looked down at her feet.

"Should I take my shoes off?"

"Take off anything you like," he winked at her.

Katie blushed brightly and looked away.

"Sorry," Finlo was quick to apologize. "The carpet is easier to walk on if you take your shoes off, but you don't need to if you don't want to. I'm not worried about you getting things dirty." As he was speaking, Finlo kicked off his own shoes and Katie felt she should follow suit.

She slipped out of her sneakers, grateful to give her feet a rest after a long day of sightseeing. Then she followed Finlo into the kitchen. Katie gasped as she entered the room, first from the sheer size of the space and then from the amazing array of complicated appliances that were scattered around the plentiful quartz countertops. Finlo smiled at her.

"Yeah, it is a pretty good kitchen," he agreed. "Too bad I don't cook."

"You should be ashamed of yourself, living with a kitchen like this and not cooking," Katie told him, only half joking. "You should learn, and learn fast."

"Maybe I've just been waiting for the right teacher." Finlo gave her another suggestive smile and then laughed as Katie blushed again.

"Sit down and make yourself comfortable," he told her as he dug around in the various cupboards, coming up with plates and then serving spoons, forks and knives. Finally he brought out some very extravagant wine glasses. Katie sat carefully at the large table, with six chairs that took up a corner of the room.

Finlo opened all of the food containers across one section of the countertop. "Help yourself," he suggested as he headed to a container in the corner. 'Red or white?' he asked her as he opened the state-of-the-art wine cooler.

"Oh, goodness," Katie felt totally out of her depth as she filled a plate with small servings of just about everything he had ordered. "Whatever you prefer," she answered, afraid of showing her ignorance about wine by making a bad choice. Mark had taken a couple of classes in wine tasting and he used to mock Katie when she picked a white wine to go with something that he'd learned only went with red or vice versa.

Finlo only smiled and then selected a bottle. He poured them each a glass and then took his own plate and filled it. He sat down next to her at the table and tapped her glass with his own. "To enjoyable company," he said, looking serious for once.

"Cheers," Katie answered as she took a sip. The wine was delicious and Katie suddenly found she was starving as well. She took a few bites and smiled at Finlo. "This is good," she told him. "Everything is wonderful. But it seems different from the Chinese food I get at home."

"I suppose it is English Chinese, rather than American Chinese," Finlo answered her.

"I didn't think there would be any difference," Katie said thoughtfully, "but I suppose there must be influences from the outside that change how the food is made. I wonder if English Italian food is different from American Italian as well."

"I know that this Chinese restaurant is first generation. That is, the owners have come here from China in the last ten years. And I know a lot of the local Italian restaurants are the same. I'm not sure if that is the case in America."

"Well, the Chinese that I go to is about fifth generation, so I suppose after all those years, recipes get changed. And my favourite little Italian place has been there since 1943, so I guess they aren't exactly first generation, either."

The pair ate hungrily, talking about inconsequential things and Katie found herself relaxing and enjoying herself more than she thought she would. Finlo avoided flirting, instead showing his charming side, drawing Katie out and finding out all about her past. She was happy to tell him about her childhood. She'd been a much-loved only child who was still close to her parents. As the night wore on, she found herself telling him about Mark as well.

Finlo told her about his own upbringing as well. He had been an only child, too, and they were in total agreement that neither wanted to raise an only child themselves.

"I want at least three children," Katie declared firmly. "A boy first, because I always wanted an older brother, and then a girl and then a third that can be either."

Finlo laughed. "That seems a bit demanding," he told her. "I've never really thought about how many children I would like. I just know I want more than one."

After they'd both finished eating and Katie had insisted on helping to load the dishwasher, they headed back into the main room and settled on opposite ends of the incredibly comfortable couch. Finlo lowered the lights and opened the blinds on the large windows, so that he and Katie could watch the sea far below them as it crashed in and out along the beach. He kept the conversation flowing smoothly, introducing new topics as others fizzled out, and Katie was suddenly shocked to realize that it was past midnight.

"I need to get home and get some sleep," she said, leaping up from the couch.

"No problem," Finlo told her, rising himself and heading towards the door. "Pop your shoes back on," he smiled at Katie. "Would you like to walk home, or should we take the car?"

"Is it safe to walk?" Katie asked, thinking again about the elaborate security system in the building.

"Of course it is. I told you the island is one of the safest places in the world. It looks like a lovely night out there," he added, "let's walk."

"Okay," Katie was happy to agree. She enjoyed walking and she wasn't eager to get back into the intimate confines of Finlo's tiny sports car, either. Outside, Finlo took her arm and they walked in silence, listening to the waves as they met the shore. Once past the apartment complex, they had to walk by a number of pubs and bars and Finlo kept a tight grip on Katie's arm as they threaded their way through the men and women who were celebrating the weekend.

Some of them had clearly been celebrating a bit too much and one man leered at Katie and shouted something at her, but Finlo upped his pace and they were quickly away. It was quieter in front of the hotels and boarding houses and they slowed their steps again to enjoy the warm night. As they reached the steps to the institute, Katie found that she was walking still more slowly. In spite of how tired she was, she wasn't in any hurry for the evening to end. She couldn't remember the last time she had enjoyed herself as much as she had that day and she was grateful to Finlo for showing her such a lovely time.

She used her key to open the back entrance to her apartment and then turned to face Finlo.

"I suppose I better leave you here," Finlo said. "Otherwise I might struggle to keep my promise from earlier."

"I had a really lovely day," Katie told Finlo sincerely. "It was great seeing the sights and you were wonderful company."

"Thank you," Finlo told her, his eyes serious. "I can't remember the last time I enjoyed a day so much. You were terrific company and I hope we can spend another day together again soon."

His eyes darkened and Katie felt herself tense. She knew what was coming and she found she was holding her breath in anticipation. Finlo's head dipped towards her and she raised her head, meeting his lips with her own.

"Katie, is that you?"

A voice in the darkness startled both of them and Katie leapt away from Finlo and turned to see who was calling her. William was just walking down through the alley between the buildings, presumably heading for his car. Katie hadn't noticed that it was parked in its usual spot. She hoped that he hadn't seen what he had just interrupted.

"Oh, sorry, I didn't realize you had company." William looked from Katie to Finlo and back again. Katie knew that her blush told him what he had broken up.

"No problem. We just got back. Finlo and I went sightseeing today.

And then we came back here with Chinese, but the institute was really busy. So we went to Finlo's. But now we are back. And it is really late. I need to get some sleep," Katie knew she was babbling but she couldn't seem to stop herself.

William smiled tensely at her. "'I'll let you go, then. Sorry I disturbed you. I was just locking up after the meeting and heading home."

He headed towards his car and then paused. "Finlo, can I give you a lift home?"

An awkward silence followed. Katie didn't know what to say and she could feel both men watching her closely. Finlo finally stepped in and rescued her.

"You won't keep getting saved from my kisses. Next time I will make absolutely sure of that," he told Katie very quietly as he turned towards his cousin.

"Come on, William, give me a ride home, then."

Katie closed the door behind herself and stood still, listening to their footsteps and then the sound of William's car engine. Her head was swimming from the combined effects of wine and the second aborted kiss.

Back in her apartment, she quickly got ready for bed and climbed in. In spite of her preoccupation with Finlo, her last conscious thought was to wonder again about the woman she'd seen at Castle Rushen.

❧ 8 ❧

Katie woke up early on Monday, her body clock still not totally reset. At least that gave her a little bit of time to get ready for her meeting with Ealish. She had planned to do that on Sunday evening, never intending to be out so late. She quickly went through the books and papers she had brought with her, refusing to allow her thoughts to drift towards Finlo, which was more of a struggle than she wanted it to be.

She finally headed down the stairs at about quarter to nine, carrying a pile of books and papers. She blushed fuchsia as she ran head first into William, dropping books and papers all over the floor and then tumbling over herself in surprise.

"Oh dear, I'm sorry," she gasped out as she stumbled to her feet. "I wasn't expecting there to be anyone here yet. I thought I would just leave all these books outside of Ealish's office and then go and make myself a quick cup of tea."

"I think I should be the one apologizing," William grinned at her. "We do seem to keep bumping into each other quite literally, don't we? Let me open Ealish's door and you can put the books down in her office. That will save you having to move them later."

William quickly unlocked the door to the office while Katie gathered the books and papers and then maneuvered past him through the open door. The hallway was tiny and Katie caught her breath as she brushed up against William on her way past. A shock of something like electricity shot through her and she nearly dropped everything a second time.

"All set?" William asked, seemingly unaffected by their brief contact.

"Yeah," Katie mumbled, setting the books down on the now empty guest chair in the corner. She turned to leave the room and was uncomfortable to find William in the doorway watching her.

"It looks like Ealish tidied up a bit for this morning," he told Katie. "Are you settling in all right in your little flat?"

"Yes, fine, thanks," Katie answered tensely. For some reason William was making her nervous this morning.

"Did you have a chance to see all of the sights with Finlo, then?" he continued, seemingly oblivious to her discomfort.

"We went to the House of Manannan and Peel Castle and then Castle Rushen," Katie answered.

"So you missed Rushen Abbey?" William frowned. "I know it dates from before the time period you're investigating, but it is worth a visit."

"I'm hoping to get there before I have to go home," Katie answered. "But we just didn't have enough time to do everything in just one day."

"We start digging there again next week," William told her. "I'd be happy to take you out with me one morning. You could have a look around the site and the dig and then I could run you back at lunchtime."

"That sounds great," Katie said, delighted at the chance to see the site. "Finlo said you might even give me a chance to do some digging one day, if I can find the time," she added.

"You're more than welcome," William told her with enthusiasm. "We're always looking for willing volunteers. Let's plan on my taking you down one day next week and then you can have a good look and see if you really want to try out a bit of digging."

"Great," Katie answered. "Is there a day that is better for you next week than any other?"

"I have to stop here every morning and I have to be at Rushen Abbey every day, so it makes no difference to me. If I were you, I would go for the first day that is sunny."

They both laughed and Katie looked out the office window where a steady rain was falling.

"Seriously," William smiled. "Why not see how your research is coming? If you work hard all this week, you will probably need a short break next week anyway."

Katie nodded. "Too much hard work, not enough sunshine, will make me a grumpy wreck."

William grinned. 'So it's a date," he told her. "Now I'd better get some work done. If I'm going to be out of the office all next week at the abbey then I need to get a lot done this week."

He turned around and opened his own office door, smiling back at Katie as he walked into the room and turned on the light. He left the door open, but immediately picked up his phone, dialing into the voice messaging system. Katie took the hint and headed down the rest of the stairs, William's words echoing in her ears. "It's a date," he had said. What was she supposed to make of that?

She headed down to the ground floor kitchen and made herself a cup of tea while she waited for Ealish. She stood in the middle of the comfortable room, leaning against the counter, sipping her tea and resisting the temptation to grab a biscuit as well. After a few minutes, she heard the front door open and stuck her head out the kitchen door.

"Hey, Ealish," she said as the woman bounced in, "I was just getting tea while I was waiting for you."

"Sorry if I've kept you," Ealish answered. "I stopped at the shops for some biscuits and a few other bits," she explained as she shut the door behind her to block off the grim weather.

"No problem. I had a cup of tea and if you had been much longer, I would have had a biscuit as well," Katie laughed.

"Let me just find a new hiding place for the biscuits and then we can go up to my office and get started."

Ealish walked into the kitchen and unpacked her shopping. She put a box of chocolate-covered biscuits behind a row of books that ran along one wall of the kitchen.

"Out of sight, out of mind," Ealish sighed as she shut the cupboard door, having put the coffee and tea away. "I swear William can smell them when he comes down here, and once they're open, I can't resist them," she patted her hips and sighed again. "I really need to stop eating chocolate biscuits," she said to Katie.

"Nonsense," Katie answered stoutly. "Life is too short to deny yourself chocolate," she told the other woman firmly.

Ealish laughed. "My sentiments exactly," she agreed as she fixed her own cup of tea. "Okay, let's head up to the office and get down to work."

Katie followed Ealish up the stairs, focusing her mind on her work, rather than on her desire for a chocolate biscuit. As they walked into Ealish's office she found her eyes wandering over to William's door and she blushed as he caught her eye. He winked at her and waved a hand. He was still on the phone, or on it again, so he didn't speak to them. Katie moved her books off the visitor's chair and sat down.

Ealish interrupted Katie's thought gathering with a question. "So, did you have fun on Sunday with Finlo?"

"It was great to see some of the sights," Katie answered cautiously, not sure what she should or even wanted to say about her relationship with Finlo.

"What was your favorite bit, then?"

"Castle Rushen, for sure, by miles," Katie answered with a huge smile. "It was amazing and I could have spent hours just sitting in the throne room soaking up the atmosphere of the place."

Ealish laughed. "It is atmospheric, I suppose," she agreed.

"I loved the staff in period costume as well. I saw this woman...." Katie hesitated, unsure of what to say about the mysterious woman she had seen crying in the throne room.

"A woman? In period costume?" Ealish sounded intrigued. "What did she look like?"

"I didn't get much of a look at her, really," Katie confessed. "I was just sitting there and I must have shut my eyes, because when I opened them, she was standing there. I said something to her and she turned around, but she was crying, and it didn't seem polite to stare."

Ealish was looking at Katie open-mouthed. After a long silence, she stood up and grabbed a book from a shelf behind the door. She quickly flipped through the pages and then stopped. "Did she look like this?" Ealish showed her a picture from the book.

Katie looked at the picture for a moment. "Sort of," she answered. "I didn't get that close of a look at her, but she did have her hair like that and the dress is similar. I was surprised at how elaborate her dress was, for a staff costume."

"It wasn't a staff costume," Ealish answered slowly. "It was a ghost."

Katie started to laugh, but then broke off when she realized that Ealish was completely serious. "A ghost? Come on, I'll wave to the Little People and avoid black cats, but ghosts?"

Ealish shook her head. "There have been sightings over the years, but I never actually met anyone who has seen her," she told Katie. "I always thought people were making it up or dreaming it, but you didn't even know she was supposed to be there."

Katie frowned. "Who was supposed to be there? Who is it that I'm supposed to have seen, then?"

"Charlotte de la Tremouille, the wife of James Stanley, the Seventh Earl of Derby."

Katie was shocked. "Hang on, that's the Earl who was here during the Civil War. What is his wife doing haunting Castle Rushen then?" Katie still didn't believe a word of it, but she was curious in spite of herself.

"She was at Castle Rushen, reportedly sitting in the throne room, when she received word that her husband had been killed. It was particularly cruel, because the Parliamentarians arrived in Castletown Harbor and demanded that she surrender the island to them. They sent in a letter and within it they mentioned 'the late Earl of Derby', which was how she found out that her husband had been executed. She was said to be devastated, as theirs was a true love match. That is why she is said to haunt the Castle. She is still hoping that Derby will come back to her, even though she knows he can't." Ealish shivered and Katie burst out laughing again.

"All of this is very dramatic, but I don't believe a word of it," she told Ealish.

"The history is all totally true," Ealish defended herself. "And I never believed in the ghost until just now. But you saw something there, didn't you?"

Katie was forced to nod, in spite of herself.

"And you said that she was crying. According to local legend, if you see her and she is crying then whoever you came to the castle with is not your true soul mate," Ealish told Katie. "If you see her and she's smiling then the man you are with is your one true love. I guess that is bad news for Finlo, then."

Katie struggled not to laugh again. "What nonsense," she declared.

"There is a local story that there was a girl who saw the Countess crying one summer and immediately dumped the man she was dating, the one who had brought her to see the castle in the first place. She spent the next year on her own, and then one day she was at the castle with her best friend, who happened to be a man. When he went down the stairs ahead of her, she turned around and saw the Countess smiling at her. She married him the next month and they lived happily ever after."

Katie shook her head. "It's a lovely story, but surely no one really believes it?"

"It's been years since anyone has reported seeing the ghost," Ealish told her. "But in the early years of the twentieth century, after the new prison was built in Douglas, it was traditional for girls to make their intended take them through the castle the month before their wedding. They would walk together through the throne room and then the boys would be sent down the stairs while the girls would sit and wait to see if the ghost would cry or smile. Of course, the vast majority reported seeing her smiling. No one wanted to admit that they didn't actually see anything. Some might have actually imagined seeing her because they wanted to so badly."

Ealish frowned at Katie's skeptical look. "Of course a few did claim to seeing her crying, and then broke off their engagements. I suspect that some used it as a good excuse to get out of their engagements where they were having doubts." Ealish smiled at Katie. "Anyway, the practice died out with the coming of the first World War. Perhaps it seemed too frivolous to worry what a long-dead Countess thought of your fiancé, when you had to worry that he might die in the war?"

Katie shook her head. "I don't know. It all seems really farfetched to me."

"But you did see something," Ealish reminded her. "I bet the local paper would love to hear about this. Not to mention Manx National Heritage. If they could sell people the idea that we had a real live ghost, tourism would boom."

"Live and ghost don't really belong together, do they?" Katie giggled, "but I would rather that we just keep the whole thing to ourselves, if we can, please."

Ealish nodded. "I won't say anything to anyone," she agreed, "but if you decide to tell people, I'm happy to confirm your story that you mentioned it without knowing anything about it."

Katie shook her head. "That's not going to happen," she insisted. "I don't want to talk about it anymore, ever. I'm going to forget it happened and just get on with my life. I know I haven't found my soul mate anyway. And I'm not trying to find him at the moment, remember?"

Ealish only smiled. "Let's get down to business, then."

The pair spent a long time discussing the various directions that Katie's research could take.

"Really, you need to get started, dig around a bit and then decide what you want to focus on," Ealish suggested. "There is a lot of material, and no one expects you to look at everything for the whole Civil War period to do an in-depth analysis. You need to look for something interesting or a special hook to hang your chapter on. Preferably something that doesn't require you to do too much transcribing of old documents, as that can be terribly time-consuming."

Katie had to agree, but she didn't, as yet, have that magic hook. "Can we quickly take a look at the documents that Marjorie gave me? She felt that they were particularly important ones. Things that she or other researchers had come across over the years that she had put aside for the day that someone finally did some research into the period."

"No problem, let's take a look," Ealish took the pile of photocopies and looked through them quickly. "Most of these appear to be Acts of Tynwald and other government documents. There are a few relating to the price of bread and ale. That might be significant if you look at the economy or issues in that area."

She paused as she shuffled through the papers again. "This one looks the most interesting to me," she told Katie, holding out one photocopy. "It is fairly neatly written, I'd bet you can transcribe this one yourself."

Katie took the copy of the document back and took a closer look. She had gone through all of the sheets after Marjorie had given them to her and she hadn't felt that she could read any of them. Now she studied the document carefully and thought maybe she could make out some of it.

"Considering..." she read out slowly, looking at Ealish for confirmation.

"Yes, I think that is right," Ealish smiled. "It sounds like something serious was going on."

Katie continued reading, surprise growing on her face. "But this is extraordinary," she said to Ealish. "According to this there was wide-spread famine on the island and those that had bread are ordered to share it with those that don't. Did this sort of thing happen a lot on the island?"

"The wording of the Act has echoes in the English Poor Laws that were in effect throughout the sixteenth and seventeenth centuries," Ealish answered, reaching for a book on the shelves behind her desk. "Here, have a look," she suggested, showing her a page in the book.

Katie took the book and quickly read through some of the old laws. "Did the same laws apply on the island?" Katie wanted to know.

"No, the island had its own government, so it had its own laws. I'm not sure if anything similar was put into effect earlier than this date or not," Ealish frowned. "I can't think of anyone who has done much research in that area, but I'll make a few phone calls and see what I can find out. Meanwhile, this could be just the hook you need. An analysis of the parish registers might just tell you how serious the famine was. And while you are at it, you might get a feel for the number of Royalists who were living on the island. Everyone speculates that a number of them fled here during the war, but no one has ever satisfactorily figured out how many that might have been. If they were here, with their families, they might have been having babies baptized or some may have been buried. I doubt many would have married during the war period, at least not on the island, but you never know. It is something to keep in mind while you are studying the registers anyway."

Katie nodded excitedly. This might be just what she needed. "You did say that the registers have been transcribed, didn't you?"

"Yes, ages ago. They're all on microfilm and if Marjorie has copies of the film, you can bring them back here to work on as we have a couple of readers in the extra office. If she doesn't, you will have to work on them in the museum library. Then again, it might be better to work there. That way you have to quit at five every day. If you have the stuff here, you seem to be the type that will work into the small hours if you feel as if you're making progress."

Katie nodded in acknowledgment of the fair assessment. "I'm sure I would," she agreed, "but it would be nice to be able to work on my own time, rather than being constrained by the schedule in the museum."

"Well, you can only talk to Marjorie and see what she says. Run the whole idea past her and see if she thinks you're going in the right direction. If she agrees, I would spend a couple of weeks or so looking at the registers. Try to see if there is enough information in there for you to draw any conclusions. If not, at least you can write about that, and we can talk again about other possible ideas to be included."

Katie smiled. "I'm getting really excited about this," she confided to Ealish. "I like the idea of finding out just how serious this famine was."

"Wait until you've seen the sources," Ealish cautioned. "I don't know how many parish registers survive from that period, but there might not be many and they might be really incomplete. It's great that you are excited, but a lot of research on the island is very frustrating because just as you find something really exciting, you find out two out of three documents that might help have gone missing over the years or simply can't be found. The library has thousands of documents and it would take a team of ten their whole working lives to properly sort and catalogue it all. And that doesn't take into account the fact that more stuff is being deposited there every year."

Katie frowned. "No one told me all of this before I agreed to write a chapter for the history," she moaned.

Ealish laughed. "Don't worry, we don't expect the impossible from you. We all know the limitations of the library and of a single researcher. Chat with Marjorie and if she's happy, give it a go. We can meet again next Monday at nine and you can let me know how you think it is going."

Katie smiled at her and took that as her cue to leave. "Thank you so much for all of your time this morning," she told her, "I really appreciate it."

"No problem," Ealish insisted. "I've got meetings most of today and tomorrow, unfortunately, but how about we have lunch on Wednesday? We can talk informally about your progress, or not, if you would rather leave it for Monday. And regardless, we can have a nice lunch."

"That sounds great," Katie agreed, happy to continue building her friendship with the other woman.

"Right, so if I don't see you between now and then, let's meet downstairs at noon on Wednesday and we can walk to one of the hotels for lunch. Shall I ask Jane as well?"

"Oh yes, please do," Katie agreed enthusiastically. "That sounds fun and less dangerous than another night of drinking too much wine."

"This isn't a substitute for that," Ealish laughed. "Just a mid-week alternative. I'm still hoping for a repeat of last Friday one week very soon. Just not this week, because I've got a hot date on Friday night."

"You can tell me all about him on Wednesday," Katie grinned, "and then next week you can tell me how it went."

She and Ealish both laughed as Katie gathered her books and papers and walked out of the room. She glanced back over her shoulder to say another quick "bye" to Ealish and noticed that William was watching her. She smiled and ducked her head in his direction and quickly headed back up to her apartment. He was making her very uncomfortable and she wasn't sure why.

❧ 9 ❧

The week rushed by for Katie. She spent most of her time buried in the microfilm viewing room at the museum library. Marjorie had agreed that the document was significant and that the matter might be worth pursuing, so Katie had steamed ahead. What Marjorie didn't have was copies of the films that could be taken back to the institute for further study.

Still, Katie found that if she started at ten every morning and spent the day looking at the films, she really needed the break by five. Most nights she ended the day with a couple of pills for the pounding headache that working with the microfilm for so many hours gave her and an early bedtime.

Even on Wednesday, when she took a long lunch break to eat with Jane and Ealish, her head was still pounding by the end of the day. Lunch had been a great break, though, full of the latest gossip about Ealish's love life and the great new guy Jane had met and was cautiously letting through her armor. The week continued to be rainy and Katie could only hope that the following week would be nicer, for the sake of the Rushen Abbey dig, if nothing else.

She found herself feeling disappointed when, by Friday, she'd heard nothing at all from Finlo. She'd expected, after their day out, that he would be back in touch soon, but he hadn't called or dropped in to see her once during the whole week. When five o'clock on Friday arrived, she pushed back her chair at the museum and sighed. Her head was aching again and she bent it left and right, trying to ease the tension in her neck.

Unexpectedly, she felt hands descend on her neck and begin to rub gently. Within seconds, she could feel the tension lifting and her headache dissipating. She struggled to suppress a soft moan of relief as the hands moved on to her shoulders, releasing the muscles that had been bent over microfilm and notepaper all day. For a long delicious moment she relaxed and let herself enjoy the massage, then she dragged herself back to reality and turned in her chair. She wasn't sure what she felt when she found William standing behind her.

"That felt wonderful," she told him honestly.

"You shouldn't spend too many hours a day hunched up over your work," William told her seriously. "You'll find yourself burned out and fed up before the end of June. You need to make sure you take frequent breaks. From the feel of your neck and shoulders, you didn't take too many today."

"I stopped for a while for lunch," Katie told him, flushing guiltily. She knew that she needed breaks, but she hated to take them. She was in a hurry to get this burst of research done so she could get on with analyzing what she was finding.

William shook his head. "One break isn't enough. You need to try harder next week to stop more often. It doesn't have to mean stopping your research. You could take a break and look at a couple of books or something, but too much time with the microfilm will give you a headache and make your eyes hurt."

Katie couldn't argue with that sound advice and she smiled up at William. "You're right. I guess that is why you're the boss." She turned away from him and began to gather up her papers and notes that were scattered all over the tiny space.

William spoke again behind her. "I do know how easy it is get obsessed with your research and forget about the rest of the world. That isn't good for anyone," he told her. From the corner of her eye,

Katie saw William shake his head as if trying to get rid of a memory he would rather forget.

"I'll try harder to take breaks next week," Katie smiled at him. "I suppose Marjorie will tell on me if I don't!"

William looked at her with his head tipped to one side. "Marjorie will only tell me if she is worried about you. We all like to take care of our special visitors," he paused for a moment and then took a deep breath and plunged on, "With that in mind, do you have any plans for tonight?"

Katie was surprised and spoke before she thought. "No, nothing," she answered quickly and then frowned. She was still secretly hoping that Finlo would call or stop by and invite her out.

"You're frowning. I'm not sure what that means," William was looking at her closely.

Katie blushed under the scrutiny. "It doesn't mean anything," she answered him, "I don't have plans, no. I was just thinking that it's a bit sad that I don't."

"Well, sad or not, I don't have any plans either," William smiled at her. "Would you like to take a walk along the promenade and have dinner? The sun has finally come out and it looks like it will be a lovely evening. I know a great little Italian restaurant along the promenade. It is really casual, so we wouldn't have to change, and they don't take reservations, so we can just drop in when we get there."

Katie glanced down at her smudged jeans and old T-shirt. For the first few days she had stuck to her habit of wearing business clothes each morning, but as the week had gone on and she found herself spending yet another day alone with the dusty microfilm boxes she'd started to dress down.

She looked back up at William and smiled. "That sounds nice," she told him sincerely. "Let me drop off my things back in the apartment and run a brush though my hair and I'll be ready."

"I'll meet you at the front of the institute in ten minutes," William replied. "I need to have a quick word with Marjorie about some papers she was finding for me and then we can head out."

"Great," Katie answered. She rushed out of the library with a real spring in her step, excited at the prospect of a walk and a nice meal.

She was also looking forward to getting to know William better. He not only seemed nice, he could help her a lot in her work, if she could just stop feeling so unsettled around him. She didn't want to think about anything more than friendship with him. She was having enough trouble figuring out her feelings for Finlo. She didn't need any other complications.

She dashed across the street and up the stairs to her apartment. Once inside, she piled her notes carefully on the desk and headed to the bathroom for a quick chance to fresh up. She carefully brushed her hair and powdered her nose and then added a fresh layer of bright pink lipstick. A squirt of perfume completed her primping and, after changing into a clean T-shirt and a slightly nicer pair of shoes she was back down the stairs and waiting by the front door with two minutes to spare. She sat down on the steps to wait, reveling in the unexpected sunshine, head back and eyes closed. She felt someone sit down next to her.

"Hadn't you better get changed?" A voice spoke soft and low in her ear. Katie jumped and then stood up to look down at Finlo.

"Changed?" she choked out, feeling wrong-footed.

"I've booked us the best table at the best restaurant in town," Finlo told her with a smooth smile. "Drinks at seven, dinner at eight, dessert and breakfast at my place."

Katie bristled at his presumptuousness. "Sorry," she told him haughtily, "but I already have plans for tonight."

Finlo only laughed. "Girls' night out, is it?" he questioned. "Come on, Jane and Ealish won't mind if you cancel. They'll understand."

"My plans are none of your business," Katie told him, still furious.

Finlo smiled at her. "You're mad because I haven't rung, aren't you?" he asked her, seemingly still believing that she would come around eventually.

"I'm not mad that you haven't called," Katie told him. "You can do as you like. But if you don't call, then you shouldn't just turn up and expect me to fall at your feet either!"

"If I tell you that I'm really sorry, will you just forgive me and go and get changed?" Finlo was beginning to sound a bit exasperated.

"No," Katie answered, shaking her head. "I really do have plans for tonight," she told him. "And I won't cancel at the last minute. You should have called and asked me earlier in the week if you wanted to go out tonight."

Finlo shook his head. "Katie, I'm so sorry," he told her, giving her sad puppy dog eyes and his best "forgive me" smile. "I've had the week from hell at work, flying sick kids back and forth to Liverpool for emergency treatment nearly every day. Yesterday we lost one." His eyes filled with tears and Katie couldn't feel angry with him anymore.

"Anyway," he continued, "the only thing that kept me going was the idea of having dinner with you tonight. I made the reservation last week because I wanted to take you somewhere really nice. I just forgot to let you know. Isn't there any way you can change your plans?"

Katie felt torn in two and didn't know what to say. "I'm sorry about the sick kids," she told him, "but I really do have plans for tonight. Can't we go out another night?"

She didn't want to upset William by cancelling, even though their arrangements had been last-minute, but she felt sorry for Finlo, and he had made the reservation earlier, even if he had forgotten to mention it to her.

Finlo sighed deeply and gave her a wounded look. "I suppose I can try to change the booking," he began.

He stopped suddenly as he spotted William approaching. "Hey, cousin," he called to the other man. "'Want to go to dinner with me? I wanted to take Katie, but she has other plans. I hate to give up a booking at Maurice's when they are so hard to get."

William smiled and swung an arm around Katie. "Sorry, cousin, but Katie has plans with me tonight. You'll have to dig out a name from your little black book this time."

Finlo narrowed his eyes and looked from William to Katie and then back again. William smiled smugly at him.

"So that is how it is going to be?" Finlo snarled at his cousin.

"Looks like it," William answered, pulling Katie closer to him.

Katie frowned. "How what is going to be?" she demanded, looking from one to the other.

"We're both attracted to you," Finlo answered, "and William ought to step aside. I met you first, after all."

"Hang on here," Katie demanded. "I've told you," she said to Finlo, "and now I'll tell you," she said to William, stepping away from him, "I'm not looking for a boyfriend. I had one and it didn't work out and now I'm done with men for a while. I'm here for three months to do my research and write my chapter, and then I'm going home. I don't even want to think about dating for the next three months. I'm happy to go out with both of you, or either of you, or whatever, but just as friends. I expect both of you to respect how I feel."

Finlo chuckled softly. "I do respect how you feel, Katie. How you really feel, though, not how you say you feel."

He looked deeply into her eyes and Katie could feel herself blushing as she remembered how his lips had felt on hers.

"For tonight, I'll do the mature thing and bow out gracefully. I've got a big charter tomorrow night, but I'll be in touch about rescheduling our dinner soon," he turned and headed back down the steps. "Good night, Katie," he called back over his shoulder. "You won't win, William," he added, before disappearing down the alley next to the neighboring building.

Katie stood stock still, staring after him. She had no idea what to say next or what to do. William made an impatient move next to her and then cleared his throat.

"Sorry about that," he told Katie sheepishly. "I shouldn't have dragged you into all of this. He took you out first and I should have steered clear. But it is so unusual that I actually meet someone that I'm attracted to that I couldn't resist asking you out. He's never been slowed down by the idea that I was seeing someone first."

William was talking out loud, but he almost seemed to be talking to himself, arguing with his own conscience, and Katie kept quiet. "How many women has he stolen from my arms? Hell, some he even took from my bed. All I wanted to do was have a chance to get to know you better. You seem like a great woman, smart and good company, and you're so pretty. Too pretty for me, I guess. A woman like you belongs with someone like Finlo, but then he is all flash and no substance." William sighed deeply. "I'm no flash and all boring archaeologist, as Finlo keeps reminding me as he jets off with yet another of my girlfriends."

Katie was astonished by the monologue and took a breath to steady herself before she spoke. "Look, William, you seem like a nice person. If my situation were different, I would love to go out with you and see where things went. But I'm only here for a few months and I've just had my heart comprehensively broken, so I'm not looking for a boyfriend. And that means I'm not interested in Finlo either! What I could use is a friend or two, someone to spend some time and explore the island with, so if you are interested in that position, great."

William smiled at her. "I could use a friend as well," he told her. "Finlo is right about me spending too much time digging in the dirt, when I should be living my life. And you're in real danger of spending too much time staring at microfilm. We need to force each other to get out more, starting right now! A walk on the promenade and dinner is just what we need."

Katie smiled happily and the pair made their way down the stairs to the sidewalk in front of the institute. William took her elbow to guide her to the nearest pedestrian crossing. Katie ignored the sudden shock she felt when William touched her. They had agreed to be friends, and that was all that she wanted, so there was no point in looking for trouble.

"I am sorry that you missed dinner at Maurice's tonight," William told her after they crossed the road and were wandering slowly down the wide promenade, watching the seagulls and the waves. William had let go of her arm after they had negotiated the crossing and Katie was torn between being grateful and being disappointed.

Katie shook her head at him. "It doesn't matter. Finlo is definitely looking for more than friendship. A romantic dinner for two somewhere expensive would probably give him the wrong idea."

"Kissing him like you were the other night will give him the wrong idea as well," William muttered the words, but Katie heard them clearly and blushed. She was unable to think of a suitable reply. A small child on a skateboard saved her by running squarely into her legs.

"Ouch," she blurted out in surprise. The little boy fell off the board and sat down hard on the paved surface, his face scrunching up, ready to cry loudly.

William grabbed the skateboard, which had continued down the promenade on its own after its owner had fallen off, and he surprised the boy by leaping on and doing a complicated move. Katie and the boy both watched, open-mouthed, as William rode the board a short distance, performing a series of tricks that seemed to hugely impress the child, who had by now completely forgotten to cry.

"Wow," he said as William handed back his board, "that was amazing. How did you learn all of that?"

"Lots and lots of practice when I was young," William told him. "The most important thing to learn, though, is to not run into anyone."

The boy looked down and flushed. "Sorry," he mumbled and then ran back to his mother who was just now getting close enough to see what was happening. She and the boy had a quick chat and then she waved at William and Katie before the pair turned away and headed back down the promenade.

William turned now to Katie. "Are you okay?" he asked in concern. "Did you get hit with the board?"

Katie shook her head and giggled. "Where did you learn to do all of that?" she asked, echoing the child's earlier question.

William was still worried about her, however. "First things first," he told her. "Are you sure you are okay?"

"I'm fine!" Katie told him. "It was more shock than anything that made me shout. I was watching the family down there, building that sand castle, and I never saw him coming."

William looked to where Katie was pointing and then he laughed. "That is the sorriest sand castle I've ever seen," he whispered to Katie as they began their stroll again. They both burst out laughing.

"Seriously, though, William, where did you learn all those skateboard tricks?"

"We rarely went anywhere during the summer holidays," William answered, his eyes reflecting his memories. "In those days there weren't as many sports programs for kids, so it seemed like there was never anything to do. My best mate, Simon, and I used to ride our skateboards all over the place. We would take a bus somewhere and then ride around for hours. It was just a way to fill in the time, really. If you think I'm good, you should have seen Simon. He could do tricks I could only dream about."

"So where is Simon now?"

"He went to medical school across and then settled in London. Last I heard he was a big shot cosmetic surgeon on Harley Street or something like that. He doesn't even get back to the island for Christmas with his family. Last year he flew his mum and dad to Ibiza for Christmas. They hated it, but apparently Simon and his wife were in their element."

Katie frowned. "Christmas in Ibiza doesn't sound very, well, Christmassy to me," she told William. "Of course, I'm from a snowy part of the world. Christmas should mean a couple of feet of snow and having to bundle up warm and lots and lots of hot chocolate to drink."

William smiled. "That sounds lovely. We don't get much snow here, but it is cold, certainly colder than Ibiza! But to me, Christmas is about stirring Christmas cake and too many people being crowded into one house and fighting with all the cousins who always came to our house for dinner and broke my new toys."

Katie laughed. "How awful," she said. "Everyone always came to our house as well, but my mom always hid my best new things so no one could break them."

"My mother always said that Christmas was about giving and sharing and I wasn't allowed to put away anything. Finlo always managed to break my favorite new toy, every year." William frowned. "I didn't mean to bring Finlo up again."

Katie just laughed. "That sounds about right," she grinned. "I had one cousin, Diana, who always managed to figure out what toy I liked best and then somehow broke it every year. It was after that happened twice that my mother started letting me hide things. But Diana always broke something that I really liked anyway. She was terrible! It is only now that I can look back and realize that she was a really unhappy child and I think she was really jealous of my life. I was an only child and my parents lavished attention on me. She had four brothers, all younger, and I doubt she ever got much time with her parents."

William nodded slowly. "Finlo had a very different upbringing to mine." He spoke as if thinking out loud again. "I suppose he could have been jealous of some aspects of my life. He had lots of material things, but his parents both worked and he was sent to boarding school quite young. Maybe he was jealous that I got to stay at home with my parents for school."

Katie smiled. "Enough talking about our childhoods! We are talking far too seriously for such a lovely night! Tell me what that man is doing over there." Katie pointed.

William looked where she indicated and then shook his head. "I've no idea what he is doing," he told her, looking again. "It looks like he is trying to bury himself in the sand, but I've no idea why he would want to do that."

Katie and William looked at each other and burst out laughing, enjoying the warm sunshine, the wonderful views and each other's company. They walked in silence for a while, watching the water, the birds and the people who were still scattered around the sandy beach.

Occasionally they stopped to look more closely at something, talking quietly and laughing together. Katie felt relaxed and happy in William's company in a way that she hadn't when she had been with Finlo. With Finlo she was constantly aware of the bubbling sexual tension between them. She didn't feel the same pressure between herself and William, in spite of the definite attraction she felt towards him.

After about an hour of slow walking, they reached the far end of the promenade and stood for a long time watching the waves rolling into the large rocks. Katie looked up the road at the large hill that rose steeply from the promenade's end. She could see houses and office buildings along the road, and also the tracks for the electric tramway.

"What is it like on the electric train?"

"A lot like riding any train," William answered. "The carriages are small, but they transport a fair few passengers in the summertime. We could take the train up to Laxcy one Saturday if you would like. We could even go all the way up Snaefell if that interests you."

"There are just so many things I want to do," Katie exclaimed impatiently. "I don't think three months is going to be anywhere near enough time to fit in everything." Taking the train to the top of Snaefell, the island's tallest mountain, had been one of the things she had wanted to do.

"Well, we can see about extending your grant," William answered her outburst seriously. "But I'm not sure how much we can do."

"No, no," Katie rushed a reply. "I have to be back at my desk for work on the fifth of September. Maybe I'll just have to figure out a way to come back soon."

"You've really only just arrived," William reminded her. "I'm sure you'll find the time to do most of the things you want to do. Try not to get too worried yet. I'll help you find time to fit things in and help sort out arrangements and tickets and whatever."

Katie smiled at him. "Thank you," she told him gratefully. "I told you I needed a friend."

"And I need some food," William grinned. "I can hear my favorite garlic bread calling to me from here."

"Garlic bread?" Katie suddenly realized that it had been many hours since she had grabbed that limp sandwich for lunch, and she was starving. "Let's go!"

The pair walked back along the promenade with a purpose now, heading to William's favorite Italian restaurant. They still chatted and laughed together, but their pace was much quicker and only a few minutes later they found themselves at the door to the restaurant. William held the door for Katie and then led her down the stairs to the small dining room. It was dark inside after the dazzling sunshine and Katie stood still at the bottom of the stairs for a moment, letting her eyes adjust.

A man rushed forward. "William," he said in a thick Italian accent, "how nice of you to join us tonight. And you have brought a very beautiful lady friend. Please, come and sit in the corner where you can have a nice romantic meal." As he spoke he led them to a small table in a dark corner along the back wall of the room.

William smiled. "Katie is a work colleague," he told the man, "but this table will do nicely anyway, thanks."

They sat down and the man handed them each a menu, offering William the wine list as well, and then rushing off to greet a large party that had just walked through the door.

"Should we get a bottle of wine?" William asked Katie.

"I don't know." Katie didn't want to do anything to make the evening feel any more 'date-like' than it already did, but a glass of wine might help calm the nerves that were suddenly plaguing her.

"Oh, let's go for it," William smiled. "I usually come on my own and stick to a single glass. Sharing a bottle is far more friendly."

Katie studied the menu for a long time and then sat back with a sigh.

"Everything sounds good. This is your favorite restaurant. What should I have?"

William smiled and rattled off several suggestions to Katie. Katie was happy to agree with his ideas and William called the waiter over with a look and ordered the wine and food in perfect Italian.

"Is it only food you pronounce, or do you speak Italian properly?" Katie demanded.

William blushed. "I speak Italian properly," he answered, looking shy.

"I'm terrible with languages," Katie told him. "I can't seem to learn anything but English and I'm not even great at that!"

"Languages come fairly easily to me," William told her, looking sheepish. "I started French in primary school, of course, and then took that and Spanish and Italian at O and A level, studying all three at university as well, just to give me a break from the archaeology. I travel a good deal as well, digging all over Europe, and it helps if you can speak to the locals in their own language."

"Well, I'm impressed," Katie told him. "As I said, I just can't do languages."

"Maybe you just haven't had the right teacher," William suggested, blushing again as he did so.

Katie only laughed and then changed the subject. "So how long has this restaurant been here?"

The pair chatted easily about the restaurant and then more generally about favorite foods as they shared three delicious courses of wonderful, freshly prepared Italian food. Somehow a second bottle of wine got opened and drunk and Katie found herself feeling incredibly giddy and a little bit drunk as they left the restaurant. She tripped down the stairs at the front and stood, breathlessly at the bottom, giggling at herself.

"Oops. I missed one of those steps," she grinned up at William, wondering why she had never noticed how attractive his eyes were before.

"Careful," William frowned. He took her arm gently and led her back across the road to walk along the promenade again. "Let's take another short walk before I take you home," he suggested. "I think some fresh air will do you the world of good."

Katie giggled again. "I'm not that drunk," she told him, "I'm just feeling a bit giddy and silly." She laughed again and then looked at him with a sideways glance. "Can we walk on the beach?" she asked pleadingly.

William laughed. "Of course we can, if you like," he answered and they headed down a ramp from the promenade towards the sand.

"The tide is coming in, so watch your step or you'll get wet," William told her as they made their way over rocks and onto the sandy shore.

Katie took off her shoes and socks and rolled up the legs on her jeans. She stood still for several minutes in the shallow water, enjoying the feeling of the cold water splashing against her legs. A larger wave grew out of the water and Katie backed away quickly, nearly knocking William over as she stumbled backwards. He grabbed her waist and they stood together on the still warm sand, arms intertwined, for a moment.

"Sorry," Katie spoke first as she moved away from William. "I didn't know you were behind me and I was trying not to get too wet."

"No problem," William answered.

They walked slowly down the beach, collecting odd shells and skipping the occasional stone. The sun was still sitting low in the sky and Katie felt as if she had been transported to some magical world where it never got dark. The night air was growing cold, however, and Katie suddenly realized that her feet were freezing. She sat down on a convenient rock and put her socks and shoes back on.

"Maybe we should head back," she said reluctantly to William. "It's getting cold out here."

"Here," William pulled off his sweatshirt and handed it to Katie. "This should keep you warm enough for the walk back." He turned towards the institute and Katie followed slowly, pulling William's shirt over her head as she walked.

It was warm, and smelled of the sea and Italian food and William's cologne. Katie inhaled the delicious scent deeply. She caught up to William and he smiled at her and took her hand. They walked hand in hand back to the front door of the institute, neither speaking, both simply enjoying the moment.

"I guess this is good night," Katie said slowly, as she looked up at the building in front of them.

"Let me walk you around to the back door," William suggested. "I'm parked there and it saves having to unlock and then relock all the doors in the building."

They walked quietly down the short alley, both reluctant to end the evening.

"Well, I guess *this* is good night, then," Katie laughed, looking up at William, now lit by streetlights as much as by the sun.

William stood very close to her and smiled. "I suppose so," he answered looking deeply into her eyes, as if searching for something buried in them.

He turned to go and then turned back again quickly. "Before I go, I just wanted to say, um..." William took a deep breath. "Right, you aren't looking for anything more than friendship, and I'll respect your boundaries, but just so you know, I would very much like to think about being more than friends."

The words had rushed out and William blushed with the effort but now he stopped and looked again into Katie's eyes. He sighed and then pulled her closer.

His lips brushed hers gently and Katie told herself to pull away, but her body wouldn't listen to her brain. Instead, her body leaned into his and she found herself deepening the kiss. When William finally lifted his head, Katie was breathless and confused. They stared at each other for a long time, neither knowing what to say.

"I didn't mean..." Katie started.

"I didn't either," William answered.

"I'm sorry," Katie told him, not sure what she was apologizing for, but feeling she should.

"I am too," William told her, seemingly equally confused. "Anyway, I think I had better go. You need to think about what you want. If you just want to be friends with men, you need to stop kissing them like that."

Katie knew he was thinking about her and Finlo as much as their own kiss and she blushed as she turned away and tried to open her door. Her fingers wouldn't work properly and after a short struggle, William leaned around her and turned the key in the lock for her.

"Thanks," she muttered, embarrassed about how the evening had turned out.

William grabbed her hand as she started through the door. "Thank you," he told her, "for a really lovely evening."

Katie blushed again. "No, thank you," she replied, "I'm sorry about the kiss and everything, I mean…"

"Stop," William smiled. "Let's just leave it at that," he told her and then he leaned in again and kissed her very softly on the lips.

"Sleep well, Katie. And remember that the first sunny day we get next week, I'm taking you to Rushen Abbey."

With that, he released her hand and Katie stepped inside and shut her door. For a long time she stood just inside the door, leaning against it, with her mind in turmoil. She was startled to hear William's car engine start after a while, and she wondered how long he had stood on the other side of the door doing his own thinking. Finally, she made her way up the stairs and into her apartment, stripping off her clothes and climbing into bed without even washing her face. She was exhausted now, mentally at least, and she fell at once into a deep and dreamless sleep.

❧ 10 ❧

atie woke up on Saturday morning determined to keep both
Finlo and William at arm's length. She needed a break from
men, and she was going to get it, in spite of feeling a growing
attraction to both men. She spent a quiet day, enjoying some time to
herself.

A great deal of effort was devoted to studying and analyzing the
data that she had spent the previous week collecting. She was counting
the events that were recorded in the parish registers, looking for some
evidence of the famine that was suggested in the document that Ealish
had helped her transcribe. By looking at trends in baptisms, burials
and weddings during the period, she was hoping to prove that the
famine had actually taken place.

Demographic study was new to her, but she was determined to do
her best to find out what she could about the island during the period.
She was also eager to learn more about the Derbys, especially the
Countess, whether she had actually seen her ghost or not.

The idea that the Derby marriage was a true love match intrigued
Katie. Such a thing would have been fairly unusual in their social class
at that time and Katie was curious to find out more about the couple.
She was surprised to find that, as yet, she was not terribly homesick.

She missed her family, of course, but she missed them just as much when she was in Maryland at her own little house.

She was also surprised that she didn't miss her old life the way she thought she might. She didn't feel that she was missing out on anything being on such a small island, either. Katie wasn't much of a shopper, so she wasn't pining for the large malls that dotted the landscape around where she lived. So far the island had proven to be a very pleasant surprise, with breath-taking scenery, lovely people, and great food.

For Sunday she had arranged to go with Ealish on a trip to the wildlife park in the north of the island. The day dawned sunny and bright and Katie found herself as excited as any small child going to the zoo for the day. Ealish was right on time and Katie jumped into her small car, eager to get on the road. They drove up the mountain road, following another part of the course for the TT races. Katie was delighted by the stunning views as they climbed the mountain.

"That's Snaefell, the highest peak on the island," Ealish told her, indicating one of the mountains they were driving through. "It's the one with the towers on the top."

"It doesn't look any bigger than any of the others," Katie told her with a frown.

"I'm assured that that is just an optical illusion and Snaefell really is the tallest," Ealish grinned, "but I always think that too."

They drove on, past the tram tracks that carried passengers to the top of Snaefell. "If you look back, you can just see Laxey, in the valley below," Ealish offered as they rounded a bend. Katie strained to see the small village, but only got a fleeting glimpse as they sped onwards.

"What is the speed limit up here?" Katie asked, a bit breathless from the twists and turns that seemed to be flashing by quite quickly.

"There's no limit on the mountain road," Ealish answered with a grin. "You should try riding in Finlo's flashy car up here. He flies along at an amazing rate."

"I think I might skip that, thanks," Katie answered, feeling dizzy at the prospect. "You're driving faster than feels safe."

"I can slow down if you like," Ealish offered instantly. "I don't want to frighten you. I drive the mountain so much that I forget that some people aren't used to it."

"No, you're fine." Katie answered "I'm just used to flat roads that are a lot wider and don't have sheep grazing right next to them!"

Both women laughed at this because there were a large number of sheep grazing right next to the fence that they were passing. They drove around another bend in the road before Ealish spoke again.

"There she is, Royal Ramsey by the Sea," she said.

Katie drew a breath. In front of the car the mountain dropped away dramatically and below them she could see a small town dazzling in the sunshine. The town was built along the sea front and Katie smiled as she watched sailboats chasing each other in the calm water.

"It looks magical," she told Ealish as they made their descent into the town.

"Ramsey is lovely. It gets more sunshine than anywhere else on the island. I've lived there my whole life and I'd move back if Douglas wasn't so convenient for work," Ealish grinned. "Of course, I'm lucky I bought my flat ten years ago, before house prices went totally crazy. Today I wouldn't be able to afford a flat in Douglas, or anywhere on the island for that matter."

"Are houses expensive?" Katie had never given house prices on the island much thought.

"They are now," Ealish answered. "As the finance industry moved in, more and more people moved over from across and that has driven up house prices. It isn't quite that simple, of course. There are other reasons why prices have gone up, but that is one of the reasons. The sad thing now is that many Manx people can't afford to own homes on their own island. Like I said, I was lucky. My parents insisted that I buy as soon as I was able and they gave me the down payment. Not many people my age have that advantage."

Katie frowned. "I suppose it doesn't help that the island is a pretty small place. There's only room for so many houses. It would be a shame to spoil all of the lovely scenery with lots of housing."

"Yes, it's tricky balancing the needs of people who want to buy homes with the need for farmland and green space. I don't envy the politicians who have to make the tough decisions. That is why I study history instead of being involved in making it."

Ealish and Katie both laughed at that. Katie wasn't keen to make history either, though she loved studying the subject.

They made their way down through the Ramsey hairpin turn and Katie spent a moment trying to imagine racing a motorcycle though that difficult corner. Then they drove though Ramsey, with Katie trying to look at everything at once in the small and picturesque town. They were quickly through Ramsey and across the island to the wildlife park.

Katie and Ealish chatted about everything from the weather to shoes and handbags as they drove along in the sunshine. Katie was expecting something like a large zoo, so she was surprised at the small sign that marked the turnoff to the park's parking lot. She and Ealish walked from the car to the small gift shop that served as the entry point to the park and paid their admission. Back outside, Ealish turned to Katie.

"Which way first?" Ealish asked. "The park is a big circle, so it doesn't really matter. We can start with mongooses and end with penguins or vice versa."

"Isn't it mongeese?" Katie laughed. "I think penguins sound more exciting, so let's leave them for last," she suggested.

Ealish grinned. "I always leave them for last as well," she told her friend. "Unfortunately, they aren't often actually doing anything exciting, but we can hope."

The pair turned and walked through a large gate. They stopped for a moment to look at a lazy mongoose that was sunning itself on a large rock. Then Katie read the sign on the next gate out loud. "'Please stick to footpaths. Please do not eat in the enclosures. Some animals are unrestrained. Please treat their home with respect.' Unrestrained?" she asked Ealish.

"Don't worry, the lynx are fed often enough that they don't usually eat visitors," Ealish told her with a mischievous grin. She laughed when Katie looked worried and then reassured her. "Nothing that's dangerous is allowed to roam about, but you will see for yourself. Don't worry." Katie didn't look convinced, but followed Ealish through the gate slowly.

"We don't have free-ranging animals in zoos back home," Katie told Ealish. "I've never actually heard of such a thing. Maybe they do have them in zoos somewhere in the U.S., but not any zoo that I've ever been to."

"Well, you came to the island for new experiences, didn't you?" Ealish challenged, as she made sure the gate was shut tightly behind them before walking onwards.

"Yes, I suppose I did," Katie answered bravely, trudging off along the footpath, looking at the large grassy area and the small pond that were separated from the path by a fence that was only about eight inches high.

Katie followed the path around a bend and found her way suddenly blocked by half a dozen large white birds, a few of whom looked up from their nap in the sunshine as if to see who had disturbed them. Katie took a step backwards into Ealish.

"Eek," Katie said softly, not knowing what do next.

Ealish laughed. "They're just pelicans," she told Katie. "They aren't small, but they are harmless, unless you're a fish!"

Ealish carefully picked her way through the birds, ignoring their outstretched heads as they inspected her progress. Katie followed quickly, thinking that their beaks looked very sharp. Katie skirted around the last one and hurried a few more steps down the path before she stopped and looked back at the birds.

Most had now put their heads back down and were resting, but one had stood up and was watching the two women. Katie didn't need any further encouragement to leave the enclosure, and she walked quickly down the rest of the path to the next gate. Ealish followed at a more leisurely pace, but even she sped up as the bird began to gain on her. The pair slipped through the gate and shut it tightly behind them, laughing together as the pelican gave them what appeared to be an angry look and then slunk back to his friends.

"We weren't in any real danger," Ealish assured her friend.

"No, of course not," Katie tried to sound confident as she agreed.

"Still, time to move on," Ealish pulled Katie along towards the next enclosure. "I think we've seen quite enough of the pelicans for one day."

They passed a lemur area and then saw a pair of strikingly beautiful cranes before passing through another gate. This let them into another large section and Katie found herself looking anxiously around for free-roaming animals. Ealish noticed her searching looks and grinned.

"There isn't anything roaming in here," she told her. "At least there wasn't the last time I was here."

"Good," Katie answered. "I like the idea of the animals being able to have a lot of space to walk around in, but I'm not so keen on sharing that space with them."

They headed through yet another pair of gates into the children's farm area and a pair of lambs enchanted Katie as they "baa'd" plaintively at her and Ealish. "Aren't they sweet?" she asked Ealish.

"I suppose," Ealish answered. "I grew up near a sheep farm," she explained to Katie, "so lambs aren't really that exciting to me."

"Well, I grew up in a city. We never saw a lot of baby animals. I think they're lovely."

Katie leaned over the fence and gave the nearest sheep a small pat. The sheep looked startled and then walked away to join his brother on the opposite side of their pen. "I guess he doesn't like me," Katie laughed and moved on.

She watched chickens and geese fighting with wild ducks for food and was enthralled again by a baby donkey sharing hay with his somewhat larger parents.

"You keep making a fuss over the baby animals, and I'm going to think you are broody," Ealish told her.

"Broody?"

"Wanting a baby," Ealish answered. "Don't you use that term in the States?"

"No, we don't. I don't know that we have just one word for wanting a baby. Broody is a lovely way of putting it. It sounds like a hen, fussing over her eggs. That is one English word I'm going to put to good use once I get home."

"It is a good word. Lots of meaning in just the one word," Ealish agreed. "But that doesn't answer the question of whether you are or not."

Katie smiled. "I suppose I am a bit," she answered slowly. "I was supposed to be getting married yesterday and Mark and I had talked about trying for a baby right away. I was sort of planning on a honeymoon baby. There didn't seem to be any reason to wait. We had been together for so long already. So yes, I guess I am a bit broody, because I thought by today I would have already started trying for a baby."

"Oh my gosh, I'm so sorry, Katie. I forgot about your cancelled wedding. I should have taken you out last night for dinner and drinks to help you forget. I'm so very, very sorry," Ealish said, clearly feeling awful that she'd forgotten.

"It's okay," Katie rushed to reassure her. "Friday night I had dinner with William and then yesterday I spent the day working on my research. Last night I treated myself to some amazingly good food from the takeaway down the street, and had a glass of wine. I really didn't even think about the wedding or Mark all night."

Katie was shocked when she realized that it was true. She hadn't given much thought to her called-off wedding or her former fiancé yesterday. She'd been less successful in not thinking about Finlo or William, but they were another matter.

"Still, I should have been there for you, not out with yet another loser," Ealish smiled at her friend. "No matter how cute he was."

Katie laughed out loud. "Go on then, tell me all about him," she encouraged as the women walked slowly through an indoor exhibit of snakes and turtles that neither was particularly interested in.

Ealish filled Katie in on all the juicy details of her date while they walked, clearly taking care to edit her conversation as they caught up to groups that included small children. Katie nearly choked with laughter as Ealish struggled to tell the story without offending anyone around them.

They left the small building and made their way into an outdoor exhibit that celebrated the uniqueness of island wildlife. Katie avoided still more snakes but watched a handful of turtles climbing around a large pen. As they studied some small mammals that Katie had never heard of before, Ealish turned the conversation back to her.

"So, you went out with William on Friday night?" she asked, trying to sound casually disinterested, but failing miserably. Intense curiosity was evident in her voice and Katie laughed again.

"Strictly as friends," she assured Ealish. "We walked up and down the promenade and then had dinner at this little Italian place with wonderful food. It was really nice."

"Just friends?" Ealish smiled. "Actually, I'm surprised that Finlo wasn't around to ask you out. I thought he seemed really keen the last time I saw him with you. I'm not trying to pry, mind you, but I am curious."

"Finlo did stop by," Katie admitted, "but I had already agreed to have dinner with William."

"I bet that went over well," Ealish frowned. "Those two don't need much encouragement to fight over something."

"Well, they aren't going to fight over me," Katie answered firmly. "I'm only looking for friends, and they can both be friends with me."

"Ha," Ealish laughed at her. "William is probably too nice to push things, but you won't catch Finlo leaving you alone. If he's decided he wants you, he will be putting everything he can into the chase. You can bank on that."

"Well, he's going to be disappointed," Katie answered sternly. "I've had enough heartbreak this year. Unless he wants to follow me home and keep trying there, he is going to be out of luck."

"Finlo can be very persuasive," Ealish warned, "but I would go for William if I were you. He is a wonderful guy and he deserves a good woman."

"I'm not going for either of them," Katie answered. "I am not interested in men right now."

Ealish grinned and changed the subject as they walked into a darkened enclosure. "Did you see the bats?"

Katie looked quickly through the glass wall that separated her from the animals in the room. "Bats?" Now that she knew what she was looking for, it was evident that there were several bats hanging from the nets and ropes that were strung around the room.

"They're fruit bats and they are harmless," Ealish told her.

"If they're harmless, how come they aren't free to fly around with us?" Katie teased.

"You haven't seen the whole exhibit yet," Ealish replied, pointing to the door in the far side of the room. Katie read the sign on the door that explained that, in the next room, the bats were indeed able to fly freely around the visitors.

"Maybe we should go back the way we came?"

"No way, the bats are really wonderful," Ealish told her. "Come on, trust me."

Katie followed Ealish reluctantly, thinking that that the bats were a better alternative than talking any more about Finlo and William. In the next room she stopped short and looked around quickly. The room was large and there was a small fenced area for people to stand. The room was full of plants and lined with netting and ropes as well as the small trees. Katie looked carefully around and spotted a bat high above them, pulling itself along some netting.

"Wow." She was enthralled in spite of herself. "I've never seen that before," she remarked to Ealish, watching carefully.

Movement beside her caught her eye and turned to see two more bats in the tree near her. She stepped back a short distance, but found herself mesmerized by their behavior. They were eating from a long stick that had been stuck through with a variety of fruits and vegetables. Katie watched as one bat nibbled some banana while another seemed to be enjoying an apple slice.

She looked up again to watch a bat fly from one side of the room to the other and then move easily along the netting along the far wall. Katie wasn't sure how long she stood there, but it was only when a large group with several small children flooded into the room that she and Ealish moved on.

"That was amazing," she told Ealish as they walked through a small area with pens along one side. She wasn't really paying any attention to the cages. She was too busy talking to Ealish about the bats. "I've never seen anything like it, they were fascinating and I feel like I could have watched them all day."

"I told you so," Ealish laughed.

"I thought bats only came out at night," Katie questioned.

"Actually, that isn't true at all," Ealish replied. "Those fruit bats are usually out and about at dusk and sometimes even in the day. I think they are my favorite animals here, though the lemurs are pretty good, too."

She said this as she held open a door for Katie. Katie passed through it and into a large grassy outdoor area. There were trees and ropes here as well and Katie wondered what animals lived in it as she looked around. She didn't have to wonder for long as a pair of lemurs made their way towards her curiously.

"Hello," she said to the small furry black and white animals as they leaped over a low fence and stood on the path in front of her.

"They come from Madagascar," Ealish told her. "Apparently they were replaced by monkeys through evolution everywhere else in the world, but not there. Aren't they cute?"

Katie had to agree that they were very cute as they climbed the fence and looked at her carefully. "How many are there?" She was sorry now that she had missed out reading the signs in the previous area.

"I think there are six," Ealish replied. "One pair of each of three different kinds. At least, there were the last time I was here."

They walked slowly through the enclosure, trying to spot the others, but they failed to find them. They carefully opened and closed doors behind them, making sure that no lemurs were escaping with them. Across from the exit was a small train station and Ealish explained that the trains only ran on certain days during the height of the summer season. It was a tiny miniature train that ran around a small area of the park on very small rails.

"The railway is all run by hugely dedicated volunteers and I doubt there is anything else like it in the world," Ealish told Katie.

"It's a shame it isn't open, then," Katie answered.

"We'll have to try to come back later in the season," Ealish smiled. "Maybe I'll invite Finlo and William to join us and we can watch them fight over you. Could be fun, like watching peacocks strut their stuff."

Katie blushed and shook her head. "I really don't want them fighting over me. I've had enough man trouble for now, really."

Ealish laughed. "I shouldn't tease you," she told Katie, "but it has been a long time since William was interested in anyone and I would like to see him happy."

"Well, I hope he finds happiness soon," Katie answered, "but he shouldn't be looking at me!"

She strode off, determined to leave the subject alone from there. The women walked past the lynx, which were sunning themselves on their platform. Katie was relieved to find that they were well and truly behind glass and fencing.

The next area was labelled "Australia" and Katie was delighted to find wallabies bouncing around freely throughout the large space. She was less enamored of the piles of wallaby poo that covered some sections of the path, however. Next it was through a large walk-through aviary where Katie saw several birds she had never seen before. A quick walk through the trees took them past some North American otters. Katie had to laugh when she saw the raccoon enclosure.

"Back home they are just pests," she told Ealish.

Then the path led them right to the doors of a small café.

"It's the perfect time for a lunch break," Ealish told Katie.

They ordered sandwiches and drinks and settled at a table outdoors that overlooked a small lake and some animal enclosures. While they waited for the food to arrive, they played "spot the animal", studying the signs that were spread along the wire fence that separated the dining area from the animals. Katie was delighted to see several birds and a few other small creatures in the area immediately in front of their table.

Sandwiches and drinks finished, the women treated themselves to ice cream cones made with fresh Manx ice cream before they headed back out into the park.

"Let's have a walk through the woods," Ealish suggested, leading Katie behind the café to a path through the trees. They walked for a short time and then came to a tall wooden tower.

"Come on then, up we go," Ealish told her. They climbed the steep steps to the top and stood on the platform, looking down at the land below them. "The curraghs are a unique conservation area," Ealish told Katie. "Curragh is a Manx word for a boggy woodland, by the way."

"Do many people speak Manx these days?" Katie asked curiously.

"The last native speaker died in the 1970s, but the language has been having something of a revival in the last few years," Ealish answered. "More and more people are taking classes in it and there is even a Manx language school now where you can have your children taught entirely in Manx."

"Is that a good thing?" Katie wondered out loud. "I mean, they have to live in an English-speaking world most of the time, don't they?"

"The school is based on Welsh and Scottish models and those have proven to be very successful," Ealish answered. "So far the children seem to be thriving and happy and they certainly benefit from very small classes and lots of individual attention. You should ask William about it. He knows several of the teachers there."

"Maybe I will," Katie answered.

The women climbed back down the tower and headed back along the path to the rear of the café. Back in the park itself, they passed spider monkeys playing on their own island, and then headed through another set of gates into an area full of capybaras and ducks.

A walk through a wooded area revealed varieties of tiny monkeys, some with their even smaller babies clinging to their backs. Katie was captivated by the way that the babies managed to hold tight to their mothers as the mothers climbed all over the trees and swung from the branches. The women walked through the flamingo area, where a pair of new-born chicks looked out of place in their grey feathers among their brightly colored family members.

Last, but not least, were the penguins, and Katie and Ealish arrived at feeding time. They watched, delighted, as the penguins dove through the water to catch fish that were being thrown into the pool by one of the keepers.

"That was fabulous," Katie said as they made their way out of the park. "I feel like a kid again."

"Zoos are great for that," Ealish answered with a smile. "I always bring my nieces and nephews, which is why I know so much about all the animals and everything. Now, what time is it?"

Katie looked at the watch she was actually wearing for a change. "Just after three," she answered.

"So, a bit too early to go out drinking, I guess," Ealish grinned.

"What else is there to do on a sunny Sunday?"

"How about a trip to the park? We can keep on feeling like kids by going on swings and climbing frames and playing some crazy golf."

"That sounds great," Katie answered eagerly, enjoying her day off from real life and grown-up responsibilities.

Once in the car, Ealish had a short chat with herself about the various parks on the island before deciding on the one in Onchan for their afternoon visit.

"There are several others that are very good too," she told Katie, "but Onchan should have just about everything we want and it is close to home for when we get tired."

Katie was happy to agree, as she knew nothing about the different parks. Ealish enlivened the drive back across the island by telling Katie a series of Manx folk stories that were both fanciful and funny.

Onchan Park was everything that Ealish had promised and the pair annoyed mothers and their children by hogging the swings for several minutes, each trying to get higher than the other. They then played a fiercely competitive round of crazy golf with Ealish winning in the end by only one stroke. A spin around the boating lake left them both feeling a bit seasick, but another pair of ice cream cones didn't seem to bother their stomachs.

"I can't remember the last time I've had this much fun," Katie told her friend. "Mark didn't really enjoy doing silly things like zoos and parks, and we were together for years and years."

"I think everyone needs a day acting like a child once in a while," Ealish told her. "It's easier once you have your own children, of course, because you can just act silly and tell everyone that you are doing it to keep them happy."

They both laughed at that as they walked through the park, noting several parents who were pretending to be monsters or sliding down slides under the guise of entertaining their children.

It was nearly six o'clock when they left the park and Ealish insisted that Katie come back to her apartment for dinner. She lived in a lovely old Victorian building that had been broken up into two separate apartments. Katie loved the high ceilings and the original features that had been maintained when the house had been remodeled.

Ealish threw together a quick spaghetti Bolognese and Katie enjoyed the food and the company a great deal. She returned back to her own apartment full of good food and feeling happier with life than she had in a long time. She went to bed full and happy and was grateful later that she hadn't checked her emails before bed.

❧ 11 ❧

Katie woke up Monday morning feeling happy with the world. She'd made it through the weekend that should have been her wedding weekend surprisingly easily. She'd enjoyed a nice night with William and a great day with Ealish, and she'd made progress on her research as well.

She climbed out of bed and looked out the window at another rainy day. That was probably a good thing, because it gave her the perfect excuse for avoiding William today. It was a shame that he and the others would get wet digging at Rushen Abbey, but it let her off the hook. She was eager to get back to her research anyway.

After she'd showered and gotten dressed, she ate a quick breakfast before firing up her laptop. She wanted to check her emails before she headed over to the museum. She usually checked them every day, but she'd missed doing so yesterday because of her day out with Ealish.

Sending a quick note to her mother at least three times a week was the least she could do, as she knew that her parents worried about her being so far away. She smiled as she saw a message from her mother drop into her inbox. The first half of the message was her mother's usual chatty note about the things going on in her parents' life. They'd had dinner with their oldest friends, had found a great new restaurant that had just opened near them, etc. The last paragraph made Katie frown, however.

"By the way, on Thursday we got a phone call from Mark. He said he was thinking about you because it was coming up to your wedding weekend. He wanted to make sure that you were okay, but you didn't give him any contact information after you sold the house. We had a lovely chat. You know I always liked Mark. I know you won't like my saying so, but I did think you were rather hard on him after that unfortunate incident. Anyway, he asked how you were and what you were doing and I couldn't see any harm in telling him that you were on the Isle of Man doing some research. I don't know if he will try to get in touch or not, but if he does you should think long and hard about giving him another chance. Everyone makes mistakes, after all, and you don't know if you will meet someone else or not. You aren't getting any younger, after all."

Katie re-read the final paragraph and shook her head. She knew that her mother had always liked Mark, but she hadn't realized that she also saw him as her daughter's last chance at marriage.

She frowned again. Her mother had been very upset when Katie had cancelled the wedding, but Katie had assumed that she'd understood. Mark had betrayed her, personally and professionally, and Katie wasn't about to forgive that with "everyone makes mistakes." As far as Katie was concerned, her relationship with Mark was over, whether her mother understood that or not.

Her high spirits dampened, Katie had a quick chat with Ealish about her research and then headed over to the museum for another long day in the microfilm room. By five she was feeling headachy and grumpy and she stomped back to her apartment and locked herself in tightly. She ate a quick snack and composed a carefully controlled reply to her mother, then spent a few restless hours searching the television for something to watch. Finally, she took herself off to bed, still feeling cross with the world.

Tuesday was equally rainy and Katie stormed over to the museum and tried to bury herself in her work. By lunchtime she'd finished her initial counts of the registers for the period around the "famine" and she decided to treat herself to an afternoon off. She gathered up her papers and headed back to the institute, determined to find something fun to do with the rest of the day. Unfortunately, it was still raining, which limited her options. She climbed the steps and stuck her head into the office to see if Jane had any suggestions.

Ealish was standing near Jane's desk, and a huge bouquet of flowers dominated the room. Katie was instantly intrigued.

"Well, aren't you popular?" she asked Jane, admiring the colorful blooms.

"I wish I were," Jane smiled wryly, "but the flowers are for you. They were just delivered."

"For me?"

Katie was suddenly afraid that they were from Mark, and she didn't want to open the envelope.

"Aren't you going to see who they are from?" Jane asked curiously. "I could guess, but I could be wrong," she muttered under her breath.

Katie realized that Jane thought the flowers must be from Finlo and the idea gave her the courage to open the envelope. She wasn't sure what to say to Jane as she read the card.

"Please, will you do the me the honour of having dinner with me on Friday at 7:00p.m.? Thinking of you, Finlo."

"They're from Finlo, aren't they?" Jane recognized the confusion in Katie's eyes as she looked up from the card.

"Yes, I'm sorry," Katie answered, not sure why she was sorry, but feeling that she should be.

"It's not your fault," Jane answered. "Anyway, I'm over him. I told you about the great guy I met a few weeks ago, right? He's much nicer than Finlo, though not nearly as rich!"

Katie laughed. "Money can't buy happiness," she told Jane. "Congratulations on the new man. I was afraid the flowers were from my old one," she admitted to Jane and Ealish.

"Mark?" Ealish was surprised. "Does he know you're here?"

"He does now. Apparently he called my parents and my mother told him where he could find me. She thinks that he wants to get back together, but I bet he just thinks I have something that belongs to him or something." She shook her head.

"Anyway, he used to send me flowers now and again for no reason, just because he loved me, and I just thought..." she trailed off there and Ealish and Jane exchanged looks.

"Are you disappointed that they're from Finlo, then?" Ealish asked gently.

Katie thought for a moment. "I don't think so," she answered slowly. "I'm certain that I don't want to get back with Mark, but I suppose it would be flattering to think that he wanted me back. But flowers from Finlo probably mean that he is still not listening to me when I say that I just want to be friends. How did my life get this complicated?"

"You should just enjoy it," Ealish told her. "Now you have William, Finlo and Mark fighting over you. We should all be so lucky!"

"I don't want any of them," Katie insisted. "What I want is some idea of what to do with my afternoon. I've finished the stuff I was working so hard on and I thought I'd earned a break. Any ideas?"

"It's a shame it's raining," Ealish answered. "Maybe you should check out the Douglas library? There won't be anything there to help with your research, but they have lots of great fiction."

"That sounds perfect," Katie agreed. She had been working so hard that she had forgotten the simple pleasure that reading fiction provided. Money was too tight to allow her to buy many books, so a trip to the library was just what she needed. "Will they let me take out books even though I don't really live here?"

"Just give the institute as your address and you will be fine. If they give you any trouble, have Vivian call me. She is the head librarian and a good friend," Jane told her.

"Thanks so much." Katie was delighted and dropped her research and her flowers off in her apartment before getting directions to the library that was, fortunately, within easy walking distance, even in the miserable weather.

A few hours later she was back with a pile of books and a spring in her step. She'd spent an enjoyable hour browsing through the library and chatting with Vivian about various authors, and then she had treated herself to a cup of tea and a slice of cake at a coffee shop just down the street from the institute. Once done, she carried her books up to her room and settled in for a long relaxing read.

The half-day off work refreshed her spirits and she woke up on Wednesday feeling in a much happier frame of mind. Even better, the sun was shining and that meant that she could join William at Rushen Abbey for the day.

Katie worried a little when she realized how excited she felt about spending a day with William, but then she decided that she would feel much the same about spending the day with Ealish, and that made her feel less conflicted. She got dressed in old jeans and a T-shirt, put on her nearly worn-out sneakers and grabbed a jacket. She raced down to the offices and popped her head into William's office.

"Yoo hoo," she called, "is anyone here?"

William looked up from a pile of paperwork and smiled brightly at her. Katie felt a flood of warmth that filled her from top to toe and made her blush.

"Good morning. All set for a day at the abbey, then?"

"All set," Katie answered, trying to tone down her obvious enthusiasm.

"Great. I just need five minutes to sort out a few papers and we can be on our way."

William continued flipping through the papers on his desk as Katie hovered in the doorway. She wasn't sure if she should go downstairs or just wait there, but William put her out of her misery by finishing quickly.

"Right, off we go," he said just a minute or two later.

William was dressed in a similar fashion to Katie in old and well-worn clothes, and he had old but durable work boots on his feet. He grabbed a tattered jacket that was hanging on his door and collected his mobile phone from a charging unit on his desk.

"Essential tools for the modern archaeologist," he joked to Katie as he tucked the phone into a jacket pocket.

"Technology is changing the way everything works, isn't it?" Katie remarked as they headed down the stairs and out of the building.

"We still dig the old-fashioned way," William smiled, "but now when we find something we don't recognize we can take a photo on my phone and send it to a dozen experts instantly. Within minutes we can have a half-dozen opinions on what it is, where it used to take months to get any answers. Not that the opinions, once gathered, are any more likely to be right, but at least we get them faster."

William led Katie around the corner to his battered car. He held the passenger door open for Katie and then shut it carefully before opening his own door and climbing inside. Katie did up her seatbelt as she tried to find a comfortable place for her feet among the clutter on the floor in front of her.

"Sorry about all that," William frowned as he leaned down and gathered up some of the books, papers and assorted flotsam that filled the passenger's footwell. "I don't usually have passengers, so I tend to just throw all sorts down there."

Katie smiled. "No problem, I just hope I don't step on anything important."

"That's not likely. I'm actually very careful with the important stuff. The stuff that gathers down there tends to be copies of my books and notes from articles I'm writing, that sort of thing."

Katie leaned down and picked up a book that remained. "Your books aren't important?" she teased as she looked at the cover of a book that he had written about Neolithic pottery.

"Not to me, I suppose they might be to some unfortunate under-graduate who has to study them, but I have all the notes and material from writing them, so I'm not too bothered about the published texts."

William took the book from her and threw it onto the floor at the back of the car. Then he started the engine and smiled at her.

"Hold on," he teased as he eased the car out of its space and down the short alley. "This car once hit forty going down hill with a tail wind, you know!"

Katie laughed and felt her worries about Mark, Finlo and her research fading away. Today was a day to learn more about the island and about archaeology and she wasn't going to spoil it by worrying about anything. The drive to Rushen Abbey took them south and Katie was delighted to have another chance to wave to the Little

People as they drove along. William shared some of the stories that he had heard about the dire consequences of not acknowledging them.

"Has anyone ever compiled a book about all the horrible things that happen to people who ignore the Little People?" Katie asked.

"I don't think so," William answered. "There are books on Manx folklore, but I don't think there is one specifically about the perils of slighting the Little People at Fairy Bridge. It would have to be a very long book, at that, because everyone I know has a different story."

Katie and William both laughed at that.

The parking lot at Rushen Abbey was about half full of tour buses and cars and Katie grinned as William pulled into a special spot labelled "Chief Archaeologist" near the entrance.

"Wow, a special parking space and everything."

"I need it for carrying all the bits in and out," William defended himself. "Besides, I need to be able to come and go throughout the day and still have a parking space when I get back. It doesn't always work, though. You do get cheeky tourists who park in the space in spite of the sign."

He led Katie through the parking lot and up a path into the main entrance of a modern building.

"Hey, Sue," he called to the woman on the reception desk. "This is Katie. She's doing some research on the Great Derby and the Civil War period, but she is having a day off to take a look around here."

"Yeah, 'lo," the woman looked up from a book she was reading and gave Katie a slow nod. She looked to be about twenty-five and was wearing a sullen expression to go with baggy jeans and a T-shirt emblazoned with "Manx National Heritage". She wore her hair straight with bangs that were falling into her eyes. Her makeup seemed to consist only of a dash of bright pink lipstick that had been chewed off in the center, leaving only a vicious ring of pink feathering at the edges of her lips. Katie smiled at her, thinking that with a little effort the girl could be lovely. Replacing the sullen expression with a smile would have gone a long way.

"I'm going to take Katie around the site quickly before I hit the dig. Is there anything going on that I need to know about before I start?" William smiled at the woman and she seemed to light up under his gaze.

"No sir, Mr. Corlett, there isn't anything going on. John stuck his head in as he came in and said that he would get everything started. I haven't seen anyone else this morning yet. Did you want some coffee or anything before you go?"

The woman was on her way across the room to the coffee machine before she had finished speaking, but William stopped her. "No, thanks anyway, Sue, but I want to make sure I have plenty of time to show Katie everything and still have time to grab a proper lunch hour today. Thanks anyway."

William turned and smiled at Katie. "The tour starts this way," he told her, offering his arm.

Katie took it with a smile and they turned towards the beginning of the exhibit. Katie was sure that William missed the grumpy look that Sue cast at her as she walked off with him. Sue clearly had a thing for William, and it seemed that he was oblivious to it.

As soon as they were out of earshot, Katie broached the subject. "Sue seems nice," she started, even though it was patently untrue.

"She's a nice kid," William answered absently, pointing out another thing in the exhibit that he didn't want Katie to miss.

"She seems really fond of you," Katie persevered, stopping to read another sign about life in the abbey when the monks were living there.

"I suppose," William frowned. "I'm not interested in Sue and I'm not likely to be," he told Katie softly. "So if you were thinking that we would be a good match you can forget it."

Katie laughed. "I wasn't thinking that at all," Katie assured him. "She didn't seem like your type to me. But I do think that she might not agree!"

William looked startled. "Sorry, are you saying you think she likes me?"

"Yep! In a big way, if I'm any judge," Katie grinned. "Haven't you noticed how she looks at you? She practically flew to the coffee machine to get you a drink."

"I just thought she was being nice," William frowned. "I haven't encouraged her, really I haven't."

"I doubt you would have to do much to encourage her," Katie answered. "She looks like she is pretty shy around men. I suspect that just being nice to her is providing her with all the encouragement she needs."

"Should I say something to her? Make sure she knows I'm not interested?" Clearly, William had no idea how to handle the issue.

"I don't think you should. Some things are best left unsaid. Just keep treating her nicely, but not too nicely and hopefully she'll find someone else soon."

William grinned. "I think I might be able to help with that, actually. Matt, who helps with the digging, has a bit of a thing for her. I've been ignoring the whole issue, but maybe I'll encourage him to ask her out. He is a great guy and would be just right for her!"

Katie grinned. "Right, that's two people's love lives sorted out, anyway."

William took her around the rest of the site, showing her the remains of various walls and explaining how the buildings would have looked hundreds of years earlier. His depictions were so rich and colorful that Katie felt she could almost see the old buildings rising up before her and she began to wonder if maybe she'd specialized in the wrong era in history. They completed their tour of the abbey with a walk through the re-created herb garden and Katie almost felt as if she had walked back through time.

"Now for the really interesting stuff," William told her as he led her through a gate and into a fenced-off area where several people were digging in a couple of large holes.

"This year our excavation is centered on what was, we think, an ancient burial site," he told her. The next few hours flashed by for Katie as she was introduced to half a dozen men and women who were involved in the dig in different ways.

There were a handful of students from various universities as well, but Katie forgot their names as soon as she'd heard them. William showed her a sampling of the things that had been found earlier in the week and even gave her a go with a trowel for a few minutes. Katie didn't manage to do any more than scrape away at some soil, but she felt delighted with herself and the whole experience.

"Having fun?" he asked a short time later when he returned to her side in the pit.

"It's amazing," Katie answered, "and I haven't even found anything."

"It is never too late to take up archaeology," William told her, half-seriously.

"It is a tempting thought," Katie answered. "But I think I'll stick to what I do best."

"Well, you know that you are always welcome to come and have a go at digging. Now would you like to get cleaned up and grab some lunch before I take you back to the institute?"

Katie took his hand and he pulled her out of the hole. She felt a rush in the pit of her stomach as he held her close for a moment to steady her as she emerged. They exchanged glances and Katie could feel the heat in William's gaze. She stepped away quickly but carefully and shook her head.

"Just friends," she muttered sternly to herself as she headed to the nearby building where finds were being catalogued. The building boasted toilets and plenty of hot running water and Katie felt much better as she scrubbed away several layers of soil and mud. She was amazed at how quickly she had become filthy. It must be awful digging in the rain, she thought.

William had taken time to clean up as well and he smiled at Katie as she joined him again.

"There is just time for a quick lunch before we head back to Douglas," he told her as they waked back out into the sunshine.

Katie grinned as she noticed Sue having lunch with a man that she was pretty sure was the Matt they had been talking about. They were talking quietly and seemed to be enjoying each other's company. Katie hoped that was the end of her crush on William.

Back in the car, William turned towards Douglas, but stopped not far from the abbey at a large pub.

"I hope this is okay," he said to Katie. "The food is good and it isn't too expensive. Most importantly, they are pretty fast, as I have to get back for a meeting at two."

"I'm sure it will be great," Katie reassured him as they walked through the parking lot. She was pleased to find that she was right, as the food was homemade, tasty and fresh. An hour later they were back in the car, having enjoyed the meal and each other's company a great deal.

William drove Katie back to the institute and she hopped out quickly so that he could get back to the abbey.

"Thanks so much. I had a great time," she called to William as he prepared to drive away.

"I did, too," he smiled at her. "Any time you want to do it again, let me know."

Katie smiled as she skipped back up the steps to the institute. She would love to do it again some time. She had had a wonderful day, enjoying William's company and doing something completely different.

William had been wonderful, friendly, but not flirtatious. At least he was listening to her, even if Finlo wasn't. She raced up the stairs to her apartment and grabbed her research notes. If she hurried, she could still get three hours of research time in as well.

❦ 12 ❧

By Friday Katie felt sure that she was making real progress on her research. She'd learned a lot about the island during the seventeenth century and she thought she was getting somewhere with trying to work out the extent of the famine.

Because she didn't have a phone number for Finlo, she decided that she had little choice but to join him for dinner that evening. She gave up working on her microfilm an hour earlier than normal and headed back to her apartment to have a long soak in a hot bath before he arrived. She'd worked her way through fifteen of the seventeen parishes now and she felt that she was well on the way to finishing with that particular job.

Back at her temporary home, she ran a hot bubble bath and sank in gratefully, closing her eyes tightly. She was tired. The mental work was as exhausting as physical activity could be. She laid back and let her mind wander. June was already drawing to a close, but she was fairly confident that she would finish the first part of her research by the end of the month. Once she had, it was time to analyze the data, and then she could decide what direction she wanted to go in next.

She knew there was no way she was going to be able to research everything that she wanted to while she was there for such a short time, but she was sure now that she would have more than enough material to complete her chapter for the book. Having satisfied herself that her work was going well, Katie ran some more hot water into her bath and let her mind shift to personal matters.

It had been a least a week since she had let herself think about Mark and Katie was amazed to find that she could now think about him without feeling the once-familiar stab of pain. She wiggled in the warm water and tried to dredge up her emotions, but no matter how hard she tried she could only find disappointment and a lingering sense of regret. The anger had left her and she was surprised to find that she no longer felt broken-hearted.

She was sad that things hadn't worked out the way they had always planned, and disappointed that Mark had not turned out to be the man that she had long thought he was, but she no longer felt that she hated him or that he had ruined her life. In fact, her life had now taken a very interesting and exciting turn and Katie found that she was feeling something like gratitude to Mark for the way things had ended up. She just wished she could have avoided some of the unhappiness that she had been forced to endure to arrive at today.

Mark was thus dismissed from her mind and Katie spent a moment thinking about William. He was such a nice man and he had been friendly and kind to her. He was good-looking as well and Katie enjoyed his company a great deal. He wasn't a bad kisser either, Katie reminded herself with a giggle. If she were staying longer than three short months, she might have allowed herself to try to get a bit closer to him. Of course, Finlo might have objected to that. Ah, Finlo. Katie sank still deeper in the bath and let her mind focus on her date for that evening.

Finlo was a real problem. He seemed determined to make a play for Katie and he refused to believe that she was serious about not getting involved. William seemed to understand and had been behaving perfectly, but Finlo was a different matter. Flowers and a romantic dinner didn't seem "friendly." They were something else altogether and Katie wasn't sure that she could convince him to just remain friends.

"One dinner," Katie spoke out loud, surprising herself. "Dinner tonight and then that is it! I shall just tell Finlo that I don't want to see him again."

Katie stood up quickly and wrapped herself in a towel. She meant it. Tonight was the last time that she would be going out with Finlo.

"I'd better make sure I have fun," she laughed to herself as she padded into the bedroom and dug into the wardrobe for something to wear. Within twenty minutes she was dressed and ready to go, half an hour early for her date. She sat down at the little desk and began to do some adding up and recording of events into the table she had started earlier in the week.

She looked up suddenly when she heard someone knocking on the back door to her apartment. A glance at the clock showed her that she had been working for over thirty minutes and now she jumped up and grabbed her bag and headed down the stairs quickly. As she suspected, Finlo was waiting at the bottom, looking incredibly handsome in a dark suit. For a moment her determination to end the fledgling relationship faltered, but Katie forced herself to focus.

"Hello, you look beautiful," he greeted her with a huge and confident smile.

"Hey," Katie mumbled, feeling uncomfortable from the start.

"Hey? Is something wrong?"

Finlo took her arm as she turned from locking her door and looked inquisitively at her.

"Just feeling a bit overwhelmed," Katie answered. "Look, flowers and a romantic dinner are over the top. I told you that I just want to be friends, remember?"

Katie sighed, glad to have been honest with the man, even if it did mean that she had to miss out on the expensive meal.

Finlo just laughed. "I know all that, really I do. Look, I work hard all day and at night I like to relax and enjoy good company, okay? Just because I'm taking you for an expensive meal doesn't mean that I expect anything at the end. I know you are still getting over your former fiancé. I promise, no pressure, okay?"

Katie smiled gratefully. "Thanks. I think the flowers threw me," she admitted as she climbed into Finlo's gorgeous little car.

"I like to send flowers to beautiful women. It makes me feel more alive," Finlo told her, leaning across the small space to check her seat-belt in spite of Katie's efforts to deflect him. "I have to keep you safe," he told her, his face only inches from hers, the smell of his expensive aftershave filling her nose.

Katie shut her eyes and held her breath, afraid that if she looked into his eyes she would want to kiss him. Finlo might be saying all the right things, but he was still acting as if he was looking for more than friendship. She was fairly sure that he had no idea how inexperienced she really was with men. He was far too sophisticated for her and she knew that she would have to be very careful tonight or he might just get her to change her mind about ending their relationship before it had a chance to get started.

Finlo chuckled softly as he sat back in his own seat and started the car. "I only bite if you want me to," he told her as he rolled smoothly away from the curb.

Katie didn't even want to think about that remark, so she forced herself to look out the window and concentrate on the waves that were rolling slowly onto shore. A short drive took them through central Douglas and then up, further along the seafront and up a large hill. Finlo reversed into a space in a small parking lot and they got out of the car.

"Have a look," he told Katie, turning her to face the sea.

Katie took a deep breath and tried to speak, but failed to find words. They were standing high above Douglas, with the seafront spread out below them. Katie stared at the beach below as it curved gently around towards the Sea Terminal. The sun was just beginning to set and it glowed across the water, making the sand sparkle and the windows from the buildings glitter.

Katie felt as if she could stand there forever, watching the tide as it rose and fell, watching the people and the traffic as they bustled about on the streets and beach below. Finlo stood behind her, encircling her waist with one arm and Katie realized that she was relaxing into the embrace. She quickly pulled away and broke the spell.

"Come on, our table will be waiting," Finlo smiled at her, an almost arrogant confidence flashing over his face as he turned towards the building.

He obviously had no doubt that he was breaking down her resistance. She suspected that he was prepared to be patient for a while longer, his eyes firmly fixed on the prize. No doubt his determination was increased by the knowledge that William was also interested.

Inside the restaurant, Katie immediately felt underdressed in her often-worn little black dress. "I should have dressed up more," she whispered to Finlo as they passed the bar area.

"Nonsense, you look fabulous," Finlo told her, as the host led them to a small table in a dark corner of the room. Floor-to-ceiling windows allowed diners to take in the amazing view, and Katie sank into the comfortable chair and feasted her eyes on the sea below.

A waiter rushed up quickly. "Mr. Quayle, so nice to see you again, and your lovely friend. Can I get you both something to drink?"

Finlo looked questioningly at Katie. "Shall we get a bottle of wine?"

"Um, I wasn't going to drink tonight." Katie felt like she was spoiling Finlo's evening.

"Why ever not?" Finlo asked, even though he had to know exactly why Katie was reluctant to drink in his presence.

"I've just been having a lot to drink lately and I'm not used to it," Katie answered vaguely, not wanting to admit that she was worried about how she might behave if she got drunk.

"Half a bottle of wine isn't much," Finlo insisted, taking the wine list from the waiter. He quickly ordered a bottle of something that sounded expensive to Katie.

"If you really don't want to drink, I'll order you a soft drink when the waiter comes back," he told Katie in a soft voice. "I don't want to do anything that might upset you tonight."

Katie was relieved. "I suppose one glass won't hurt," she admitted. "I'll just have to make sure that I eat enough to soak it all up."

Seconds later the wine was poured and Katie and Finlo were studying their menus. Katie had heard of such places, but she had never actually been in a restaurant where some of the menus didn't have prices on them. She tried to peek, discreetly, around her menu to see the prices on Finlo's, but he held his just far enough away that she couldn't see anything. Katie sighed. She would just have to order something that didn't sound too expensive.

Two hours later Katie felt more stuffed than she had in a long time. Somehow Finlo had persuaded her to eat three courses of the fantastic food that the kitchen supplied. The appetizer had been large enough to be a main course, at least in Katie's opinion, but she still managed to eat nearly all of her main course and an amazing chocolate dessert.

She had also drunk nearly the entire bottle of wine herself. Finlo only had one small glass, reminding her that he was driving later. With a deep sigh, she sank back against the plush back of her chair and smiled.

"That was the most amazing meal I've had in a long time," she told Finlo.

"I'm glad that you enjoyed it," Finlo told her with a big smile of his own. "You can see why I like to eat here often."

"It must get expensive."

"Some things are worth the expense," Finlo told her.

"I suppose," Katie said with doubt in her voice. "I've always had to be so careful with money. It goes with being an academic."

"You just need to find the right man," Finlo answered smoothly. "You need a man like me, who loves to spoil the woman in his life."

Katie thought for a moment before she answered, not wanting to say the wrong thing. If she had drunk a bit less of the wine, she probably would have found that easier.

"If only this was taking place in about a year's time, when I was really and truly over Mark and ready to move on."

Finlo laughed. "Then again, if you are looking to get over an old boyfriend, maybe you need a meaningless fling with a man who will treat you well."

Katie thought again, wondering if Finlo might be right. A meaningless fling with someone like him might restore her confidence and help her get over Mark even more quickly. When she realized that she really wanted to believe it, she started to worry.

"Really, Finlo, I'm not the meaningless fling type," she told him, suddenly wanting the evening to be over.

"I used to specialize in meaningless, but lately I've been thinking that maybe it's time to settle down," Finlo told her, looking deeply into her eyes, obviously trying to convince her that she was the cause of his newly professed desire to find the right woman.

"Hm," Katie looked away. "I wish I knew whether to believe you or not," she spoke almost unconsciously and kept her eyes firmly focused on the sea, rather than her date.

"Give me time to convince you," Finlo said pleadingly, taking her hand. "Just tell me that you are willing to give me a chance, that you'll forget all this 'just friends' nonsense and give a relationship with me a try."

Katie shook her head. She knew she had had too much wine and that she wasn't thinking clearly. "Finlo, you need to give me time to think. Time when I'm not full of wine! Let's have this conversation another day."

Finlo used his free hand to cup her cheek and turn her face towards him. His eyes met hers and he stared at her for a long time. "That is the first tiny bit of real encouragement you have given me," he told her finally. "You won't regret it."

Katie frowned. She hadn't meant to encourage him, had she? The waiter interrupted whatever Katie was going to say by coming to clear away the last of their dessert dishes. Katie shook her head to the offer of coffee and then rose somewhat unsteadily to her feet. "I need the, um, I need to, um."

Finlo laughed. "The loos are at the back," he told her. "If you walk along the row of tables and then turn left at the end, they'll be right in front of you."

Katie followed his instructions and spent several minutes freshening her makeup and brushing her hair. She was reluctant to spend any more time with Finlo while she was still trying to figure out her feelings. Finally she shook her head at her reflection and headed back to the table.

"I thought you might have decided to hide in there all night," Finlo chided her gently when she returned. "I've sorted out the bill, so we can leave whenever you are ready."

"I'm ready," Katie answered, feeling that fresh air would do her a lot of good. They walked back down the stairs in silence and back outside. A sudden gust of wind almost took Katie's breath away and she stumbled on the uneven ground as the wind blew around her.

Finlo quickly took her arm and steadied her, then pulled her even closer. Katie knew she should resist, but she loved the feeling of being held by this gorgeous and sophisticated man. He kept her tightly at his side as they walked through the parking lot and then he gently helped her into the car.

He did his usual check on her seat belt and Katie had to struggle hard with her resolve as he leaned in close. It took every ounce of self-discipline she had to resist pulling him close for a kiss. He buckled up his own belt and then eased the car out of its space. "Straight home or would you like to go for a drive first?"

"A drive might be nice," Katie answered.

Right now all she could think about was a good night kiss, a long and passionate good night kiss. She hoped that a drive might let some of the alcohol work through her system and distract her from her own desires. Finlo turned the car north as they headed through Douglas and followed the coast road towards Laxey. The views were spectacular in the fading light and Katie thought that she had never seen such a beautiful place.

They drove past the Laxey Wheel and Katie watched it turn lazily in the moonlight. It was getting late and Katie was planning on spending another day at the museum on Saturday, so she reluctantly suggested to Finlo that they head for home. Finlo obliged immediately, turning back towards Douglas.

The trip to Douglas seemed to take only a few moments and Katie felt disappointed that the evening was ending. She was certain that she wanted the evening to end with Finlo heading home alone, though. She wasn't ready to sleep with anyone new, least of all someone as urbane and experienced as Finlo. The drive had cleared her head and helped her think about things. What she still couldn't decide was whether or not she wanted to encourage Finlo to keep up his pursuit. Finlo stopped smoothly at the back door to the institute and parked his car.

"Are you going to invite me in for a nightcap?" he asked, running his hand along her arm, sending shivers through her entire body.

"I don't think so," Katie answered, trying to think clearly and ignore the desire that was coursing through her. She had loved Mark, but even in the early days of their relationship he had never made her feel so alive.

"I won't push you," Finlo told her gently. "Not yet anyway. But I want to keep taking things further. If you agree to keep on seeing me, I don't want any more talking about just being friends. We are both consenting adults and I want to take things along their natural course."

"You need to let me think about it," Katie told him softly. "I just don't know. Mark and I only split up a few months ago."

"From what I've seen," Finlo told her, 'you are already well over him. I don't think you were ever properly in love with him, you just thought you were."

Katie couldn't answer for a moment. She had been thinking along similar lines herself, lately. "Regardless of Mark, I am only here for a few months," she argued. "What happens after that?"

Finlo shook his head. "You really do like to borrow trouble, don't you?" He stroked her cheek. "Let's not worry about what happens at the end of August, when it is still only June! A month ago we had never met and look at where we are now."

Katie smiled. Finlo was right about one thing. Her life had looked very different only a month ago. Then she had been suddenly single and feeling like she was being left on the shelf, broken-hearted by her lying and cheating ex. Now she had two men vying for her attention and she had never felt more desirable. Katie closed her eyes and allowed herself to revel in the moment, with one of Finlo's arms around her, and his other hand gently stroking her cheek.

Finlo wasn't the type to miss an opportunity, and while her eyes were shut, he leaned in and kissed her gently. When Katie didn't resist, he deepened the kiss. Katie thought about resisting for only a moment and then found herself responding with a growing passion. It was several minutes later that Finlo finally pulled away.

"Maybe we should go upstairs?" he murmured softly, in a sexy voice. "Or we could go back to my place. I've got a king-sized bed, after all."

The words were like a bucket of cold water washing over Katie and she pushed away quickly.

"I'm so sorry," she began, "I didn't mean to respond like that. I mean, I was just, that is…" she trailed off, knowing that she was sending out very mixed messages and hating herself for doing so.

Finlo only smiled. "No worries," he assured her. "I didn't for one minute think that I was going to get you into my bed tonight. It was worth asking, though, just in case you might have had a major change of heart."

Katie sighed in relief. "I am sorry. I shouldn't kiss you like that and then stop. I feel like a sixteen-year-old girl again. You'll think I'm a tease, or worse."

Finlo laughed. "I know that you have a lot of emotional stuff to work through," he told her, "and I don't want to rush you into anything that you aren't ready for. But you're right, you are sending out very mixed signals. You keep saying stop but your body is saying 'yes, please' and that's hard for men to figure out. We're simple creatures. If we want something, we go after it. We're pretty straightforward.'

Katie sighed. "I don't mean to be difficult," she insisted. "I came here determined not to get involved with anyone, so that I could make sure I was over Mark. But I've never met anyone like you. You are miles more sophisticated and worldly than any man I've ever known. I really enjoy spending time with you, but you scare the hell out of me as well. I know you could just be playing with me and that once you win me over you'll sleep with me and then dump me and this time my heart might be really broken."

Katie frowned. She hadn't intended to say all those things. They had just spilled out.

Finlo went back to stroking her cheek. "I'm flattered that you think I'm worldly and sophisticated, but that just shows how few men you must have been with before you met me," he told her. "I don't think there is anything I can do to convince you that I'm not just playing with you, other than to keep doing what I'm doing and let my actions speak for me. I just hope that, given enough time, you will learn to trust me and maybe, if I'm really lucky, let me into your life and your heart."

Katie picked up her bag from the car floor. "'I think we'd better leave things there for tonight," she told Finlo, opening the car door. She knew she was enjoying his touch far too much and that she had to get away from him in order to think. "Thank you for an amazing evening," she told him as she moved towards the door to her apartment.

Finlo climbed out of his car and walked lazily towards her. She already had her apartment door open and was ready to leap inside and lock it behind her.

"Let me come up and make sure everything is okay," Finlo told her. "I promise not to try anything."

Katie tried to laugh, but found her throat closing at the thought of him coming up to her apartment. "I'm sure that isn't necessary," she told him, holding the door half shut as a shield between them. "I'll just say good night and lock up behind myself."

"Good night, then, Katie," Finlo told her, stepping around the door and taking her arm gently. He pulled her close and kissed her very softly, leaving her desperate for more.

"I've got to go away for a week, on business, but I'll call you the minute I get back so we can continue this exactly where we left off," he told her.

Katie frowned. "A week away?" She hadn't meant to sound so disappointed, but the words were out before she could stop them.

Finlo smiled. "I'm afraid so. Will you miss me?"

Katie knew there was no right answer to that question, so she ignored it. "You can leave a message for me at the institute," she told him, "and if you leave your number, I can return your call."

"Have I never given you my number?" Finlo frowned. "How terribly remiss of me," he said.

He took a pen from his suit pocket and a business card from his wallet. He flipped it over and wrote neatly on the back.

"There you are, my home number and my mobile number. You can even ring me on the mobile number next week while I'm away if you miss me too much," he teased her. "Otherwise, I'll ring you when I get back so we can pick up where we left off. I'm not sure if I'll be back on Friday or Saturday, otherwise we could try to fix something up now."

"Never mind," Katie told him. "Just give me a call when you get back." She was trying hard not to mind that he was going away, but she wasn't succeeding.

Finlo grinned at her. No doubt he knew exactly what she was thinking. "Good night then, my beautiful American girl."

"Good night," Katie echoed, shutting the door before she could change her mind about inviting him to stay the night.

She leaned against the closed door and breathed deeply. She could hear Finlo whistling softly to himself as he walked the short steps back to his car. She listened to the car engine start and the sound of it fading away and then climbed the stairs slowly.

She had left earlier determined to make Finlo understand how she felt, but now she was afraid that he understood her only too well. All thoughts of keeping things "just friends" between them were gone and she was now worried about how quickly things might be moving forward. Still, she had a week to figure out what she wanted to do. She needed to do some serious thinking during that week.

13

Katie spent the rest of the weekend counting and analyzing and crunching endless series of numbers for births and deaths and marriages from the seventeenth century. By Monday morning she felt she might actually be making some progress. What she really needed was to run her thoughts and ideas past someone that could look at them critically and give her advice on the best way forward.

Ealish was one possibility and William was the other. Katie spent some time debating which was the best bet before electing to let fate do the deciding for her. Whichever one arrived at their office first would get to have her thoughts bounced off them, assuming that they had time to listen, of course.

She opened the door at the bottom of her apartment stairs into the main institute building and sat at her barely used desk, listening for the sound of approaching footsteps. She wasn't sure how she felt when she heard William's heavier footsteps coming up the stairs before nine o'clock. Gathering her growing pile of notes and papers, she headed over to meet him before he got busy on his own work.

"Hey, have you got a minute?" she asked as she knocked on his door.

William stopped on his way to his desk and turned towards her. "I always have a minute for you. Maybe even two, but not much more, I'm afraid. I'm due at Rushen Abbey in half an hour and then I've got a paper to finish for a conference this weekend. But I wanted to talk to you as well, so I'm glad you dropped in. You go first."

"Thanks," Katie smiled at the warm greeting. "I just need to bounce some ideas off someone, that's all," she told him. "I've been working all weekend, crunching up numbers and drawing some tentative conclusions and now I need to talk to someone about what I think I've found."

"That ties in well with what I wanted to talk to you about, actually," William told her, grinning broadly. "How would you like to have a chance to talk about what you've found to a whole conference full of experts?" he asked her.

"I'm not sure I'm ready for that level of help," Katie gasped.

"Don't worry, I'm not throwing you in with the lions or anything," William laughed. "I'm giving a paper on what we've been finding at Rushen Abbey at a conference in London later this week. The budget has room for one more person to go with me and I thought you might like to come. While there will be a lot of archaeologists there, the idea of the conference is to bring archaeologists and historians together to discuss recent findings. One of the guest speakers is an expert in demographics and his work always generates a lot of interest. I'm sure that a lot of experts in the field will be there, and you know how historians are, always happy to bore one another about their work."

Katie laughed. "I suppose you are right," she agreed, "but I still don't think I'll have enough done to be ready to talk to experts."

"We don't have to leave until Thursday afternoon. That gives you a bit more time. Have a think about it and let me know later today if you want to come or not. We need to get flights and hotels booked if you are coming. In the meantime, I suggest you bounce your ideas off Ealish, as I really have to go. If she is too busy, then catch me later and I'll have a listen. I should be back here before five and will probably be here until quite late tonight working on my paper. I wanted to make sure I included all the most recent finds, so I've left writing anything until the last minute."

Katie laughed. "You mean you waited until the last minute to write it, but at least now you can include all the latest finds," she teased, recognizing William as a first class procrastinator.

William laughed as well. "Okay, you are probably right about that, but my way sounds better. Anyway, I really do have to dash. I promise we can have a proper chat later, though. I'll knock on your door when I get back and you can pop down for a talk."

While he had been speaking, he had quickly flipped through his pile of mail and scanned the phone messages that were stacked on his desk. Now he grabbed his raincoat from the corner and shrugged into it. "I'll see you around five," he promised Katie, as he headed back out of his office.

"See you then," Katie answered, feeling totally overwhelmed by the short conversation that certainly had not turned out at all like she had expected. She was still standing on the landing gathering her thoughts when Ealish bounced up the stairs a few moments later.

"Hey Katie, how are you?" Ealish called, opening her office door. Katie shook her head, trying to refocus her mind. "Katie? Are you okay?" Ealish asked in concern.

"I'm fine," Katie grinned, "just a bit befuddled by a meeting with the boss, that's all."

"He has that effect on people," Ealish agreed. "His mind works at warp speed and he expects everyone else's to do so as well. Give it half an hour and you will probably catch up to wherever it was he left you."

Katie laughed. "I think I'm afraid to catch up this time," she told Ealish. "He wants me to go to a conference with him at the end of the week to talk to some experts about my work."

Ealish smiled. "Good! We were talking about that conference last week. I often go to such things, but I've got plans this time and besides, I'm not doing anything new or interesting in my own research at the moment. I'm too busy with institute business. Anyway, it is much better suited to your work, what with Demo Dave being there and everything."

"Sorry," Katie said, "but Demo Dave?"

"Dave Anderson. He is an expert in demographic history. I'm sure you will have come across some of his work."

"I have, yes. And I couldn't possibly talk to him about my stuff. He is much too important," Katie blushed at the idea of talking to one of the world's foremost experts in the subject about her own tentative attempts at demography.

"He's a pussycat," Ealish laughed. "I always call him 'Demo Dave' to his face as well as behind his back! But then we're really good old friends, if you know what I mean," she winked exaggeratedly at Katie and Katie's eyes grew wide.

"You mean you've slept with him?" Katie was agog, but Ealish only laughed.

"Lots of bed hopping at these conferences," she told Katie, "but you must know that. You must have been to tons before."

Katie shook her head. "I've been to lots of conferences, but I've never, um, you know, at them."

Katie thought for a minute. "Actually," she continued slowly, "Mark always came with me when I went to conferences, but he never wanted me to go with him to his. I never gave it any thought before, but maybe he was cheating on me at conferences and making sure I didn't get the chance to do the same."

Ealish patted her arm. "No point in worrying about it now," she told her, "that's ancient history."

Katie had another thought. "Um, Ealish, you don't think that William is thinking that we could, um, get together at this conference, do you?"

Ealish shook her head firmly. "William isn't like that. If he invited you to the conference it is because he thinks it will be helpful for your work. I bet it hasn't even occurred to him. Finlo would be a different story, but I don't need to tell you that!"

Katie nodded slowly. If Finlo had been the one asking, she would have been pretty sure of his true motives. "So do you think I should go? Will I be able to hold my own with a bunch of really clever British demographic experts?"

"Come into my office," Ealish suggested. "You can tell me all about what you have been doing and what you have found out and then I can help you sort out your thoughts and ideas."

"That was exactly what I wanted to do anyway," Katie told her. "I need someone to tell me whether my thoughts and ideas are making sense or if I'm getting myself into a mess."

The next hour flew by as Katie bounced ideas and preliminary conclusions off of the other woman. They both agreed that it was time well spent at the end of it. Ealish now had a good understanding of Katie's work and how well it was progressing. Katie felt afterwards that she was doing better than she'd realized.

She felt more confident in her ideas and thought that maybe, just maybe, she could talk to the experts and not be totally out of her league. She put off a final decision about the conference until her meeting with William. That would give her time to see how much more she could get done that day. Really, though, it seemed too good an opportunity to miss.

Katie retreated back to her apartment to get some work done. By five o'clock Katie was fairly sure that the work she had done so far would make up the first part of her chapter, but now she needed to figure out what else was going to be in that chapter.

"Something else to discuss with William," she told herself as she tidied her papers and got ready to go down to talk with him. She dashed into the bedroom and ran a brush through her hair, slicked on a fresh coat of lipstick, and sprayed on a blast of perfume.

"Just trying to look professional," she told herself, ignoring the little voice that knew that she wanted to look nice for William for personal reasons. She jumped when she heard a quick knock on the door at the bottom of the stairs.

William had made his way into his office when Katie stuck her head in a few minutes later, and he turned from his desk and greeted her with a huge smile. "'There you are," he remarked as he stood up and quickly cleared off the visitor's chair at the corner of his desk.

"I don't want to take you away from your work," Katie answered him, worriedly looking at the huge pile of papers he had in the middle of his desk.

"Please, interrupt as long as you can," William pleaded. "I'm really not in the mood for working on this paper and I'm happy to have something to distract me," he confessed with a sheepish grin.

Katie laughed. She knew exactly how he felt. "Someone talked you into giving a paper and you don't really feel that you have anything to say," she guessed.

"Exactly," William smiled again. "Every year I get talked into doing these stupid things and I never feel like I've got anything to say."

"You must be pretty interesting, though, or they wouldn't keep asking you to do it again and again," Katie argued.

"Ha! I wish I could believe that," William countered. "Have you ever organized one of these conferences?" he asked Katie.

When she shook her head he continued. "You start out full of optimism that lots of people will be keen to talk about whatever the theme of the conference is, then you sit back and wait for papers to be submitted. Sometimes you get lucky and you get far more than you need. Usually you get a small trickle of papers from the same people who always want to give papers at these sorts of things. Then you get a few from folks that are desperate to be seen to be busy by their departments. Of course you always get one or two from amateurs who are just bored and looking for something to do on a weekend away. About a month before the conference, you start trying to fit everyone into the schedule and you realize that you are about five papers short of filling your schedule so you start calling all of your friends and begging them to take part. If you are lucky, you get enough to agree that you can go ahead. If you are unlucky, you end up giving half-a-dozen papers yourself."

Katie laughed. "I've been to conferences where the organizers have given most of the papers. I just assumed that they had very high standards and didn't like any of the papers submitted."

"I suppose that might happen as well, but in my experience most conferences will let just about anyone talk, as long as they are vaguely talking about the conference theme," William grinned. "Of course, most conferences have such woolly and vague themes that just about anything would qualify. This one is called "New Ideas, Old Techniques or Old Ideas, New Techniques?" which pretty much gives the speakers carte blanche to talk about anything."

Katie smiled. "I'm sure you will do a wonderful job and I, for one, am looking forward to hearing what you have to say."

"Does that mean that you are coming, then?"

"Oh, yes, sorry. I would love to come if you are sure the budget can afford it."

"The budget isn't a problem for a change. I was really hoping you would come, so much so that I already had Jane book your flights and hotel. I hope you don't mind, but it is much easier to cancel them than it would have been to find you a room in London once the conference hotel is fully booked."

"I don't mind at all," Katie assured him. "But it could have been expensive if I'd decided not to go."

"I was pretty sure I could persuade you," William grinned wickedly for a moment. "Besides, hotels don't charge if you cancel at least twenty-fours before you are due to arrive and Finlo charges by the charter, not by the number of passengers."

"Finlo is flying us to London?" Katie tried to keep the surprise out of her voice. "I thought he was away this week."

"He might be, I don't keep track of his comings and goings," William looked concerned that Katie was clearly doing just that. "But he has six planes and ten pilots at Quayle Airlines. I just rang and booked the plane. His office manager will sort out who actually flies us to London. Finlo probably doesn't even know that we're going."

Katie was silent. The conversation was getting close to uncomfortable territory for both of them and she didn't want to add to the building tension. William finally broke the silence.

"We fly out on Thursday, at three, so we need to leave here about half-one, if that is okay with you?"

Katie nodded.

"The conference starts on Friday morning and runs until Sunday afternoon. I've booked our flight back for six on Sunday night so we will have time to grab something to eat before we have to get to the airport. We should be back here before eight on Sunday night. Does all that sound okay?"

"I didn't realize that we would be away all weekend," Katie answered slowly, thinking about her tentative plans with Finlo.

"Did you have plans for the weekend?" William sounded disappointed, no doubt guessing that she was most likely planning to spend time with Finlo.

"Nothing important," Katie told him, and herself, firmly. "The conference plans sound great and I'll be looking forward to it."

"Good." William smiled brightly, perhaps feeling that he'd won a small victory over his more sophisticated cousin.

"Now, before I go," Katie continued, "can I just bounce a few ideas off of you?"

"Of course," William was quick to agree. "How about we go down and have a cup of tea and some biscuits in the kitchen? It is more comfortable than my office and I'm sure there are some chocolate biscuits down there. I haven't had anything to eat since lunch and I'm starving."

"Nothing since lunch? And now you are planning on working all evening with only tea and biscuits to keep you going?" She shook her head at him. "What are you thinking?" she asked, exasperated.

"I don't want to take the time to go out for something to eat," William defended himself. "And I don't have time to go home and fix myself something either. I can't very well drag all of the samples and paperwork back to my house so that I can work from there."

Katie frowned at him. "Right, come on up to my apartment and I'll cook something for both of us while we have a chat about my work. I'll just do spaghetti or something quick so I won't be keeping you too long, but you can have something a bit more nutritious than chocolate biscuits."

William cocked his head and looked at her curiously. "You really don't have to go to all that bother," he told her. "I'm used to living on biscuits when I've got a paper to write."

"You can live on biscuits the rest of the week," Katie laughed, "but for tonight, I need to talk to you and I haven't eaten either, so you might as well join me for dinner. You can have a chocolate biscuit for dessert if you eat everything on your plate."

William laughed.

"This is very kind of you," he told her as they climbed the stairs to her apartment.

"Not at all. I need to talk to you and I'm hungry as well. While I love chocolate biscuits too, I tend to eat my proper food before my dessert."

William laughed again as she unlocked her door and let them into the apartment.

"At least let me help with the food, then," he insisted.

"Can you cook?"

"You'll just have to wait and see," he told her with a grin.

As it happened, he didn't get a chance to prove his skills in the kitchen. Katie insisted that he sit at the table while she threw the meal together. While he watched and waited, she filled him in on where her research was at and then quizzed him on where he thought she should go next. By the time they sat down to eat, Katie was happy that her research was going well and that her friendship with William was growing as well.

"Enough about work," she insisted as she put plates on the table. "Let's talk about something more interesting."

"Right, then, tell me all about you," William grinned.

"I will if you will."

"Sounds fair," William answered as he tried a bite. "This is delicious, by the way. Go ahead, then, and tell me your life story."

"There isn't much to tell, really. I grew up in a small town, went to college, fell in love with one of the upperclassmen. With his encouragement, I eventually earned my doctorate, and just before we were due to get married I found out that he was cheating on me." She stopped and took a big drink of fruit juice. William hadn't wanted any wine because he had to get back to work and she didn't really want to drink on her own.

"Wow, that is short and not very sweet," William smiled gently. "Are you still getting over your ex then?"

Katie thought for a minute. "I don't think so," she answered slowly. "I thought it would take months or even years, but maybe the total change has helped to speed the process. I still feel badly that it didn't work out, but I don't feel devastated that we aren't still together. At least I found out what he was really like before I married him."

"You were smarter than I was, then," William told her.

"You've been married?"

"For about ten minutes," William answered curtly. Then he shook his head and frowned. "Sorry," he said in a softer tone, "I guess I still have a bit of residual anger about the whole thing."

"Go on, then, tell the whole story," Katie urged, and then backtracked. "Only if you want to, of course. I don't want to pry."

"No, it is my turn," William smiled at her, "and I don't really mind giving you the basics. I grew up on the island. My family has lived here for hundreds of years and I was expected to stay here forever as well. I got a place at University in Liverpool and did my time there, always expecting to come back here when I finished. And that is just what I did once I had my doctorate. I came back and, after a year or so, I married my childhood sweetheart. She was from another old Manx family and everyone had always assumed that we would marry when we were old enough to do so. Certainly my parents were keen to see us unite the two old families, as it were. Anyway, about three months after the wedding she announced that she had landed her dream job in London and was leaving immediately. And that was the end of that."

"Wow." Katie couldn't think of anything else to say.

William shrugged. "Yeah, wow. She hadn't bothered to tell me, or anyone else, that she was looking for a job in London, but she had been applying for jobs there for a while. After she left I kept getting letters from other places where she had applied. I still don't know why she bothered to marry me at all. I suppose it was something to do while she waited for her big break."

"Didn't she want you to go to London with her?" Katie was confused.

"She didn't bother to ask. I suppose she knew better. I wasn't about to leave the island, not when I'd only just got back. The institute had just been established and I was hired as the Assistant Director. I was happy here, doing what I loved. Living in London was out of the question."

"I guess I'm really lucky I never made it down the aisle," Katie told him.

"I wish I hadn't," William answered fervently.

"Were you desperately in love with her? Did she break your heart?"

William smiled. "Don't hold back, don't worry about my feelings," he told her.

Katie blushed. "I'm so sorry. I didn't mean to be so blunt. I was just ..." she trailed off. Clearly she was just being nosy but she couldn't bring herself to admit that.

William laughed. "It's been years," he assured her. "I'm still angry that things turned out the way they did, but I'm not still nursing a broken heart. At the time I did think that I loved her a lot, and yes, I suppose she did break my heart, but it has been years since I've seen her and I've had plenty of time to get over it."

Katie shook her head. "I just can't imagine getting married without meaning to go through with it," she told William.

"Neither can I," he told her. "When I'm feeling charitable I imagine that she never really thought she would get a job in London, that she was just applying for jobs to keep her dreams alive. I suspect that if that job had never materialized we might still be married with a couple of kids by now."

Katie was suddenly very glad that this unknown woman had taken off to London all those years earlier. If William were married, there was no way they would be having this conversation, and Katie was very much enjoying his company. The conversation turned to lighter subjects, and William and Katie enjoyed a fierce but friendly debate about the relative merits of American versus British television. Dessert was a handful of chocolate biscuits and then William had to get back to his paper.

"If I don't see you until then, I'll see you here on Thursday afternoon. We can drive down to the airport in my car," he told Katie. "Pack business-like stuff for the conference sessions and casual clothes for the evenings," he suggested. "But then you must have been to dozens of these things before."

"I have," Katie agreed, "but never in London. It's always helpful to be sure of the dress code. I'll see you on Thursday, then."

William walked with her to the door and turned. For a moment, as their eyes met, Katie thought that he was going to kiss her, but then the moment passed.

Instead he gave her a quick hug and brushed her cheek with his lips and then quickly headed down the stairs, calling "bye" as he disappeared. Katie responded in kind and then shut her door, telling herself sternly that she hadn't wanted a good night kiss anyway.

❦ 14 ❧

Thursday afternoon arrived well before Katie felt ready for it. She carried her suitcase down the stairs and was waiting for William at the appointed time, a bundle of nerves about the conference, about spending the weekend with William, and about the possibility of Finlo being their pilot.

"Have a great time," Ealish called to her from the office, as she waited.

"I'm sure I will," Katie lied anxiously.

William was only a few minutes late and he quickly put her bag in the back of his car and then opened her door for her. The trip to the airport didn't take long, and Katie even spotted the Fairy Bridge by herself on the journey. At the airport, Jack met them and greeted Katie like an old friend.

"It's nice to see you again, Katie," he told her, giving her a hug. "I'll be flying you to London today. I hope you're going to do something fun while you're there."

"Not much time for fun on this trip," Katie told him. "We're going to a conference full of academics. Fun isn't really in the plans."

Jack laughed. "I'm sure William will do his best to make the trip enjoyable, regardless," he told her. "Shall we get going?"

He led them both through the airport to a gate marked "Charters," using his pass card to get them through the door. Outside, they headed to a small plane, much like the one that had brought Katie to the island at the beginning of the month.

The flight itself was fairly uneventful. William was still making last-minute adjustments to his paper, so Katie simply stared out the window, watching the clouds, as they flew along. Things got more exciting as they came in for a landing over London, however, as the weather was clear and William was able to point out a few landmarks to an excited Katie.

"I wish we had time for sight-seeing," he told her regretfully. "Maybe another time."

"I'd love to be able to do some sight-seeing," she agreed.

The conference organizers had provided a car and driver to pick them up at the airport. They were quickly whisked to the nearby hotel and conference center.

"And that, I'm afraid, is all that we will get to see of London on this trip," William told her as the headed into the reception area of the hotel.

The hotel was large and modern with a sprawling conference center that wouldn't have looked out of place in any major city in the world. Katie sighed as she slid her room key card through the slot in her door. It was slightly disappointing to have come all this way only to find herself in a bland and anonymous hotel.

Her room was on the small side, but it was comfortable, with a large bed and a huge stack of pillows. She opened the wet bar and then checked the price list before shutting it firmly with a shake of her head. A knock on the door set into the middle of the wall startled her, but she already knew that William was in the adjoining room.

"Just wanted to check that your room is okay," he told her when she opened the door.

"It's fine," Katie assured him. "As bland and boring as any hotel room anywhere, but fine."

"Maybe some day I can take you somewhere a bit more interesting," he suggested, with a wink that made Katie blush. "There are a number of old stately homes that take in paying guests, for instance."

Katie's eyes lit up. "That would be amazing."

"Tonight's dinner is for all of the speakers and their guests," he changed the subject. "Drinks are at seven, with dinner at eight. I would love for you to be my guest."

"That sounds good," Katie answered lightly, trying to ignore the intensity in William's voice. "I should have just enough time to fresh up a little bit."

"Don't worry too much about your appearance for tonight," William reassured her. "Things will be pretty casual. Most of us are all old friends who have been doing these things for years."

Katie had a flash of panic at the thought of trying to fit in with a bunch of strangers who all knew one another well, but it seemed like William could read her thoughts as he continued.

"Don't worry, you'll fit right in," he told her. "You have the right background and you know your stuff. Besides, mostly the group is full of stuffy old academics. They'll be thrilled to have a young and beautiful woman to talk to."

Katie laughed at that, but William turned out to be right. Within minutes of their arriving for drinks, Katie was surrounded by a group who wanted to hear all about her research, both back in the States and on the Isle of Man. And Katie realized that a couple of the men hanging on her every word were interested more in her than in her research. She couldn't help but feel flattered by the unexpected attention, in spite of having more than enough male complications in her life at the moment.

When it was time to go in to dinner, William pushed his way into the group and took her arm.

"I was afraid I was going to have to beat them off with a stick," he whispered to Katie as he guided her to their place at the long table.

Katie laughed and shook her head. "I can't believe how interested everyone is in what I'm doing and how helpful they're all being."

Now William laughed. "I'm not sure most of them don't have ulterior motives, but I'm glad they're helping."

Katie just shook her head and took her seat. She had William on one side, but the chair on her other side remained empty as the salads arrived.

Just a few bites later, however, everyone in the room stopped as a whirlwind breezed in.

"Dave!"

"Demo Dave's here."

A couple of voices shouted out a greeting and a few people waved as a man built like an American football player waved and "high-fived" a few friends. Katie could only stare at him, as he looked over the room and then beamed a huge smile.

"Ah, wonderful, someone has saved me a seat next to the most beautiful woman in London," he announced to the crowd, heading towards the empty seat next to Katie. "I guess it must be my lucky day," he told everyone as he dropped down into the seat and took a swallow from the full water glass that had already been placed there.

Katie took a deep breath and then smiled timidly at the man. "Hi, I'm Katie Kincaid," she told him, trying not to stare into the stunning hazel eyes that were framed by tousled waves of golden brown hair. Really, the man was beautiful and Katie could easily understand how Ealish had fallen for him.

Dave took her outstretched hand and raised it to his lips, his eyes never leaving hers. "I am beyond enchanted to meet you, Katie," he told her with a sexy smile.

Katie burst out laughing, which spoiled the mood. Dave raised an eyebrow and then grinned at her.

"Was that a bit over the top, then?" he drawled.

"Oh, way, way over," William told him, leaning around Katie to offer his hand. After the handshake William pulled his arm back only as far as Katie's chair, casually resting it against the back in a possessive gesture that was not lost on the newcomer.

"Ah, right, well then," the man grinned at both of them. "I'm Dave Anderson, but you probably already got that," he told Katie. "You must be the researcher that William has been talking about."

"William was talking about me?" Katie wasn't sure whether she should be flattered or not.

Dave winked at her. "He asked me to try to find some time for you this weekend to talk about your work," he told her. "He told me you were doing some very interesting things with the island parish registers. He neglected to tell me that you were young and beautiful, but I guess he was hoping I wouldn't notice."

William laughed and shook his head. "No chance of that, is there?"

"Absolutely not," Dave replied, winking extravagantly at Katie. "So maybe after dinner we can head up to my room and talk about your research," he winked again, clearly teasing.

"Maybe we could talk in a quiet corner down here," Katie suggested sweetly. "I'd love to hear your thoughts on what I'm doing."

"I'd love to give you my thoughts on a number of subjects," he waggled his eyebrows at her. Dave's flirting was so over the top that Katie couldn't help but laugh.

"I think we'd better stick to demography," Katie told him.

"If you insist," he agreed easily. The man was an outrageous flirt, but he seemed to recognize the boundaries that Katie was quick to establish.

Katie felt like she hadn't laughed so much in years as the dinner progressed. Dave continued to flirt in such an exaggerated fashion that even William finally relaxed, although he continued to rest his arm on the back of Katie's chair whenever he could.

After dinner, Katie got a few quiet minutes with Dave to discuss her research, and she was thrilled when he gave her some helpful pointers and also offered to read her early draft of the chapter, if she thought that would help. She was also grateful that he stopped flirting and was all business during their conversation, waiting until they had finished everything that Katie wanted to discuss before picking back up with his outrageous behavior.

William picked that moment to join them, however, and was just in time to hear Katie laughing off yet another suggestive remark.

"I think I'm going to head up to bed," William told the pair. "I'm giving my paper at nine tomorrow morning. I think the organizing committee hates me."

Everyone laughed at that. No one wanted to give the early paper on the first day of a conference, but someone had to do so.

"I should head up as well," Katie replied. "I want to be awake enough to listen to your paper."

"Wow," Dave interjected. "I didn't realize you guys were a serious couple," he winked, "but if she is getting up and coming to hear your paper about a subject she couldn't care less about, it must be love."

Katie was annoyed to find herself blushing at the teasing remark, but William smoothly defused it.

"I'm nominally her boss," he told Dave. "She's just trying to stay on my good side."

Again they all laughed and then Katie and William headed out while Dave headed for the bar. He was giving the keynote speech on Sunday morning, so he didn't particularly need an early night.

In the hallway outside of their rooms, William and Katie said polite "good nights" to each other. For a moment William looked like he wanted to kiss her again and Katie held her breath, but the moment passed as the elevator pinged open behind them and they split into their separate rooms without a further word.

Inside her room, Katie leaned against the door and sighed deeply. Flirting with Dave had been fun and harmless, but William was a different story. She was enjoying his company too much, especially if she were considering a relationship with Finlo.

A knock on the connecting door broke through her thoughts.

"I just wanted to give you this," William told her when she opened the door. Then he leaned over and kissed her very gently on the lips. "Good night."

He was gone again, shutting the door in his own wall quickly and quietly. Katie shut the door on her wall quietly as well, wondering what she was getting herself into.

She had a restless night, finally drifting off only a short time before her alarm chimed. In her tired confusion, she accidentally turned the alarm off, rather than hitting the snooze button as she'd intended. Consequently, she only woke up when William telephoned from the next room to see if she wanted to join him for breakfast. As it was already eight-forty and she wanted to be presentable for William's talk, she declined the breakfast invitation and flew through the fastest shower on record. She had her conference clothes on and her makeup done before she was even totally awake.

"What is it about hotel blow-dryers?" she wondered as she tried to dry her hair with a feeble blast of lukewarm air. She finally gave up and bundled her still wet hair into a haphazard pile on the top of her head. She slipped into a seat at the back of the room just seconds before William started to speak.

An hour later she felt energized and excited about archaeology in a totally new way. "That was amazing," she told William when she finally got through the crowd of admirers that were talking with him after he finished. "Now I really want to do more digging in the dirt."

William grinned at her. "I told you that you are welcome any time," he reminded her. "You could always come back and study archaeology at the institute if you really get hooked."

Katie grinned, half-tempted by the thought.

"I'm sorry, but I have to run," William interrupted her, as her mind played around with the possibility of leaving behind her old life and becoming an archaeologist instead.

"I promised Mathew that I would come and hear his talk on flint and then I've got to have lunch with a couple of Liverpool undergrads and their advisor to discuss a project they want to try on the island next year. This afternoon, I'm sitting on both panel discussions, one right after the other. The last one is due to finish at five. How about we meet in the reception area at ten past and we can have dinner together?"

Katie's head was spinning from William's itinerary, but she was quick to agree to dinner that evening. She returned to the reception area to grab a copy of the day's schedule to figure out what sessions she wanted to attend. She was only half way across the room when she was swept up in a bear hug from behind.

"Good morning, gorgeous," Dave said, as he swung Katie around before setting her back down gently.

"Good morning." She shook her head, as much to clear it as to discourage Dave.

"So, what is on your schedule for today?"

"I haven't really looked yet," Katie admitted, "but I know there are some sessions that are aimed at the historians more than the archae-ologists."

"There are indeed," Dave agreed. "Come on with me and I'll make sure you get to only the very best ones."

Katie hesitated for only a few seconds. While Dave was a flirt, he was also an expert in her research area and she could use all the help she could get at this stage. In any event, she enjoyed the day, listening to a couple of talks that covered information that was both interesting and relevant to what she was trying to do. Dave insisted that she join him for lunch and she found herself in the middle of a lively debate with a group of demographic experts about the usefulness of various sources of information that only fellow historians could really enjoy.

Dave was charming and only slightly outrageous and Katie enjoyed being part of the reflected glow that came from being seen with the keynote speaker at an important conference. When five o'clock finally rolled around, she was almost reluctant to find William because she was really enjoying Dave's company. In the reception room, Dave handed her back to William with a bow.

"I have looked after her well and return her to your care only slightly over stimulated by an excess of historical drivel."

William laughed. "Do I take it that you have had a fun day, then?"

Katie's eyes were glowing with enthusiasm as she tried to explain how much she had learned and how much she had enjoyed the intellectual interplay that had taken place during the day. After listening to her babble for several minutes both William and Dave laughed.

"I thought you went to these sorts of things all the time," William questioned.

"Yes and no," Katie answered. "I've been to several conferences, but I always went with Mark and he always 'helped' me pick which sessions to attend and hung out with me in between sessions. I guess I must have missed out on a lot of opportunities for discussing my work because of him. I never realized how wonderful these conferences could be."

"I take it Mark is an ex-boyfriend," Dave checked.

"Oh yes, very much so," Katie told him.

"Well, I very much enjoyed spending the day with you as well," Dave told her. "I would invite you to have dinner with me, but I suppose you and William already have plans."

In the end, Katie, William, Dave and a few other conference attendees all had dinner together at a large table in the hotel's main dining room. Dave ended up sitting across from Katie, and lacking an opportunity to flirt with her, spent the night getting better acquainted with their waitress. As the meal wrapped up, Katie watched as Dave made plans to meet the waitress after her shift finished. She tried not to be shocked at the casual way he chased women, or with the ease with which some chose to be caught.

William saw what she was watching and smiled at her. "I don't know how he does it," he told her quietly.

"He is charming," she told him, "but so clearly a player."

"A lot like Finlo," William replied.

Katie felt stung as she considered the remark. Was Finlo truly that bad? Was she foolish to believe that he wanted more than just a casual relationship with her?

Their little group hung out in the bar for a short time before Katie and William agreed that it was getting late. Katie wanted to get to an early session the next day, and William was chairing a round table discussion that started early as well. They said their polite "good nights" again at their respective doors. Inside her room, Katie waited to hear the knock on the connecting door, but it didn't come. Disappointed and relieved at the same time, she got ready for bed.

The next morning she managed to grab breakfast with William before they headed off in different directions. They waved to each other at lunchtime as William was swallowed up by a large group of people who had more to say about the morning's topics. Katie ended up eating with Dave and some of his demographic researchers. After lunch, William found Katie and they grabbed seats together to listen to Dave's keynote address. Dave was an excellent and fascinating speaker and Katie found herself fired up with renewed enthusiasm about her own research as a consequence.

In the taxi on the way back to the airport, she continued to bubble over with excitement.

"William, I can't thank you enough for including me in this conference. You were totally right that it was exactly what I needed. I learned so much about what I'm trying to do and I made some amazing contacts that all seem willing to help as I go along. It was just about the perfect weekend."

William grinned at her delight. "I'm so glad that you enjoyed the weekend," he told her. "I think I might have enjoyed it more if I had been able to spend a bit more time with you, but other than that it went well for me, too."

"Your talk was wonderful and I heard lots of great comments from different people all weekend long about the institute," Katie told him. "What you guys are doing is very well respected."

"Well, at least in our little community of academics it is," William chuckled. "Beyond that I doubt very much if any one much cares."

"I live in an academic bubble anyway," she told William, "so that is all I really care about."

"Unfortunately, I have to worry about funding as well," William sighed, "and being well-respected is great but I would almost rather be well-funded."

"How can you afford to have me over, then?"

"We were lucky to get a large grant to get a series on the island's history written," William explained. "A large portion of the grant money is earmarked for bringing in visiting professors to research and write parts of the different volumes. It is a great pot of money for the books, but I would love a few more pennies in a few other areas as well."

Katie sighed. "Sorry, I'm just a starving professor. I can't offer to make a huge donation to the institute any time soon."

William grinned at her. "You are making a huge donation. You're writing part of one of the books, that's very huge. If you weren't here doing that, we would probably lose part of the grant money that is paying for you to be here."

Katie shook her head. "Why does it all have to be so complicated?"

William laughed. "I'm not sure, but it always is."

As they neared the airport and hit a huge traffic jam, he questioned Katie.

"So what would have made the weekend totally perfect for you?"

Katie frowned. "I'm not sure. Nothing special, really, but nothing is ever totally perfect, is it?"

William smiled at her in the back of the stationary taxi. "I know one thing that would have improved it for me," he said quietly.

Katie looked at him in surprise and then, when she saw the look his eyes she turned away, worried about what he might say next.

"Were you hoping I would knock on the connecting door last night?"

"I, um, I don't know," Katie answered honestly.

William chuckled. "So I guess I made the right choice," he said ruefully.

Katie turned her head and stared into his eyes. She felt like she could get lost in his gaze, overwhelmed by the intelligence and kindness he radiated. For a long time they simply stared at one another and then William very gently pulled her closer. The kiss was soft and gentle, more of an exploration of possibilities than anything else, but it still left Katie breathless.

They rode the rest of the way to the airport in silence, Katie nestled in William's arms, both lost in their own thoughts. Being in William's arms just felt comfortable and right and Katie couldn't bring herself to pull away.

At the airport they made their way slowly through the chaos to the chartered flights area. As they checked in at the "Quayle Airlines" gate, the clerk gave them a grin.

"You've got the boss flying you today," she told them, "and he is in a terrible mood as well."

"Oh, great," William replied.

They stepped away from the desk and took seats in the small waiting area.

"I bet I know why Finlo is in a bad mood," William said.

"Why?"

William looked at her curiously. "Surely you know," he suggested.

Katie just shook her head.

"Didn't you two have some plans for this weekend? Sorry, but that was the impression that I got."

"Only very vague ones," Katie answered. "Besides, it isn't like we're a couple or anything. We've only gone out a couple of times."

"Glad to hear you speaking so highly of me, my darling," Finlo spoke from behind her and Katie jumped up feeling and looking guilty.

"I didn't know you were there," she stammered out.

"Obviously not, although after your romantic weekend away with my cousin, I'm not sure why you would care what I think."

"It wasn't a romantic weekend, it was an academic conference."

"Really?" Finlo looked skeptically at her.

"Just because you can't imagine a weekend away without sex being involved, doesn't mean that it can't happen. Your cousin was a perfect gentleman." Katie said stoutly.

"I'll just bet he was," Finlo drawled, shooting a nasty look at William. "Come on, then. I've had a terrible week and now I have to get back home. As luck would have it, this is the only flight going, so I get to fly you two lovebirds back to your cozy little island romance."

Katie opened her mouth to argue, but then shut it again. Finlo was being completely unreasonable, and there was no point in sinking to his level.

She and William followed the still scowling Finlo out to the plane and Katie was pleased to find that Jack was there to help them climb in. She settled in a seat as far from both William and the cockpit as she could find and then pulled out a copy of Dave Anderson's latest book that he had kindly given her after the conference. She turned the pages periodically, pretending to read and ignoring everyone and everything else until the plane landed.

❧ 15 ❧

Finlo was apparently busy in the cockpit once they landed on the island, but Katie didn't mind. She got her bag from Jack and followed William through the airport back to his car. A light rain was falling and the weather seemed to match everyone's mood. The drive back to Douglas was a silent one.

"Thank you again for including me in the conference," Katie said politely when William dropped her off at the institute.

"I'm glad you enjoyed it," William answered stiffly.

Katie felt fed up. She knew why Finlo was mad at her, even if it was undeserved, but she had no idea what was bothering William. She grabbed her bags and stomped away from the old car, determined to get safely inside before she started shouting, or worse, crying.

William waited until she was safely inside and then he drove away.

Katie unpacked and had a long soak in a hot tub. A few tears sneaked out as she thought about the two men and the impossible situation they were putting her in. She relaxed back in the tub, determined not to let them get to her. She decided that she would simply avoid them both and focus on her work. Men were nothing but trouble!

With that thought firmly planted in her mind, she dried off and wrapped up in pajamas and a fluffy robe. Then she checked her emails, something she hadn't done since Thursday morning.

An email from her mom did nothing to improve her mood, or her opinion of men.

"We had Mark over for dinner last night and had a lovely time. He is so very contrite about the way he treated you and so eager to make amends. He is doing very well with his new job and doesn't miss academia at all, he says, but he does miss you a great deal. After much persuasion, he coaxed your email address out of me. I do hope, if he does take the time to get in touch, that you at least read the email and give him a chance to explain. Everyone makes mistakes in life and Mark made a huge one, but I think you owe him a chance to explain and apologize. Your dad and I miss you as well, of course."

Katie grimaced. While she was here working, her parents were entertaining the enemy. She was even more glad that she had had the chance to get away. It was much easier to ignore her mother's attempts to reunite her and Mark with three thousand miles of sea between them.

She thought for a long time about how much had changed in just the few weeks she had been gone. If she'd stayed at home, there was a small chance she might have been swayed by her mother's arguments and given Mark another chance. He was the only man she had ever really dated and when they had broken up she had briefly wondered if she would ever find a replacement.

She laughed to herself. What a difference a bit of time and distance makes, she thought. Almost unbelievably, she now had two men fighting over her, not to mention men like Dave Armstrong, who'd flirted and flattered her so outrageously. Whatever else this trip to the island had been good for, it had definitely confirmed her decision to end things with Mark. She knew there was nothing he could ever say or do now that would change her mind.

Now she flipped through the rest of her emails, deleting the inevitable junk mail and catching up on news from friends back home. She was just about to shut her computer down when her email pinged and a new message popped into her inbox. Katie stared at the unfamiliar sender's ID. The subject line was simply "hi" and Katie felt a sick feeling in her stomach when she thought that the message might be from Mark.

"Please don't just delete this. Really, please, after all our years together, do me the favor of reading this whole message. I will try to keep it brief."

Katie read that far and stopped. She pushed away from her computer and stomped into the kitchen. She realized that she was hungry and thought about sneaking downstairs for a few biscuits, but she was afraid she might run into William. She always seemed to run into him at the most awkward times and she really didn't want to see him tonight. Her emotions were too fragile at the moment to handle that sort of encounter.

She poured herself a glass of wine and then reluctantly returned to her computer. They had spent ten years together. She supposed she should at least read what he had to say. They hadn't really spoken since that terrible scene in the Dean's office when the truth had come pouring out. Katie had done everything she could to cut off all communication, deleting his emails unread, not answering the phone and moving out of the house immediately.

"Words can't begin to say how sorry I am. And I know that nothing I can say or do will ever make up for the hurt I caused you. But if you could find it in your heart to forgive me, then maybe I can at least look at myself in the mirror again. Ah, Katie, I love you so much. These months without you have been hell. I know I made a huge mistake, but we were getting ready for a wedding and I suddenly panicked. We had been together for so long already and I suddenly felt trapped. And then this beautiful young woman started coming on to me and I was flattered. And I cheated. And then she started blackmailing me in order to get good grades. And I let her instead of just confessing everything and begging for forgiveness. I was just so afraid of losing you."

Katie stopped again and downed her wine. It was all so cliché that she figured it was probably true. It was, sadly, a story that probably got played out in a lot of relationships. Katie was just sorry it had happened to her. She reluctantly returned to the last few lines of the email.

"After it all came out, it was too late to explain. You cut me off completely, and I don't blame you, but I have never stopped loving you. I want you to know that. And now you are thousands of miles away and I miss you terribly. I know you have probably moved on with your life and never even give me a thought. But I love you and I miss you and I beg you to forgive me for my stupidity. Much love, Mark"

Katie found that she was crying as she finished the email, which made her angry with herself and with Mark. Even with time and distance, he could still upset her. She shut her computer down and went to bed where she let her thoughts run freely and had a good cry.

The next morning Katie felt mad at the world. Which was fine, because it seemed to her that Finlo and William were mad at her anyway. She stomped down through the institute, calling a vague "hello" to anyone who happened to be there and then headed to the museum. The conference had been wonderful for focusing her ideas and she now knew exactly what her finished paper was going to look like. She just needed to do the necessary research in order to make it a reality.

That night she sent a two-line reply to Mark:

"I've moved on with my life and things are good. I am happy to forgive you for your mistakes."

Happy wasn't exactly the right word, but Katie couldn't come up with a better alternative.

After another full day at the museum on Tuesday, Katie was convinced that she would be able to contribute a wonderful chapter in two months' time. She found a note on her door when she returned home Tuesday evening. Ealish wanted a quick chat with her the next morning, if she could spare the time.

Katie was more than ready for the chat at nine the next morning. She was eager to find out what Ealish wanted and also to reconnect with her, since she hadn't seen her since before she went away.

"So how was London?" Ealish greeted her with a question.

"The conference was wonderful," Katie beamed. "I learned a lot and I got some great ideas and a bunch of email addresses for people who are willing to help and let me bounce ideas off of them."

"I bet Dave was one of them," Ealish grinned. "He is always very helpful to beautiful women."

Katie had to laugh. "He was charming, if a bit of a flirt," she answered.

"Yep, that's Dave," Ealish agreed. "He is lots of other things as well, but we can save that conversation for our next wine evening."

Katie laughed. "I'll look forward to it."

"Right then, down to business." Ealish put on a mock stern face. "I wasn't sure if William talked to you or not, but there are a couple of things I wanted to run past you."

"I haven't had a chance to talk to William since we got back." Katie heard her voice wavering slightly and bit her lip. She didn't want Ealish to know about the stupid argument at the airport.

Ealish raised her eyebrows but didn't push her. "Okay then, first the easy one. Friday is Tynwald Day. I'm sure you know all about it, so I won't bore you with the historical significance, but you might not know that all sorts of local organizations have tables set up at the fair."

Katie shook her head. "I know that the House of Keys, the Manx parliament, meets and reads out the new laws, and people can present petitions to the government, but I don't know anything about the fair."

"Basically, it is like a big party for the whole island. There will be a few rides for the kiddies and loads of food vendors and ice cream trucks. In addition to all of that, local organizations are allowed to set up tables to promote themselves. All the dance schools and martial arts clubs, for instance, will have tables, and so will the school board and Manx National Heritage. Anyway, the point I'm trying to get to is that we will have a table as well, promoting what we do here at the institute. I was hoping you might be able to help out for a few hours at the table?"

"Help out doing what?"

"Just talking to people about the institute, really. You can tell them about your research and the history that we are putting together. We will be selling copies of some of William's books and some of mine as well."

"I suppose I could," Katie sounded doubtful.

"Really we just need warm bodies," Ealish assured her. "For the most part it is really just a big all-day picnic and most people ignore us, but we need someone at the table all day and, while I don't mind doing a lot of the day, I would like a lunch break at the very least."

Katie laughed. "I suppose I could manage sitting around and being ignored," she told her friend.

"Great," Ealish grinned. "I was assuming you wanted to go anyway. Everything will be closed, so it isn't like you could get any work done if you stayed home."

Katie agreed. "I know the museum is closed, and besides, I really want to see the world's longest continuous parliament in session."

"If you want, I'll sort out a ride for us and we can both plan on spending the day out there. We can take turns at the table and seeing the sights?"

"That sounds great," Katie agreed easily. "What was the other thing you wanted?"

"Ah yes, the second thing is slightly more complicated," Ealish answered. "Peter Finnley was going to be editing your volume of the history of the island. I know you probably talked to him about your chapter?"

"Yes," Katie agreed. "We're going to talk in greater depth when he arrives in late August. He is due here about two weeks before I'm supposed to fly home and that should give us enough time to smooth out any rough spots in my paper before I leave."

"Except he isn't coming," Ealish told her.

"Why on earth not?"

"If I say it's because he got a better offer, it will probably sound like sour grapes, but really, he got a better offer. He is going to spend two years as a visiting professor in the Cayman Islands. Ninety-two and sunny it was there yesterday." She and Katie both looked out the window at the rain that was steadily drumming down. "Not sure I can blame him," Ealish admitted.

Katie laughed. "So who do I turn my chapter in to when it is finished?"

"That's what I wanted to discuss," Ealish took a deep breath. "We have an unexpected opening for a visiting professor," she told Katie. "It is a fully funded one-year position, with an option for a second year should the situation warrant. There are light teaching duties, one undergrad course in the autumn and a second in the spring, and a master's degree course in the spring. They can be on any subject you like, really, within some rather broad parameters. Mostly this person needs to do substantial research and write several chapters for the history and also edit the chapters from the other contributors."

"And you were wondering if I knew anyone that might be interested?"

"And I was wondering if you might be interested!"

"Me?" Katie was stunned and for a moment speechless.

Ealish interrupted her thoughts. "Before you say anything, hear me out," she told her. "I know you would have to clear things with your employers back home, but it is still early enough to do that. It would mean a year or two on the island, but you would leave with a substantial publication to your credit and some solid original research credentials. We couldn't let you stay in the apartment for a full year, but the job comes with a reasonably generous salary. You could easily afford a nice apartment nearby. And the best part is, we could have Friday night wine sessions every week for a whole year."

Katie burst out laughing at the last part. "I don't know, Ealish, it's a lot to take in," she told her friend. "I'm missing my family and friends back home, and a year is a long time. The work would be amazing, though, and it would look fabulous on my resume," Katie sighed. "I think I need to think."

Ealish grinned. "I was afraid you might say no straight away, so I'm happy."

She gave Katie the application packet, which included the application for the required visa and urged her to give the position serious thought.

"Keep in mind that you would also have some opportunity to see more of Europe as well," she reminded her. "You would have time to spend odd weekends in London or Paris or Rome...," she trailed off as Katie's eyes lit up.

"That does make it seem really tempting," Katie told her, "but it is also a huge change for me and I really need to think about it."

"What are we thinking about?" Katie jumped as William spoke from behind her.

"I'm just encouraging Katie to apply for Pete Finnley's old job," Ealish answered for her. "I think she would be perfect for it."

William looked at Katie and grinned. "You would be perfect for it," he agreed, "but that would mean putting up with us for a whole year. I wouldn't blame you if you didn't want to do that."

Katie grinned back. Apparently William wasn't mad at her anymore. "I'm going to think seriously about it," she promised them both, "and I'll start filling out all this paperwork while I'm thinking."

Katie felt amazingly light-hearted as she headed back to the museum to continue her research. William was back to smiling at her and an amazing opportunity had just fallen in her lap. Life was good.

That evening she changed her tune. Life sucked. At least sometimes. She stared again at the email that she had just opened.

"Darling Katie, thank you so much for your forgiveness. Now I just need you to give me a chance to win back your heart. I will never stop loving you. And I know you will never stop loving me. August can't get here fast enough. I will be waiting for you and I will win you back. Much love, Mark"

She rubbed her eyes and then opened them again, hoping the message would simply go away. No such luck. She had no idea what to say in reply to this nonsense. After several minutes of typing and then erasing dozens of possible replies, she closed her email and shut her computer down. There was no point in even trying to reply until she got her thoughts straight.

She needed a glass of wine, but there wasn't any left in the apartment. She threw on her shoes and a light jacket and headed to Shop-Fast. A bottle of wine and a frozen pizza would be just right for tonight. The weather agreed as the steady rain continued to fall while Katie stomped her way though the puddles and gloom to the grocery store.

She turned down the frozen food aisle and stopped as she heard what she thought was a familiar voice. Finlo was laughing in front of the ice cream display with a stunning redhead whom Katie had never seen before. Katie watched as he slipped his arm around her and whispered in her ear. Whatever he said made her giggle and wind her own arm around his waist. Finlo pulled a tub of ice cream from the freezer and then the two, still tightly interwoven, turned towards Katie.

Katie took an involuntary step backwards, nearly knocking over an elderly woman who was trying to reach some frozen peas. As she stammered out an apology, Finlo spun his companion around and the pair headed towards the front of the store. Seconds later, Katie stood in front of the pizza display, still feeling stunned.

"It isn't what you think," Finlo spoke quietly, as he suddenly appeared at her side.

"Really?"

"No," Finlo shook his head. "Actually, it's probably exactly what you think," he admitted.

Katie sighed and went back to studying the freezer case.

"Damn it, Katie, I tried to take things slowly," he said, his tone exasperated, "but then you go flying off with my cousin for a weekend without saying a word. What am I supposed to think?"

"You're supposed to think that I went to a conference for my job and that I felt uncomfortable with just calling you out of the blue to tell you that those tentative weekend plans we made might not work out after all."

Finlo sighed and ran his hand through his hair. "I've made a real mess of this, haven't I?"

Katie shrugged. "Look, it doesn't really matter. I have enough going on in my life right now without having to deal with romance. You go back to your stunning redheaded friend and I'll have frozen pizza and wine and start reading up on adopting cats."

Finlo laughed. "There is no way you are going to end up single with a bunch of cats," he told her. "Look, let me get rid of Darcy and we can get dinner somewhere and talk."

Katie shook her head. "Really, you will have a lot more fun with Darcy that you will with me tonight. My ex is begging for a second chance, my research has hit a snag and I'm considering extending my stay on the island. I have too much on my mind to spend the night dodging your way-too-smooth moves."

Finlo moved closer and whispered in her ear. "Why dodge? Why not just enjoy what we both want?"

Katie burst out laughing, suddenly feeling almost immune to Finlo's obvious charms. "Seriously, stick to Darcy," she advised him, turning back to the pizza case.

Finlo studied her for a minute and then sighed. "We have unfinished business," he told Katie, as he turned to walk away. "I haven't given up yet."

Katie rolled her eyes at his back as he walked off. Then she picked out a random pizza and a bottle of wine and headed home. Back in her apartment she downed a quick glass of wine and then fired off a reply to Mark.

"For goodness sake, don't be stupid. I forgive you, but I have no interest in ever seeing you again. I might not be back in August, and even if I am, I don't want to see you."

It was blunt and to the point, but Katie wasn't feeling like sparing his feelings. She had been behaving uncharacteristically since she had been on the island, flitting between two men and flirting with others. Now it was time to focus on the important stuff, her job here and her career in general.

Thursday was spent working hard on research, but she took a few minutes out to send an email to her department head back home. She needed to test the waters a little to see how he might feel about her taking a year or two out to continue her work on the island.

His reply was encouraging as he pointed out the advantages of the sort of work she would be doing to her overall career. Replacing her for that sort of period wouldn't be that difficult either. There were a lot of adjunct professors who would happily share her teaching load in the light of the current economic doldrums. With that in mind, she filled out the application form before bed, still undecided on whether she was actually going to submit it or not.

✿ 16 ✿

Friday morning was dull and overcast, but the forecast promised clearing later in the day and Katie was hopeful that all of the scheduled activities for the day would be able to take place without rain. The vendors were supposed to be in place by nine in the morning and the fireworks display was due to go off around eleven that night, so Katie anticipated a long and tiring day.

Ealish had assured her that jeans and a T-shirt were suitable attire, and had even given her a shirt with the institute's name and logo on the front for her to wear. Katie added her most comfortable shoes, threw her hair in a ponytail and slathered on some sunscreen before heading down to meet Ealish at the back of the building. She was surprised to find William waiting for her instead of Ealish.

"Good morning," William greeted her cheerily.

"Good morning," she replied. "I thought Ealish was supposed to be here."

William chucked. "Ealish called me this morning and asked if I could get you out to the site. She decided she wanted to be out there even earlier than originally planned, and it wasn't a big deal for me."

"She should have called me," Katie frowned. "I could have gone out earlier to help her get everything set up."

William grinned. "I think that she wanted to be out there earlier to help out a friend, rather than for institute business," he told her. "I gather she has been getting to know a Tae Kwon Do instructor from one of the martial arts schools and his school is doing one of the first demonstrations on the green. I think she went out early to help him set up before they go on."

Katie nodded. "I'm sorry that you had to come and get me," she told William.

"I don't mind in the slightest," William assured her. "Besides, you're manning the table for some of the day. I need to make sure you get there or I won't get any lunch. Hop in."

It wasn't a very long journey, and William kept her entertained by pointing out various interesting sites along the way. Some of them were the same ones that Finlo had already shown her on their sight-seeing tour a few weeks earlier, but Katie didn't mention that to William.

The parking lots were already filling up when they arrived in St. John's, but William was able to find a spot in the small lot reserved for vendors. Katie tried to take in everything at once as she walked towards the Hill. There were tents set up for various different groups and small crowds were already forming. A small cluster of children in white uniforms were stretching and bouncing around, presumably getting ready to show off their martial arts skills.

Ealish waved as Katie and William made their way across the grass. "We've got a better location this year, anyway," she told William when they reached her side.

"Last year we were in the back behind these little old dears who make homemade jam. Not only could we not see anything, but the jam attracted every fly in the whole United Kingdom," she explained to Katie.

Katie was happy to find that their table was actually at the front edge of one of the tents, where she would have a decent view of everything that was happening all day. There were two chairs behind the table and Ealish had already set out piles of the books that were for sale and brochures about the various classes and programs that the institute ran.

"Can you and William take the first shift, then?" Ealish smiled at Katie. "I really want to watch Jake's students perform."

"I don't mind," Katie assured her, "but I'm not sure where William has gone."

"Oh, he will be checking in and getting the paperwork sorted," Ealish explained. "I'm sure he will be back soon. Nothing really gets started for ages, anyway."

With that she was gone. Katie squeezed between their table and the next one and pulled out a chair. Since she would probably be sitting for most of the day, she decided to remain standing for the moment, watching the other vendors set up and keeping an eye on the little martial artists, some of whom looked barely old enough to balance on one foot.

A couple of minutes later William arrived with two cups of tea and a napkin full of biscuits.

"Wow, what great service," Katie grinned at him as she snagged a chocolate-covered one.

"I aim to please," William told her, handing her a laminated badge with a clip on it.

"Do I need to wear this?" Katie clipped the badge to her T-shirt.

"No one will care if you don't," William told her, "except at the hall across the street. Only vendors with badges are allowed in to use their loos. Without the badge, you take your chances on the 'porta-loos' across the way."

Katie wrinkled her nose. "I will take great care of this badge, then," she laughed.

Katie couldn't help but smile as she noticed the Manx National Heritage table that was set up in the row behind theirs. Sue, from Rushen Abbey, was presiding over the volunteers, including a very attentive Matt. If only she could fix her own love life as easily as she had fixed Sue's.

The morning passed quickly as she and William chatted about her research and his. Katie watched various groups of dancers, martial artists and student musicians as they performed on the green in front of their tent. She even managed to tell a few passing visitors about her work at the institute. Ealish found them just before the actual Tynwald ceremony was due to begin.

"Go on, then," she told Katie. "Go get a bit closer and watch the ceremony."

"Are you sure?" Katie asked, trying not to look too eager.

"Of course I'm sure," Ealish grinned. "Take William with you, that way Jake can steal his seat."

Katie smiled at the handsome and muscular man who had arrived with Ealish as William got to his feet.

"Let's go watch democracy in action." William offered Katie his arm.

They slipped out of the tent and Katie watched almost breathlessly as the procession of dignitaries streamed out of St. John's Church. She was mesmerized as the laws were read out in both Manx and English and then thrilled to see ordinary people presenting petitions to the head of the island's government. William stood next to her, occasionally whispering odd facts and interesting details into her ear.

When it was over, Katie was happy to head back to their table in the tent. The sun was now directly overhead and she felt quite hot after standing in it for such a long time. As soon as they got back, William disappeared again and a short time later he returned with sandwiches and ice-cold drinks for everyone.

The afternoon continued on much like the morning, with occasional interested visitors and lots of time to spend talking amongst themselves. They took turns having breaks and spending time looking around the fair. Jane arrived in the afternoon to take a turn at the table as well.

Katie figured that she had seen just about everything except the "Manx Businesses" tent, so she headed there on a break as the afternoon was turning into evening. A few steps in the door, she spotted Finlo's gorgeous redhead from the other evening. She was wearing what looked like a flight attendant's outfit and passing out tiny sets of wings to all the small children who were passing through. More than a few of their dads were lingering at the table, checking out her curves in the tight uniform.

Katie sighed and turned around. She would just head back to the table and skip this tent.

"Steady on there, Katie," Finlo was right behind her and he slipped his arms around her before she could react.

"Oh, let go, Finlo," Katie could hear the exhaustion in her voice.

"Has my cousin been working you too hard?" Finlo sounded angry as he stared at Katie's sunburned face and tired eyes.

"I'm fine," Katie grumbled as she tried to pull away. "I was just going back to sit down."

"Come and have a cold drink," Finlo coaxed, guiding her further into the tent. "I've even got a nice bottle of wine, but you mustn't tell anyone. It is strictly against the rules."

Katie shook her head. She was tired and thirsty, but wine was the last thing she wanted or needed. "If you have a cold soft drink, I would appreciate it," she admitted as Finlo steered her behind a huge display that advertised Quayle Airlines. She sank into a padded chair that was far more comfortable than the folding seats they had at the institute table.

Finlo dug into a huge cooler full of ice and dug out a can of soda for her. "Sure I can't tempt you with wine?" he double-checked before popping open the top of the can and handing it to her as she shook her head.

"I'll have some wine, lover." The redhead stuck her head behind the sign and smiled seductively at Finlo. "I'm getting really tired of handing out these stupid pins to all the little brats at the show. I deserve wine."

Finlo sighed, "Darcy, this is Katie. Katie, this is Darcy." The two women nodded at each other. "No wine for now, Darce," Finlo continued. "Later, when the crowds have died down, maybe. Meanwhile, back to work."

Darcy pouted at Finlo, but turned back around and disappeared into the crowds.

Finlo sank into a chair next to Katie and shook his head. "You wouldn't believe me if I told you that there is nothing going on between me and Darcy, would you?"

Katie laughed. "Nope."

"I was afraid of that." Finlo leaned forward and took Katie's free hand. "Regardless, I still want you to give me a chance," he began.

Katie pulled her hand free and stood up. "I'm sorry, Finlo, really I am, but I'm really not ready for a man in my life." She took a few steps back towards the crowd. "Have fun with Darcy," she suggested. "She seems like your type."

The hours seemed to go slowly now. Katie was tired and she had a headache that kept getting worse as the night wore on. Still, she tried her best to answer questions and smile politely at the many visitors that streamed past their table. It wasn't until the evening was winding down that William finally noticed that she wasn't at her best.

"Are you okay?" His concern was evident.

"I've just got a little bit of a headache," Katie answered. "I probably got too much sun earlier."

William studied her face. Ealish had left with Jake to get dinner and then see a movie, and William had sent Jane home as well when Katie had assured him that she didn't mind staying until the end of the night.

"I can't take you home right now," William said, sounding frustrated, "but I can probably get you a taxi."

"No, I'm fine. I don't want to leave you here on your own," Katie replied. "Besides, I want to see the fireworks."

"Do you take anything special for headaches?"

"Just the stuff you can buy over the counter," Katie answered.

William excused himself for a few minutes and came back with a bottle of painkillers. "The first aid tent was fully stocked," he told Katie as he handed her a bottle of ice-cold water to go with the pills.

Katie swallowed a few gratefully and then sat back in her chair. The crowds were dying down and most of the people who remained were now spread out along the green picnicking and waiting for the fireworks to start. William came around behind her and began to rub her shoulders. An involuntary moan escaped her lips as she felt herself relax under his touch. A few minutes later the headache was gone and Katie felt better than she had in days.

The sun had set some time earlier and the last band of the day was just finishing up. Katie and William packed all of the unsold books and leftover pamphlets into a couple of boxes and taped them shut. They didn't need to carry them to William's car in the distant parking lot. They could be stored in the hall overnight and picked up the next day when William could park his car right outside the door.

"Come on, then," William held out his hand. "Let's find a quiet corner to watch the show."

They walked, hand in hand, around the outskirts of the crowd, finally settling for a spot near a lamppost. The lamps were all turned off a moment or two later and everyone in the crowd murmured at the sudden darkness. William leaned back against the lamppost and pulled Katie against him. There was a slight chill in the air and Katie was grateful for his body heat as she allowed herself to relax against him.

He held her gently, making no attempts to turn the embrace into anything more intimate, as the fireworks exploded around them. Finally, as the show finished and the street lamps were relit, he took her hand and led her to his car. They drove home in silence, each lost in their own thoughts.

"I hope you feel better after a good night's sleep," William told her after he parked and walked her to her door at the back of the institute building.

"I feel fine now. Those pills did the trick," she assured him.

"Good," William shook his head. "I'm sorry I made you work so hard today."

"You didn't make me do anything," Katie argued gently, "and I had fun as well. I just should have been more careful about the sun."

"Maybe if we had a bit more sun a bit more often, you would have thought about it." William laughed and Katie joined in.

They said their "good nights" and William dropped a quick kiss onto the top of her head. She let herself in and stood with her back to the door listening to William's receding footsteps and then his car engine. She had enjoyed spending time with him today and she was only a lot disappointed that he hadn't kissed her good night.

❦ 17 ❦

By mid-July, Katie had her chapter for the book under control. She'd sent an early draft of the first section off to Dave Anderson, and he'd sent it back with fulsome praise and only a few small suggestions for improvement. She was busy finishing up the last of the research she needed in order to complete the second half of the chapter, and she was confident that she would have the whole thing drafted by the middle of August. That gave her two weeks to polish the draft and maybe squeeze in some sightseeing before she had to head home.

That was assuming she didn't get the job at the institute. She had finally finished all of the paperwork and submitted it, with her visa application, but the final decision wouldn't be made until some time in August. Ealish had told her, in confidence, that there were two other applicants, but only one of them was a serious contender. Katie hated having her future so up in the air, but since there was nothing she could do about it, she simply got on with her life.

After her last email to him, Katie hadn't heard any further from Mark. Darcy was apparently keeping Finlo busy, because she didn't hear from him, either. William was spending more and more time at Rushen Abbey as additional student groups arrived to help out, so

Katie was able to relax and get on with her work without anyone to complicate things. Which was what she kept telling herself she wanted, and sometimes almost believed.

The first of August rolled around and Katie was fed up with her research, tired of writing and ready for a change.

"I need a break," she announced to Ealish as she passed through the office on her way to the museum. "I'm taking tomorrow off. Any suggestions on what I should do?"

"I know William would love to have you back down at the abbey," Ealish told her. "The season will be wrapping up soon and I know he wanted to get at least another few feet excavated before they close things down."

"What's the weather supposed to do?" Katie was cautious.

Ealish laughed. "And that is exactly why I'm a historian and not an archaeologist," she told Katie, "but it is supposed to be cool and dry tomorrow, perfect digging weather."

Katie left a note taped to William's door asking if she could tag along to the abbey the next day and then headed to the museum. She felt happier than she had in a long time, and she insisted to herself that it was simply the prospect of a day off that had improved her mood, rather than her desire to spend more time with William.

The note on her own door when she got home made her smile even more.

" I would love to have you at the dig tomorrow. I'll pick you up around nine. It is supposed to be dry and cool so wear layers of old clothes."

Katie made herself a quick dinner and then watched some television. She was learning to love some of the British shows that she had never even heard of back home. She made sure she had an early night, however, so she would have lots of energy for the next day.

The day began as promised with gray skies but no rain. Katie layered on a T-shirt with a sweatshirt and a lightweight jacket over her oldest pair of jeans and her worn-out sneakers. She added a baseball cap to protect her head in case the sun came out later in the day. She didn't want to risk getting another headache.

William seemed to be in as good a mood as her own, and he filled the drive down to the abbey with details of what they had found in the last month. Katie couldn't wait to get into the pit and start doing her own digging. At the site, William turned her over to the day's site supervisor who spent a few minutes going back over the basic techniques and then left her under the close supervision of some of the more experienced volunteers. William found her many hours later, covered in soil, happily scraping carefully around a pottery shard.

"How's it going?" he greeted her.

"Look," Katie squealed at him in delight. "I found some pottery."

William laughed as he jumped into the pit and took a closer look. "Yes, you certainly did." He borrowed a trowel from one of the other volunteers and helped Katie dig carefully around the tiny scrap. He checked that she had properly recorded the location before he dug out the shard and took a closer look.

"Well?" Katie demanded breathlessly.

"Well," William shook his head, "I think this is something rather more modern than what we are looking for."

Katie's face fell.

William couldn't help but laugh. "How much of what we find is modern rubbish?" he asked the site supervisor who was passing by.

"Oh, I would say ninety per cent," was the reply.

Katie nodded. She understood, but she was still disappointed. She was hoping she had found something with real historical significance.

"So what is it, then?"

"I suspect once we clean it up it will prove to be pottery from the tea and strawberry days in the early nineteen hundreds rather than anything older," William told her. "Most of what we've found in this area dates to that period."

"That's still pretty old, at least by American standards," Katie grinned at him. "And I found it all by myself."

"And I'm very proud of you," William pulled her to her feet, "Now go get cleaned up and I'll buy you lunch in Castletown to celebrate."

They enjoyed a quick pub lunch before they headed back for another couple of hours of digging. William was finished with meetings for the day, so he joined Katie in the pit and they worked side-by-side scraping back layer upon layer of the old soil. As the skies suddenly darkened, William called a halt to the day's efforts.

"We'd better call it a night," he announced, looking at the skies. "We need to get everything covered up for the weekend."

All of the volunteers grabbed tarps and began to cover the holes to protect them from the inevitable rain. They had nearly finished when the skies opened and a deluge flooded down on them. Katie stood under the pouring rain and laughed as William tried to shout at her over the sound of heavy rain crashing down on dozens of plastic sheets. The noise was unreal. Finally William, laughing hard, grabbed Katie's arm and dragged her into the nearest building.

"I was trying to tell you to get out of the rain," William told her, wiping rain from his face and frowning down at his sodden clothes.

Katie still felt like laughing as she studied William's bedraggled appearance. She was sure she must look at least as bad, but she didn't care. She wiped her eyes and tried to brush some of the rain from her jacket. When that failed, she pulled the jacket off, but the sweatshirt under it was equally soaked.

William watched her efforts and laughed with her as she peeled off the sweatshirt to find that her T-shirt was also sodden.

Katie shrugged and pulled the sweatshirt back over her head. "I guess that will have to do," she sighed.

"Hang on." William stuck his head around the corner and smiled at Sue in shop. "Do you have any sweatshirts left from the winter?"

Sue went into a back room and came back with a handful of heavy sweatshirts. "We only have extra-large left," she said apologetically.

"Stick two on my account," William told her, pulling one over his own head and handing the other to Katie.

Katie slipped off her wet sweatshirt and pulled the new one over her head. It was warm and fuzzy and she immediately loved it for the Rushen Abbey logo on the front of it.

"Thank you," she told William, "that feels much better."

"Good, how about we get you home and you can get properly cleaned up and then I'll cook you some dinner at my place?"

Katie hesitated for a minute, wondering what ulterior motives might be behind the suggestion. William seemed to read her mind.

"I promise, just dinner and conversation. I know you aren't ready for anything else," he assured her.

"In that case, it sounds like a great idea."

She followed William to his car and they talked about the day as they drove back into Douglas. The sun had come back out, so William pulled up to the rear parking space, but they walked together around to the front door so that William could catch up on some notes while Katie got changed. They were still chatting easily when they reached the front door.

"Well, you two look like you got caught in the same mud bath," Finlo drawled from his perch on the institute's steps.

"We were digging at the abbey," Katie answered, refusing to let Finlo spoil her good mood.

"So I see," Finlo stood up, "and let me guess, now you have romantic dinner plans somewhere nice?"

William slipped an arm around Katie. "As a matter of fact," he began, but Katie interrupted.

"Stop it, both of you," she told the pair. "I am not some prize that you two can fight over and squabble about. All I want..."

But what she wanted remained unsaid as a taxi pulled up to the curb and a man in a rumpled suit jumped out. He had a medium build with sandy brown hair and trendy glasses and he had a suitcase in his hand.

"Katie," he shouted, "I'm so happy to see you."

The man rushed over and picked Katie up, swinging her around for a dizzy minute. When he put her down, Katie just stared for a minute before she spoke.

"Mark? What the hell are you doing here?"

Finlo and William both looked from Katie to Mark and back.

"This is the Mark who treated you so badly?" Finlo checked.

"Yes," Katie replied reluctantly.

"You hold him down," Finlo told William, "I'll beat him senseless."

"Oh, for heaven's sake," Katie shook her head. "No one is hitting anyone," she told Finlo. "And no one is having dinner with me, romantic or otherwise. I'm going upstairs alone and I'm going to drink a bottle of wine and read a book and forget that any of you exist."

She turned on her heel and stomped up the steps to the building, her dramatic exit spoiled when she had to wait for William to open the front door for her. Once inside she ignored the three men who all called her name and marched up the stairs, unlocked her apartment door and slammed it behind her.

Two hours and half a bottle of wine later, Katie was surprised to hear the door to her apartment open.

"Okay, don't shoot the messenger," Ealish called as she made her way up the stairs. "If you don't want to talk to me, that's fine, but I brought more wine and I'm begging you, as a friend, to not make me go back down there."

Katie laughed. "What's going on?"

Ealish shook her head and poured herself a glass of wine. After a healthy swallow she answered. "Finlo and William are torn between punching each other and joining forces to beat up Mark. And Mark won't shut up. I don't think he's so much as taken a breath in the last hour and a half. He just keeps babbling on and on about how much he loves you and how he is going to make it all up to you and on and on and on." She finished her glass of wine and poured another.

"For the sake of everyone's sanity, I think you need to hear him out," Ealish suggested.

She held up her hand as Katie began to sputter a protest. "I still think he's an idiot and I don't think you should take him back or anything, but he came all this way and he isn't going to leave until he speaks to you. You may as well get it over with and get rid of him before Finlo or William really do start throwing punches."

"I don't want to talk to him," Katie whined to her friend.

"I don't blame you," Ealish smiled, "I can't figure out what you ever saw in him, but he isn't leaving if you don't, and we all want him gone."

Katie shook her head. "I don't want him up here."

"Take him for a walk on the promenade," Ealish suggested.

"But I love the promenade," Katie giggled. "He'll ruin it for me."

"Only if you let him," Ealish said sternly. "Now go send him back to the states and then you can get back to choosing between Finlo and William."

Katie blushed and started to protest, but Ealish wasn't done. "Of course, I'm rooting for William, but I guess it isn't really my business."

Katie rolled her eyes. "Stick around and after I talk to Mark we can drink more wine and you can try to convince me," she suggested with a giggle.

"So go get rid of Mark. I'll try to persuade Finlo and William to take off while you're gone."

Katie washed her face and ran a brush through her hair, clearing away the mud and rain from earlier. After a quick argument with herself, she kept her new sweatshirt on. It was warm and cozy and it reminded her of William, all good things at the moment.

Downstairs all three men tried to talk at once, but Katie held up her hand and silenced them all.

"Finlo, William, please just go for tonight. I need to talk to Mark." She turned to Mark. "Okay, you want to talk? I'll give you ten minutes. Let's go."

"Go?" Mark looked confused. "Upstairs?"

"Nope," Katie ushered him towards the door, "we can talk and walk on the promenade." She headed out the door with Mark protesting behind her.

"I wanted some privacy and a chance to pour my heart out. This isn't what I had in mind."

Katie ignored him and made her way to the nearby crossing, waiting to be sure that the traffic would stop before she crossed over to the wide promenade. Mark followed, still complaining.

"Okay," Katie said, turning to face him once they had crossed the road. "You've ten minutes and then I want you gone." She started a slow walk along the seafront.

Mark sighed. "Katie darling this isn't like you," he told her. "Please give me a chance."

"I'm giving you ten minutes," she replied, "or rather nine and a half now."

Mark shook his head. "I'd better keep this brief then." He stared at her for a few seconds, seemingly unsure of where to start. "I guess it's simple, really," he said finally. "The last couple of months have been hell and I miss you so much I can't sleep or eat or do anything. I love you and I want you back."

Katie shook her head. "Mark, if you're telling the truth then I'm sorry, but I've moved on and I'm at a different place now. I'm doing interesting research and working with great people and I don't want to go back. I'll always have a special place in my heart for you, but we were finished as soon as you cheated."

"Katie, please," Mark pleaded with her, "let me try to explain. Give me a chance to win back your trust." His voice broke as he looked into her eyes. "I can't live without you."

Katie turned away with a shrug. "A couple of months ago I was worried that I couldn't live without you. But you know what? I'm happier than I've been in years." She shook her head. "I think we stayed together out of habit, not love. And you cheated on me because you weren't happy either, you just couldn't tell me."

Mark shook his head. "I cheated because I was stupid and my head was turned by a sexy young woman who saw me as an easy way to get ahead. I never stopped loving you," he insisted.

"It doesn't really matter," Katie said sadly. "We broke up for good reasons and it's over. I'm sorry you came all this way just to hear that."

"It's Finlo, isn't it?"

"What's Finlo?"

"Who you're sleeping with. Why you won't get back together with me. I thought maybe it was William, because of the way he looks at you, but Finlo seems more likely to have given you this uncharacteristic burst of self-confidence. Don't tell me you're sleeping with both of them?"

"I think you better go now," Katie told him, anger in her voice.

"Really, Katie, is that what you need to do to help yourself get over me?"

Katie turned around and swung her hand at his face, wanting to slap him for suggesting such a thing.

As she swung he caught her hand and used her momentum to pull her close. He wrapped his arms around her and them tipped her head up.

"I can't tell you how much I've missed you," he told her as he lowered his mouth to hers.

Katie stood absolutely still. Shock and anger coursed through her, but she didn't struggle. She just stood completely unresponsively until Mark finally raised his head.

"Damn it, Katie," he swore, "don't be like this."

"Like what?" Katie was surprised how easily she kept her voice calm. "We broke up because you cheated. That was months ago. That you now think you made a mistake is not my problem."

Mark shook his head sadly. "I still love you."

"I'm sorry," Katie stared at the man that she had loved for most of her adult life. "But I just don't love you anymore." She was shocked at how true the words really were. She felt sad, but she also felt liberated. She was truly over the man.

Mark looked into her eyes for a long time, presumably hoping to see a glimmer of something that might give him hope, but, if so, he was disappointed. With a sigh, he turned and they walked together back along the promenade.

"I thought coming here would be a big romantic gesture. That you would fall into my arms. That we could really have our happily ever after."

Katie could only apologize again. Back at the institute, Ealish was sitting alone on the front steps. She stood up as they approached.

"I guess I need you to call me a taxi," Mark told Ealish reluctantly. He turned to Katie. "So is this good-bye?"

"I hope you find happiness, Mark, I really do," Katie told him. She gave him a quick hug and then climbed the steps to the institute.

A taxi pulled up to the curb and Ealish handed Mark the suitcase that he'd left in the office earlier. Katie turned and waved as he climbed into the taxi. She watched silently as it pulled away and disappeared down the promenade, a single tear sliding down her cheek.

Ealish cleared her throat as the taxi vanished. "Are you okay?"

Katie turned to her friend and then smiled sadly. "I'm fine," she assured her. "That was really hard to do, especially after all our years together, but there was no way I was going back."

"Good for you," Ealish grinned and the women climbed the steps into the building.

"Coming up for a drink, then?" Katie asked her friend.

"Oh, yeah," Ealish smiled. "We have lots to talk about."

They curled up on opposite ends of the couch in Katie's living room, a glass of wine each. Before they got too comfortable, Katie quickly ordered a pizza. She didn't want to drink too much on an empty stomach, and lunch seemed like a distant memory.

"At least you got rid of Finlo and William," Katie remarked. "I don't think I could have handled dealing with them after that."

"I didn't do anything, actually," Ealish told her. "They both left when they saw you and Mark kissing."

"Oh, no," Katie groaned. "We weren't kissing. Mark tried kissing me and I didn't respond. That's all it was."

"Well, the guys didn't like it and they both took off," Ealish told her. "Never mind, you can clear things up when you see them next." She paused. "Was it weird kissing him after everything he put you through?" she asked eventually.

"What was weird was that I felt nothing," Katie shook her head. "I felt like I was kissing my brother or something. There was no spark, no chemistry. And then I realized that it had always been pretty much like that, not at all like kissing...," she broke off, blushing.

"Please don't tell me you were going to say Finlo," Ealish groaned.

Katie giggled. "Finlo is a great kisser," she teased and then got serious. "But I was thinking William."

"Woo hoo, score one for the nice guy," Ealish shouted. The pizza delivery guy interrupted her celebrations, but she still had lots more questions for Katie as they ate.

"So does William know how you feel?"

"I don't even know how I feel," Katie admitted.

"I do," Ealish smiled at her. "You feel giddy and silly and you just want to spend as much time with him as you can. And when you are with him you feel happy, even if you are standing in a muddy pit with rain pouring down all over you."

Katie laughed. "I guess that just about sums it up."

"When are you going to tell him?"

"I don't know if I am," Katie sighed. "It is all so complicated. I'm not totally sure how I feel. Besides, I might be leaving in another month."

Ealish argued good-naturedly with Katie through the rest of the pizza and wine, but she couldn't persuade her to open her heart to William yet. Katie had enough going on in her life right now without adding any more complications.

❧ 18 ❧

August seemed to fly past as Katie worked hard on finishing her research and getting her chapter done. William was so busy at the abbey that he rarely stopped by the institute at all and aside from a few quick "hellos" Katie didn't get to speak to him at all. Katie heard through the grapevine that Finlo had gone to Italy for a two-week training course, but she heard nothing from the man himself. The institute's Board of Directors was due to meet towards the end of August to make a decision on the job that Katie now really wanted, but that was simply a waiting game.

By the middle of the month Katie had mostly finished her research and was focused on writing the chapter. After three days stuck in her apartment writing and rewriting the same page repeatedly, she decided that she needed a different perspective.

"I'm heading to Castle Rushen tomorrow for the day," she told Ealish when she went down to the kitchen for a much-needed coffee break.

"Do you want me to line up a taxi?"

"That would be great," Katie smiled. "I need one here at nine-thirty and then one at the castle at five to bring me home."

"Are you sure you want to spend the whole day there? What are you going to do with all that time?"

"Mostly I'm just going to soak in the atmosphere," Katie told her. "I want to spend some time at the castle but first I want to explore some of Castletown. I'm more worried that I will run out of time rather than have too much."

Ealish grinned at her. "Okay, I'll arrange your transportation, then. I'll get you a taxi for the morning and then see if William can bring you back. He'll be coming back from the abbey around that time, anyway. No point in paying for a taxi if he's going to be making the same drive."

Katie blushed, but didn't argue.

The next day was sunny and bright and Katie was in a wonderful mood when the taxi dropped her off outside the castle. She spent a happy morning wandering around the town, visiting other historical sites and trying to imagine how the town would have looked to the seventh Earl of Derby and his family when they arrived during the Civil War.

She bought herself lunch in a little pub across the street from the castle and then headed up the stone steps to the door.

"Hey, Katie."

She spun around and then frowned. Finlo was just climbing out of his fancy car.

"Hi," she muttered as he reached her side.

"I guess this is my lucky day," Finlo smiled at her. "I just got back from a course in Italy and I was going to grab some lunch when I saw you."

"Lucky me," Katie said waspishly.

"Oh dear," Finlo frowned dramatically, "I am hurt."

Katie rolled her eyes and then giggled at the sad face that Finlo put on.

"So what are you doing all by yourself in Castletown? I can't believe my cousin let you out of his sight."

Katie shook her head. "I haven't even seen your cousin this week," she told Finlo, annoyed with herself when she heard how forlorn she sounded as she shared that particular piece of news.

Finlo perked up. "Does that mean that I'm still in with a chance?"

Katie sighed. "No, it doesn't," she insisted.

"You haven't reunited with Mark, have you?"

"No, of course not," Katie laughed. "Did you really think I would?"

"From where we were standing, it looked like a pretty passionate kiss," Finlo teased her. "But no, I didn't think you would take him back. He was an idiot."

Katie laughed again. "Now there is something we can agree on."

"So if you aren't back together with him and you aren't dating my cousin, why don't I have a chance, exactly?"

Katie sighed. "Really, Finlo, I'm probably leaving in two weeks. The last thing I need is to start a relationship and then have to leave. I'm not a long-distance relationship type of person, and I really don't think you are either."

"I thought you were going to stay for another year? I thought a job had opened up?"

"The board hasn't made a final decision on that yet," Katie explained. "And even if I do stay, I think we are better off just being friends."

Finlo grinned wickedly. "I'll make a deal with you, my darling," he began. "I'm going to kiss you, and if, after that kiss, you can look me in the eyes and tell me that you aren't attracted to me, then I will leave you alone. How is that?"

Katie shook her head. "No games, Finlo, please. I have enough on my mind without playing games with you."

"What are you afraid of?" Finlo spoke softly now, looking into Katie's eyes. "I think you are as attracted to me as I am to you and you just don't want to admit it."

"Finlo, really, just stop, please."

Finlo shook his head and pulled her close. "Just one kiss, Katie. If you can tell me after this kiss that I'm wrong, then I will go quietly."

Katie looked into his eyes and felt her heart skip a beat. She took a deep breath and tried to steady her nerves as Finlo pulled her closer and lowered his head.

The kiss started slowly and gently, and Katie could feel her pulse race under Finlo's touch. His technique was excellent, but as the kiss deepened Katie found her mind was wandering. After a few more seconds, Finlo lifted his head and looked at her with disappointment in his eyes.

"Really?"

"I'm sorry, Finlo, but I'm really not attracted to you," Katie was relieved that she could easily look into his eyes and speak the truth.

Finlo tipped his head to one side and considered her for a long minute. "I hope William knows how lucky he is," he told her as he hugged her briefly and released her.

Katie tried to protest, but he waved her words away. "Tell my cousin that I guess the best man has won, after all," he said as he walked away, climbing into his car and zooming away while Katie stood on the steps watching.

After a minute she turned and headed into the castle, some of the excitement of the day drained by the emotional encounter. It didn't take long for the magic of the castle to reignite her enthusiasm, though. Bob greeted her like an old friend.

"We're shorthanded today, so I'll just leave you to explore on your own if you don't mind," he told her from his spot behind the admissions desk. "Paul is showing the movie and he can help you if you have any questions or need anything, but he's new, so if you have any real questions, you'll have to come back and see me."

Katie was happy to assure him that she was fine. She sat through the movie again, this time watching the entire thing without any distractions. Then she made her way slowly through the castle, pausing here and there to inspect any little thing that caught her eye.

She finally made her way to the throne room and sat down in a visitor's chair. She felt like she could sit there for hours, just soaking in the atmosphere and imagining seventeenth-century life. She dug out a notebook from her bag and jotted down a few notes about the room. She would use some descriptions of the space to make her chapter a bit more interesting.

People came and went all afternoon, while Katie sat and took notes and then explored the rest of the castle. It was quarter to five when she dashed back up the stairs to the throne room for one more look before she met her taxi. She could hear the castle's staff chasing out the last of the visitors as she took a few last-minute notes on the layout of the treasure room in the back corner of the throne room.

She was suddenly aware that the castle had gone very quiet, so she quickly made her way down the stairs to the exit door, only to find that it was shut and locked up tight. She headed back up and then followed the tourist route backwards through the rest of the castle to the entrance door. It too was shut and locked.

Katie banged on the door, listening to the echo as it bounced around the vast stone structure. She raced back up the stairs and looked out of one of the narrow windows. She could just make out Bob's shape as he climbed into his car and drove away. The castle was closed for the night and she was locked in.

Katie bit back a slightly hysterical giggle. She loved the castle, but she really didn't want to be alone in it when it got dark. She walked slowly from room to room, trying to figure out if there was any way out that she might have missed.

She sat for a long time in the throne room, trying to figure out what to do. She had thought at first that William would call Ealish when she never came out of the castle, but as the hours ticked by she figured that he mustn't have done so.

As the night wore on, she realized that no one had probably even noticed that she hadn't come home. She was going to be stuck there until the castle opened at ten the next morning. The castle staff had presumably turned off the electricity to the building as they left for the night and without electric light the castle began to get very dark even before the sun was fully set.

Katie paced back and forth through the Derby apartments, trying to calm her nerves and tire herself out so that she could sleep. There seemed little else that she could do. She did her best to ignore her rumbling stomach. Lunch seemed to have been very long ago. In the throne room, Katie struggled to find a comfortable spot to settle into. It was nearly pitch black in the room and the stone walls made the room feel damp and cold. Katie tried curling up on the chair in several different ways, before giving up and stretching out on the cold stone floor.

She shivered and curled up, trying to keep warm. She felt her emotions overload and tears began to flow freely. As the room darkened still further, Katie shut her eyes tightly and tried to imagine herself anywhere else but there.

A strange whooshing noise startled her and she opened her eyes. She could see nothing in the total blackness. She drew a deep and shaky breath and was surprised to find herself relaxing. A strange sense of peace came over her as she suddenly felt that everything was going to be fine. Help was on the way, and it was going to be coming from the one person who could make it all okay.

A few moments later Katie blinked hard as the room was suddenly flooded with light. She sat up and then stood, brushing herself off and trying to get her bearings. A second later she heard footsteps on the stairs and she turned with a smile on her face, already knowing who had come to find her.

"Katie," William cried, relief palpable in his voice. "I've found her," he shouted over his shoulder as he pulled her into a huge bear hug.

Katie clung to him for a moment, relief at being rescued mingling with a flood of other emotions that threatened to overwhelm her.

"I'm so sorry," William told her, "I promised Ealish I would pick you up at five, but when I saw you kissing Finlo, I got so angry I forgot."

"Finlo was just trying to get me to give him another chance," Katie tried to explain. "I told him no."

"And I thought you were thinking about giving Mark a second chance when you were kissing him," William continued.

"I wasn't kissing him," she told him, "he was kissing me. There is a big difference."

William shook his head, unsure of what to say next.

"You know," Katie told him, leaning in closer and talking quietly, "it seems like everyone wants to kiss me at the moment except the one man I want to kiss."

William stared into Katie's eyes. "You mean..."

Katie interrupted by leaning in and kissing him gently.

After a few seconds the kiss deepened and they only broke apart when they heard voices behind them.

"I found them," Bob was calling to someone behind him, "but I'm not sure they want to be found."

❧ 19 ❧

The weather had been surprisingly mild for October, and this day was no exception as the hired limousine pulled to a stop in front of the castle.

The past two months had been busy ones, as Katie had finished her chapter and flown home to tie up a few loose ends before taking up her two-year professorship on the island. At the moment, the plan was that after those two years William would look for a similar posting in the States and then, having tried out both countries, they would pick one to make their home.

William, having never even given a second's thought to leaving the island for his first wife's sake, had already promised that he would happily move to the ends of the earth to be with Katie. For her part, Katie was less convinced every day that the move back to the U.S. would ever happen. The island already felt like home in so many ways.

The car had barely stopped and Katie was already jumping out, stopping for only a second to fluff her skirt and adjust her hat.

"I swear you are more excited about the venue than the groom," William pretended to grumble.

Katie just laughed as she raced up the steps to the castle.

When she had learned that couples could marry on the castle

grounds, their wedding venue was decided. Having spent many months and thousands of dollars planning for her cancelled wedding, she and William decided on a quiet ceremony and the castle was the perfect place for it.

Katie raced eagerly around the castle building and came to a stop just before she reached the courtyard. Suddenly nervous, she peeked around the corner for the building. She smiled brightly when she saw the rows of folding chairs that were mostly full.

She was relieved to see that everyone had ignored tradition and that her parents were not alone on the "bride's side" of the seating. Instead, William's family and friends had spread themselves all around the seats, everyone laughing and talking together as they waited for the service to begin.

"It's not too late to change your mind," Finlo whispered to her as he came up behind her and gave her a big hug.

Katie laughed and hugged him tightly. "That is no way for the best man to talk," she chided him.

"We can be out of here and in the air before anyone realizes you're gone," he joked.

"Oh, stop," Ealish pulled Katie away from Finlo and gave her a huge hug of her own.

"You look beautiful," she told her friend, "and I'm honored you asked me to be your maid of honor."

The ceremony was beautiful and Katie was thrilled to see her parents beaming happily as she and William exchanged their vows.

William had called in every favor he could and managed to get permission to hold their reception in the banqueting hall of the castle. A huge buffet was spread across one wall and the tourist displays were taken down and replaced with tables for guests and a long bar.

A traditional Manx ceilidh followed and everyone laughed and tripped their way through the various patterns of the folk dances with more enthusiasm than skill. As the evening wound down and the guests began to trickle out, Katie turned tired but happy eyes on her new husband.

"Before we go, I just need to drop off the extra flowers," she reminded him.

He smiled at her. "No rush, Finlo won't leave without us."

For a wedding present Finlo was flying them to Paris for a three-week honeymoon. Katie joked that he might not be back to pick them up, but she and William were both relieved that Finlo seemed genuinely happy for them.

Leaving William behind for just a moment, Katie rushed to the throne room with the small bouquet of flowers that she'd ordered specially. She twirled through the room, feeling as if she couldn't be any happier. She carefully laid the flowers on one of the thrones, a little gift for the Countess of Derby.

She had never told anyone about the strange feeling that had come over her that night she had been locked in the castle, but in her heart she was convinced that it was the Countess looking out for her. Even though she told herself she didn't believe in ghosts, she couldn't find any other explanation.

Katie hurried back out of the room, not wanting to keep William waiting for more than a minute or two. At the door, she turned back to get one last look at the beautiful flowers. Katie could only stare at the elegantly dressed woman who was now sitting on the throne, Katie's flowers in her hands. As Katie looked at her, the woman raised her head and gave Katie a beautiful smile.

ALSO BY DIANA XARISSA

Aunt Bessie Assumes

Aunt Bessie Believes

Aunt Bessie Considers

Aunt Bessie Decides

Aunt Bessie Enjoys

Aunt Bessie Finds

Aunt Bessie Goes

Aunt Bessie's Holiday

Aunt Bessie Invites

Aunt Bessie Joins

Aunt Bessie Knows

Aunt Bessie Likes

Aunt Bessie Meets

Aunt Bessie Needs

Aunt Bessie Observes

Aunt Bessie Provides

Aunt Bessie Questions

Aunt Bessie Remembers

Aunt Bessie Questions

Aunt Bessie Solves

Aunt Bessie Tries

Aunt Bessie Understands

Aunt Bessie Volunteers

Aunt Bessie Wonders

The Isle of Man Ghostly Cozy Mysteries

Arrivals and Arrests

The Rhodes Case

The Isle of Man Romance Series
Island Escape
Island Inheritance
Island Heritage
Island Christmas

ABOUT THE AUTHOR

Diana lived on the glorious Isle of Man for more than ten years before returning to the United States with her family. Now living near Buffalo, New York, she enjoys having the opportunity to write about the island that she loves so much. It truly is an amazing and magical place.

Diana also writes mystery/thrillers set in the not-too-distant future under the pen name "Diana X. Dunn" and fantasy/adventure books for middle grade readers under the pen name "D.X. Dunn."

She would be delighted to know what you think of her work. Please feel free to get in touch!

Find Diana at:
www.dianaxarissa.com
diana@dianaxarissa.com